SECOND THOUGHTS

SEQUEL TO *THIRD IDENTITY*

KELSEY GJESDAL

WESTBOW
PRESS®
A DIVISION OF THOMAS NELSON
& ZONDERVAN

WestBow Press books may be ordered through booksellers or by contacting:

WestBow Press
A Division of Thomas Nelson & Zondervan
1663 Liberty Drive
Bloomington, IN 47403
www.westbowpress.com
844-714-3454

Because of the dynamic nature of the Internet, any web addresses or
links contained in this book may have changed since publication and
may no longer be valid. The views expressed in this work are solely those
of the author and do not necessarily reflect the views of the publisher,
and the publisher hereby disclaims any responsibility for them.

Any people depicted in stock imagery provided by Getty Images are
models, and such images are being used for illustrative purposes only.
Certain stock imagery © Getty Images.

Scripture quotations taken from the (NASB®) New American Standard
Bible®, Copyright © 1960, 1971, 1977, 1995, 2020 by The Lockman
Foundation. Used by permission. All rights reserved. www.lockman.org

ISBN: 978-1-6642-4526-6 (sc)
ISBN: 978-1-6642-4525-9 (hc)
ISBN: 978-1-6642-4527-3 (e)

Library of Congress Control Number: 2021919377

Print information available on the last page.

WestBow Press rev. date: 09/28/2021

CONTENTS

CHAPTER 1

"Explosives in place. Pick us up!" Matthew's voice boomed in my earpiece. I circled the aircraft back around toward the building, flying in as low as possible.

"Deploying cables in three... two... one." I pushed all three cable buttons and slowed the aircraft as much as I could. I looked down at the screen from the camera on the bottom of the aircraft. I watched as the three agents raced to the cables. Not far behind, two guards ran after them.

"Hurry—we've got company!" Matthew said. "Harness attached."

"Harness attached," chorused the other two agents.

"Pulling up," I replied, pushing the cable buttons again. I listened to hear the whiz of the cable motors and then began pulling the aircraft up.

"Inside," Matthew said.

"Copy that," I replied and pressed the button to close the aircraft door.

"Detonating explosives in three, two, one." The coms went silent, then cheering erupted. "Success!" Matthew cried.

I smiled and set the autopilot back to base. I stood up and walked into the main hangar of the aircraft. "Nice work, boys," I said.

"We couldn't have done it without you, Sarah," Matthew replied, grinning.

"That's for sure," Luke said, rolling his eyes. "Flying with Matthew in the pilot's chair is always more dangerous than the mission!"

"Hey!" Matthew punched Luke in the arm.

Luke shrugged and grinned. "Was it something I said?"

"Okay, you two, we need to contact base," Daniel said, tapping on his wrist computer. After a second, he began speaking into the computer. "Flight Crew 1 to Base."

A voice came through the computer. "This is Base."

"This is Flight Crew 1. We have accomplished mission flight 135. We are returning to base," Daniel said.

"Accomplished mission recorded. Sending info to ground crew. Well done, agents. See you back at base. Over and out."

Daniel turned off the computer. "Whew, glad that mission's over!"

"Me too! Did you see the guns those guards had? If they had noticed us sneak in any sooner, we'd have been goners!" Luke said, his brown eyes shining with excitement.

"I'm glad we were able to help stop that operation! Hopefully, our work will keep freedom alive in that country," Matthew said.

Luke sighed. "After all that running, I'm starving. But I forgot to bring snacks."

"Luke, sometimes I can't believe how much food you can eat!" Daniel shook his head. "I did bring some trail mix, though."

"Oh, yes!" Luke fist pumped. "That will tide me over."

As the guys snacked on trail mix, I walked back to the cockpit and checked the autopilot time. *Sixty-five minutes to* destination. *Plenty of time to relax,* I thought as I sat down and grabbed a book from my backpack.

🔫

"Entering Truth Squad airspace," I said into the speaker. I glanced out the window as I guided the aircraft toward the runway. We were back home at the Truth Squad campus. Our crew worked for Truth Squad, a private organization that partnered with the FBI and CIA. We took on important cases nationally and internationally that weren't the government's top priority due to a lack of resources. Our goal was to defend the truth throughout the world, especially the truth of the gospel. Looking down at our campus filled me with pride. It was wonderful to know that I was working for an organization that was making a difference in others' lives.

I set the aircraft down and pulled into the hangar, then powered it down. "Here we are," I said and opened the side door.

As we climbed down from the aircraft, my twin sister Rebecca ran up to us. "How was the mission?" she asked.

"It was awesome!" Luke replied excitedly, then launched into his own dramatic retelling of the mission, Daniel and Matthew jumping in with their own comments.

It was fun to listen to those three. They had been on many missions together and were close friends. Matthew was the leader of the squad and definitely looked like it. He was six foot three and muscular with brown hair and hazel eyes. He was one of the best agents in Truth Squad, holding the most records in training exercises of all the agents. Due to his talent, he was also second-in-command even though he was only twenty-three. Luke was my age, twenty, but didn't look

3

like it. He was tall and skinny with dark brown hair and still looked like a teenager. Luke had more energy than anyone I'd ever met, and he was constantly eating. Despite being hyper and easily distracted, he was great at inventing new gadgets, acting, and thinking outside the box. Daniel was slightly shorter than Luke with light brown hair and broad shoulders. He and Luke grew up together and were best friends. They brought out the crazy sides in each other, but overall, Daniel was very level-headed. He was the one who kept the group on track. He was trained as a detective and did private contract jobs, but he often joined Truth Squad missions that weren't in his specialty.

That's what makes working for Truth Squad so great, I thought, smiling. *You get to have experience in many different fields.*

It was interesting to watch my sister's face as she listened to Luke's story. I could tell she was analyzing everything that had happened. Rebecca and I were completely identical in looks—we both had long, wavy brown hair, blue eyes, and pale skin. We were both fairly tall, Rebecca being five foot nine, and I was five foot eight. Our personalities, on the other hand, were complete opposites. Rebecca was the logical one. I was the emotional one. She was sarcastic, and I was not. She loved the excitement of dangerous missions. I preferred the safer, less risky ones.

Once Luke finished his tale, Daniel said, "Okay, let's go get cleaned up. We still have a report to write, you know."

Luke rolled his eyes. "Yay, I love writing reports," he said sarcastically.

"See you guys later," Rebecca said with a wave as they left, then turned toward me. "How was your part in the mission?"

"Much easier than theirs!" I replied. "All I had to do was

fly the aircraft! Speaking of which, I need to do the postflight check. Want to help me?"

"Sounds good!" Rebecca said.

I ran and grabbed the electronic checklist off the wall, and began looking over the aircraft with Rebecca. It was nice to work with my sister. Rebecca had only come to Truth Squad two years before. Before that, we had been completely disconnected. Rebecca had been working as a double agent for an assassin named Richard Zaiden since she was sixteen. But Luke and I were sent on a case that involved Richard Zaiden, causing our worlds to crash into each other once again. Rebecca ended up helping us put a stop to Zaiden's work. Through the course of our mission, she accepted Christ and gave up her double agent life to do what was right. Instead of going to prison, Rebecca was able to enroll in a parole program that Truth Squad was testing out. It was exciting to have my sister in my life again. I loved working alongside her and seeing how much she'd changed since accepting Christ.

"Okay, it looks like we're set. Thanks for your help," I said, hanging the tablet back on the wall.

"No problem," Rebecca replied. We walked out of the hangar and toward the apartment buildings.

"So we've told you about our mission. What happened back here while we were gone?" I asked.

Rebecca shrugged. "Not much. I did some training, which was fun. I also got to help out with the summer drama class today since Mrs. Peterson is sick."

"I'm sure the class enjoyed that! You have such a knack for acting," I said, grinning.

"Well, when you were a double agent for two years, it comes pretty naturally," Rebecca replied with a wink.

After changing clothes, I met back with the guys in the

computer lab to write our report on the mission. After we finished and turned it in, we heard the dinner bell through the speakers.

"Yes!" Luke said, jumping up. "I've been ready for dinner for hours!" We hurried to the mess hall, joining the crowd of agents and students already there.

While it was summer, there were still a few kids from the boarding school there. Most of them were children of agents working for Truth Squad, and many of them wanted to be agents when they grew up, too.

After everyone sat down at the tables, the president of Truth Squad, John Truth, walked to the front of the mess hall. He was tall with broad shoulders, had dark hair sprinkled with gray, an angular jaw, and bright blue eyes. He grabbed a mic and smiled at the group. "Good evening, everyone. I have a few announcements to make before dinner. First of all, if you were assigned to mission 135, it was a success. Thank you for your hard work, teams. Secondly, I want to congratulate Faith Thompson for setting a new record in the junior training course today for the fastest obstacle course time. Excellent work, Faith! Finally, I want to inform you all that we will be receiving some new students this summer from our Canadian base. These will be agents who are looking for more training. They will be arriving on Monday. Please give them all a warm welcome as a part of our extended team. With that, let's pray for the meal."

After prayer, Rebecca and I jumped in line for food behind Faith and Hope. Faith and Hope were also twins, so Rebecca and I felt a strong connection with these girls. While they weren't identical, they were definitely best friends.

"Congratulations on the new record, Faith," Rebecca said, giving her a high-five.

The thirteen-year-old smiled up at her. "Thank you! I'm so excited! I can't believe I beat Jonathan's record!" Her blue-green eyes sparkled as she tucked her dark brown hair behind her ear.

Hope giggled and flipped her braided light brown hair over her shoulder. "He'll probably be mad."

"Don't worry about it," I replied. "If he is, he'll get over it quickly." The girls continued talking and giggling while Rebecca and I listened.

After a few minutes, Rebecca checked her watch and stood up. "Leaving so soon?" I asked.

"Yeah, I have a meeting with my parole officer," she replied casually. "I'll see you later."

I glanced over at the girls to see if they were paying attention, but they weren't. I breathed a sigh of relief. Some of the agents who knew Rebecca's past treated her like she wasn't to be trusted, which frustrated me. I didn't want that distrust spreading to the junior agents.

Twenty minutes later, Rebecca returned to the mess hall as we were clearing our plates. I raised my eyebrows to ask how it went, and she gave me a thumbs up. I smiled in return, knowing it meant everything went well.

Rebecca routinely met with a parole officer and Mr. Truth once a month to go over her records and progress. Since she was the "trial run" for the Truth Squad parole program, the police and Mr. Truth were watching her progress closely to make sure this program would work well for others.

We finished clearing our table and left the mess hall. "I'm glad nothing's going on this evening. I'm ready to relax after our mission today," I said as Rebecca and I walked towards the dorm buildings.

"Yeah, I'm looking forward to finishing that book I'm reading," she said, grinning.

We entered the girl's dorms and climbed to the second floor, ready to relax.

🔫

"You ready for this?" I asked Rebecca as we suited up.

"I was born ready," she said, flipping her braid dramatically. She laughed. "In all seriousness, I'm excited to finally train with you guys."

"You should have been training with us ages ago," Luke replied, snapping on his vest.

"It's only fair that I worked my way up the ranks like the rest of you did," Rebecca said, grabbing a helmet. "Besides, working my way up meant that I got to watch some of your training to learn some secrets." She winked at me.

"Oh, dear," Luke said. "What are you two up to?"

I shrugged and smiled at Rebecca. This was her first day training with Squad 4, but since she'd watched my training a few times, she had a few ideas of how to beat some of the high scores.

"Okay, agents, let's get started," Matthew said, waving toward the training room door. We lined up and followed Matthew through the door.

The Truth Squad training room was the most high-tech, full-room simulator in the world. The floor could move to simulate different terrains, an earthquake, or an explosion. Holograms were used to simulate an enemy and could "shoot" you with laser guns. The training suits contained sensors so that when you were "shot" with a laser, they would let you know you were out, either by a blinking red light, vibrating, or, on the most realistic level, simulating the force of an actual shot. As we walked in, I saw barricades scattered around the room. *This must be a team reconnaissance training,* I thought.

"Line up!" Matthew ordered. After we were in place, he numbered us off into two teams. "Team one, you are the defending team. You have this computer chip that contains important info that you don't want the other team to have." He placed it in my hand. "Your mission is to guard this chip and keep team two from obtaining it." He walked over to the other team. "Team two, you are the offensive team. Your job is to obtain that computer chip from team one. Stealth is key. If you successfully bring the chip from team one's side of the room over to the back wall on your side of the room, you win. If team one never loses the chip by the end of thirty minutes, they win."

I smiled across the room at Rebecca and mouthed, "Good luck!" She flashed a sneaky grin. Being on the defensive team was easier than the offensive team, I knew. But Rebecca had a lot of experience in this kind of work, so I knew this would be an exciting round.

Each team had five minutes to strategize. Our team captain quickly assigned everyone a role.

"In your positions!" Matthew called through the speaker. I took my place at the left of the computer chip. "Commencing in five, four, three, two, one..."

The lights dimmed, and our laser guns turned on. The offensive team exploded into action. I stayed alert for any movement sneaking up to the computer chip. Two agents tried to run for it. We shot one down, and the other retreated.

That's an odd strategy, I thought. *Most agents don't make such a risky choice. What are they covering for?* I glanced behind me and saw someone retreat behind a barricade. *Who was that?* I wondered, glancing down at the computer chip. It was gone! "The computer chip was stolen!" I yelled to the other teammate guarding the chip.

"There!" he said, pointing to the person behind the barricade. We ran at them, but when we got there, they were gone. "Where'd they go?"

"I don't know," I said, looking around. "Hold it, look on top of the barricades!" The person was running across the tops of the barricades, jumping from one to the next, and now I could see who it was. *Rebecca.*

My teammate and I ran after her, calling to our team as we went. Rebecca jumped down to ground level before we were in range to fire and was hidden behind the barricade. "You go left, I go right," I said as we snuck up toward her. We paused, counted to three, and ran around the barricade.

"I'm hit!" my teammate cried.

I rounded the corner, ready to fire, when my vest vibrated and forcefully knocked me over. "What? How am I out?" I said, frowning.

"Should have watched your back," Rebecca replied, running past me.

I sat on the ground and held one hand up to signify I was out. Looking behind me, I saw Luke laying on top of a barricade sniping. *Smart,* I thought.

A few minutes later, a bell rang. "We have a winning team!" Matthew's voice called through the speaker. "Team two has won with twelve minutes to spare. Well done, team! And best of luck to team one next time."

The lights turned on, and our laser guns turned off. The two teams lined up to shake hands. "Well played," I said, shaking Rebecca's hand.

"Thank you," she replied, grinning. "I'm anxious to see the individual scores."

We left the training room and unsuited. After putting away our equipment, we checked the scoreboard.

"Hey, I got a PR!" Luke said, doing a fist pump.

"Nice!" I said, looking down the list. I squealed when I saw Rebecca's name. "Look, you beat the high score!"

"Wow, that's impressive! No one has been able to beat Matthew's score in ages!" Luke said, high-fiving her.

"Thanks." Rebecca had a huge smile, which made me happy.

"I knew you could do it," I said, hugging her.

Suddenly, our watches beeped. "Squad 4 needed in the conference room," Luke said.

Rebecca stared at her watch, looking perplexed. "What's wrong?" I asked.

"Well, my watch says I'm needed at the conference room, but I'm not a Squad 4 member," she said.

"It might be a glitch," I began, "but it could be that they need you there too. Let's find out."

We hurried to the conference room. Mr. Truth stood outside the door. Rebecca stopped to talk to him while Squad 4 made its way into the room. I watched the door as we took our seats. A minute later, Rebecca walked in. I sent her a message on my watch, "What's up?"

She replied seconds later. "He said they may need my expertise on this mission."

"Agents, we have an urgent mission that needs completed within the next twenty-four hours. The FBI has been notified of a terrorist in our region who's threatened to bomb LA. They've asked for backup in locating him within the next twenty-four hours before this threat is fulfilled. I need

Matthew's squad for a quick research job and to get out into the field looking for this man. I need my squad on deck for tracking and monitoring our progress and the terrorist's movements. Finally, I need one more squad on backup to go in at a moment's notice if necessary." Mr. Truth looked around the room.

Agent Elijah raised his hand. "We'll take it."

"Thank you," Mr. Truth said with a nod. "All other Squad 4 members, while you aren't directly involved in this mission, you need to be on standby, but we also need your involvement in the most important way possible."

"Prayer," Luke jumped in with a nod.

Mr. Truth smiled. "Luke is correct. Let's bow. Luke, will you take this one?"

"My pleasure," he replied. We all bowed our heads. "Lord, thank You for giving us the opportunity to be in Truth Squad, fighting to defend the truth in our country and protect others. We ask You for protection and guidance in this mission. God, You can see the whole situation—You see us, You see what's going on, and You have the upper hand. Give us Your wisdom, safety, and peace. Use us for Your glory. In Jesus' name I pray, Amen."

Mr. Truth dismissed everyone but his squad, Matthew's squad, and Rebecca. "Okay, squads come up to the front," he said, nodding at Rebecca.

I stood up, and Rebecca came over to me. "I'm not sure why I'm needed," she whispered, following behind me.

"Didn't you see your high score in training?" I asked. "This mission is right up your alley."

Mr. Truth assigned each team with research. Matthew's team was assigned to look up any information we could on this terrorist and his threat, while Mr. Truth's team was assigned to research the LA area and find out why that was the target. "Does everyone understand what their team is doing?" he asked.

Rebecca raised her hand. "What do you want me to do?"

Mr. Truth looked surprised for a moment, then replied, "You're on Matthew's team for this mission."

"What?" Matthew's jaw dropped.

"Yes, Matthew," Mr. Truth replied sternly, handing him a file. "Now, we only have twenty-four hours, so get moving."

Matthew's glare at Mr. Truth was stone cold. Finally, he replied, "Yes, sir." He marched from the room, and we followed.

Why is he so angry about Rebecca joining us? I wondered as we walked toward the computer lab. *Is it because she beat his high score?*

"Luke, Sarah, you research the terrorist. Daniel and I will research his threat," Matthew said, handing Luke some papers.

"Um, you forgot another member on our team," Luke said, raising his eyebrows.

"She's not in our squad," Matthew replied coldly. Luke's jaw dropped indignantly. Before he could reply, Matthew marched away. Daniel shrugged, smiled awkwardly, and followed.

Luke stomped his foot, surprising me. "Of all the nerve! I can't believe him!"

"Luke, don't get distracted. We have a mission to focus on," Rebecca replied calmly. "Let's go!" She opened the door to the computer lab.

"You're right," Luke replied, straightening up.

We walked into the lab. I logged into a computer while Luke and Rebecca read over the papers Matthew had given him. "Rebecca, you research the name Cain Delmir. Find out whatever you can about anyone with that name."

"Got it," Rebecca said, taking a seat at the computer next to me.

"Sarah, this info says he was a drug dealer at one point. Can you look that up? See what else you can come across with him related to illegal activity. We have a blurry picture of him, so I'll scan this into our system and see if we can locate where he was last seen." Luke walked over to the scanner.

I started my search on Cain Delmir's activity as a drug dealer. "Oh, whoops," Rebecca gasped.

"What is it?" Luke asked, walking over from the scanner.

I glanced over at her monitor. "Your parole files?" I asked, surprised.

"I was trying to log in, and instead this came up. Honestly, I didn't know this was on this computer." I could see a hint of fear in Rebecca's eyes. *That's unusual,* I thought nervously.

"It's no problem," Luke replied, waving his hand. "Just close it out and try logging in again. I'll let Mr. Truth know what happened. We're all good."

Rebecca quickly retried logging in, and it worked. She breathed a sigh of relief, and her game-face returned. *I hope Luke is right about it not being a problem,* I thought, turning back to my research.

"Here's the information we gathered," Luke said, handing a USB to Mr. Truth. He plugged it into the conference room computer. "From what we discovered, Cain Delmir was formerly a drug dealer who was caught and spent some time in prison. He left the US two years ago, and in that time gone, there seems to be a connection between him and a small terrorist organization. He reappeared on the scene a month ago with the threat the FBI uncovered, and he was last spotted in Salt Lake City via a traffic camera." Luke pointed to the traffic camera picture. "And I have to say, I have some respect for this man's snack of choice."

"Is that a doughnut?" Daniel asked, grinning.

"Amen, brother," Luke said, nodding. We all laughed. "Hey, there really is no better snack, right?" Luke grinned.

Matthew stood up. "We didn't find much more information on his threat aside from what the FBI found, although we did find records of him buying different materials over the past two months that could be used to make a bomb."

"And the threat said that something explosive would take place in LA tomorrow at 10:30 PM, correct?" Mr. Truth asked.

"Yes, sir," Matthew replied.

Mr. Truth pulled up another slide on the computer. "Our research shows that tomorrow there is a large film festival going on in LA. A big part of this festival is the premiere of a live-action historical movie series depicting the history of the United States. This series has drummed up a lot of attention, and it seems to be the best bet for our man's target."

"So, what's the plan?" Matthew asked, folding his arms.

"My squad will be searching for Delmir while your squad flies into LA. Hopefully, we'll have a general idea of his location before you arrive. We'll split the search area into two quadrants. Matthew and Daniel, you'll take one half, and Luke and Rebecca will take the other. Sarah will be your pilot and your escape route should you need it. Sarah, you'll also be in contact with the FBI. Once Delmir is located, inform the FBI and aid them in whatever they're doing," Mr. Truth instructed. "Remember, the FBI is in charge of this one."

"Let's do this!" Luke said with a fist-pump.

*

I started the aircraft on a descent. "We're coming in for a landing," I said over the intercom. "This is going to be a steep descent, so I'd recommend buckling up." We were landing on a small flat ledge, half a mile from the base of the Skyline Mountains. *This needs to be extremely precise landing,* I thought, watching the gauges. I increased the angle of descent as far as I safely could while pulling back on the speed of the aircraft. As the ground came zooming toward us, I watched the dial for our altitude. *Three, two, one, pull up,* I told myself, quickly leveling out the descent. I began applying the breaks as we touched down. The aircraft came to a stop just before reaching the drop-off. "We've landed," I said.

"Coms check," Matthew said.

"Check," four voices chorused.

"Okay, we are good to go on this end. Base, do you copy?" Matthew asked.

"Copy."

"Let's go," Matthew said. "Luke, you two take the south quadrant. Daniel and I will take the north."

I watched them exit the aircraft and head down the mountain. *Lord, please keep them safe,* I prayed as I turned back to the controls.

For the next hour I circled LA, checking in on my team's progress. Finally, Rebecca and Luke checked in with good news. "We have a visual!" Luke said excitedly. He began sharing coordinates and descriptions.

I radioed our FBI contact and relayed the information.

"Thank you. We'll move in. Tell your team to stay in position," he said.

"Copy that," I replied. "Over and out." I switched back to my team. "FBI is moving in. Stay in position."

I waited for the next half hour, listening to my team as they kept tracking Delmir. Finally, the FBI contact checked back in. "We've apprehended our suspect. Please pick up your team and return to base. Thank you for your support. Over and out."

I sighed with relief. "Okay, team, meet me at the base of the Skyline, and I'll let down the ropes this time."

"Well done, squads," Mr. Truth said as we entered the conference room.

"We couldn't have asked for a smoother mission," Matthew said, taking his seat. "No hiccups."

Luke set a box of doughnuts on the table. "This calls for celebration! Please, have one!"

I smiled at Rebecca as we each grabbed a doughnut. We could always count on a doughnut celebration, no matter how the mission went.

We wrote up our report of the mission and sent our records to the FBI. It was two o'clock in the morning by the time we were dismissed from the conference room. As we stood up to leave, Rebecca raised her eyebrows at Luke. He nodded and walked over to Mr. Truth.

Rebecca and I walked out of the conference room and waited for Luke. "Is he telling Mr. Truth about accidentally finding the files?" I asked.

Rebecca nodded. "I hope he's not upset."

I'm more worried that Matthew stayed in the room for the discussion, I thought, noticing that he hadn't left the room. *He was so rude to Rebecca earlier today.*

We waited silently for Luke to come. The longer he took, the more nervous I felt. Finally, Luke walked out the door. His face was grim.

"What's wrong?" I asked.

He shrugged. "Mr. Truth said everything's cool. There's nothing to worry about, Rebecca." We both raised our eyebrows at Luke.

"You're twinning," Luke joked halfheartedly.

Rebecca sighed and checked her watch. "I'm headed to bed. Goodnight." She walked away.

I put my hands on my hips. "Okay, Luke. What's the real issue?"

He rolled his eyes. "Oh, Matthew just seems to have real trust issues. Like I said, Mr. Truth was totally cool with it. He said he understood the mistake, and the parole file shouldn't have been on that computer anyways, so he'll remove it. Matthew, on the other hand, thinks that constitutes an 'offense' and should be seriously reviewed." He sighed. "He was also still mad that Mr. Truth let Rebecca go on this mission as though she's a Squad 4 member when she's legally not allowed to be one." He shrugged. "Mr. Truth finally asked me to leave so they could talk it out."

I frowned. *Matthew can be so convincing. What if he talks Mr. Truth into seeing this as an offense? I mean, he is second-in-command. His opinions matter. A lot.*

"Quit worrying, Sarah. Mr. Truth is the president, not Matthew. And he's the one in charge of this parole test run, not Matthew. If Mr. Truth was fine with it, then we shouldn't worry." Luke smiled reassuringly.

I nodded. "Okay. I guess I'll head to bed too. Goodnight." I walked toward the dorm. While Luke seemed to have calmed down, I couldn't help but worry. *Lord, please don't let Matthew interfere with my sister being here,* I prayed.

CHAPTER 2

"You ready to meet the new agents today?" Rebecca asked as she stepped into view of the mirror.

I finished putting my hair in a ponytail. "Yup." I smiled. "It'll be cool to meet agents from another country. I've mostly worked with agents from the US."

Rebecca glanced at her watch. "It's almost eight. We'd better hurry if we want breakfast at the mess hall."

We quickly put on our shoes and headed out the door. "Do you know what time the Canadian agents are showing up?" I asked.

"Luke said he heard they were showing up around four o'clock." We picked up our pace and entered the mess hall just as Mr. Truth began the prayer. We grabbed our breakfast and sat down with Luke and Daniel.

"Good morning, slowpokes," Luke said, grinning at us.

"Oh, I don't think you can accuse us of being slowpokes. You're normally the one showing up last minute to breakfast," Rebecca retorted.

Luke tipped his chin up. "Well, that was then. We're talking about the here and now. I was early, wasn't I, Daniel?"

Daniel laughed. "If early means two minutes before eight, then, yes, you were early." He straightened. "Now, if we want to talk about who was really early, I happened to get here six minutes before eight."

As they continued their playful banter, I glanced around at the different tables. I didn't see Matthew anywhere. I sighed with relief and turned back to my food.

"What was that sigh for?" Daniel asked. I froze. *Why did he have to hear that? I* thought. Before I could reply, he continued, "Are you nervous about the new recruits coming?"

"I think it's going to be awesome!" Luke jumped in. "It's always a plus for Truth Squad members to hone their skills, especially on our amazing equipment. I have to say, I was pretty excited about some of those updates Matthew and I made to the training room. It was so awesome!" Luke's eyes were bright with excitement.

Rebecca nodded. "I was rather impressed myself."

We finished eating and cleared our table. "What are your plans for the day?" Rebecca asked as we left the mess hall.

"I have to fix one of our aircrafts. One of the pilots-in-training broke some landing gear yesterday. Isn't that wonderful?" I rolled my eyes.

"Of course," Rebecca replied with a grin. "At least it keeps you in business."

"True. What about you?"

"I have some classrooms to clean this morning, and then I have some online studies I need to work on."

"I guess I'll see you later, then," I said, turning toward the aircraft hangar.

"See ya!" Rebecca called as she headed toward the classrooms.

"Debris cleanup on runway. ETA for Jet 140—fifteen minutes." The loudspeaker clicked off.

I closed the engine hood on the aircraft I was fixing and climbed down the ladder. I watched the ground crew clearing the runway of debris as I carried the ladder to the storage room. I went to the empty jet hangar and helped finish the cleanup with the ground crew. We didn't want any debris on the runway or in the hangar. Even a small pebble could cause serious damage to an aircraft if it got sucked up into the engine.

As we finished, the loudspeaker clicked on again. "Clear the runway. Jet 140 coming in for a landing."

I walked to the far wall of the hangar, put my earplugs in, and turned to watch the jet land. Once the jet set down, it taxied into the hangar and powered down. The side door opened, and a ramp extended from the jet. The ground crew fastened the ramp to the floor, then the passengers began exiting the jet. I counted seventeen passengers, all of them dressed in blue Truth Squad uniforms with the Canadian flag sewn onto the left shoulder. Two security guards joined the group and began looking at IDs.

As I turned to walk away, I noticed one of the visitors staring at me. He had bright red hair and glasses. Not sure how to respond, I smiled awkwardly and looked away.

Weird, I thought as I left the hangar. *Maybe he was looking at someone else, and it just seemed like he was looking at me.* For some reason, I couldn't convince myself.

Mr. Truth introduced the visitors before dinner that evening. "We are excited to welcome seventeen agents for the next eight weeks. First, I'll introduce the director of our Canadian base, Agent Trammell." A man who looked to be in his fifties stood and waved. "With him are six Squad 4 agents.

Three of them attended Truth Academy many years ago, siblings Samuel, Elizabeth, and James Marks. The other three Squad 4 agents are Priscilla Chen, Noah Mills, and Joshua Smith." Each agent waved as their name was called.

"The other ten agents joining us are Squad 2 and Squad 3 members who are hoping to pass the test to move up another level this summer. Please use this dinner time to get to know one another," Mr. Truth encouraged. He prayed over the meal and then dismissed everyone to get in line.

Rebecca and I sat at our usual table with Luke and Daniel. A couple minutes after we sat down, two of the new agents walked over to our table. My eyes widened, recognizing the red-haired man from that afternoon.

"Can we join you?" the red head asked. He was short and muscular with bright green eyes. His hair was styled with a slight faux hawk, and he had black-rimmed glasses. He looked well put together compared to the agent next to him whose blond hair looked like it hadn't been brushed for days and whose uniform was disheveled.

"Sure!" Luke said excitedly, waving to the empty space next to him. "I'm Luke Mason."

"Ethan Cole," the red head replied, shaking his hand.

The blond-haired man paused before shaking Luke's hand. "Uh, Ryan Brown." He sat down quickly and started eating without making eye contact.

Luke motioned to Daniel. "This is my good buddy Daniel Reid. And these are the Sanders twins, Sarah and Rebecca."

Ethan sat down and flashed a crooked grin. "A pleasure to meet all of you. I must say, you two ladies are the most identical twins I've ever met."

I smiled. "We get that a lot."

"So, which squad are you guys in?" Daniel asked.

"We're both in Squad 2. We're hoping to move up to three while we're here, though," Ethan said, nodding. "I'm new to Truth Squad—joined the group in April, actually."

I raised my eyebrows. "That's a fast transition to Squad 2."

Ethan nodded. "I was formerly working for the Canadian government, so part of my training passed over."

I glanced at Daniel and raised an eyebrow. He shrugged. I hadn't heard of anyone being able to "pass over" training from a former job. Mr. Truth had always required people to go through training anyways. *He must mean he was able to pass tests quickly, not that he skipped them,* I thought, trying to give him the benefit of the doubt. *I mean, Rebecca went through the tests quickly herself. Not that quickly, though.*

Luke kept up the conversation easily, answering any questions Ethan had about our Truth Squad base while Ethan described the Canadian base. All the while, Ethan continually glanced over at Rebecca and me.

***

Over the next few days, Ethan and Ryan sat by our group at every meal. I noticed as the days went on that Luke and Daniel became less and less enthusiastic for the two to join us. While Ryan never spoke unless asked a question, Ethan dominated the conversation, aiming it primarily at Rebecca and me. Each morning at breakfast, he would have to clarify who was who. "You keep changing your outfits, and then I have to start all over again," Ethan would joke. By the third day, it was obvious that the handsome red head had his eye on Rebecca.

Thursday evening Luke and Daniel were late for dinner. "We thought you weren't coming," I said when they showed up at our table.

Daniel shrugged. "We had a deadline to meet for one of our projects." His smile looked forced.

"What was the project?" Rebecca asked, looking at Luke.

Luke's answer was unusually short. "Fixing some glitches in the training room." His normally cheerful face was grim as he attacked his food, eating each bite deliberately.

Ethan flashed his crooked grin at Rebecca. "We did our first training session today. I noticed your name on the high scores list. That must make you feel proud." Out of the corner of my eye, I saw Luke glaring at Ethan with a look I'd never seen before.

"Oh, thanks," Rebecca replied with a slight smile. "I wouldn't have gotten the score without my team, though. We had an elaborate plan that worked like a charm."

Luke's eyes lit up, and he smiled at Rebecca. "That was a fun training session! Rebecca had the idea to climb over the tops of the barricades instead of only staying on ground level, which was a game-changer."

"I'm amazed at your problem-solving skills," Ethan said, keeping his eyes on Rebecca. I saw Luke roll his eyes. "If you don't mind my asking, why don't you have a Squad 4 insignia on your uniform?"

I caught my breath. There was a look in Ethan's eye that felt out of place. *Why does he want to know so much about my sister?* I thought, nervously.

"I just haven't been at Truth Squad long enough to pass the Squad 4 test yet," she replied good-naturedly. *Well, that is technically true,* I thought.

Ethan raised his eyebrows. "But Sarah is in Squad 4."

"Uh, our parents were divorced," I jumped in. "She lived with Dad in another state, and I lived with mom near Truth Academy."

"I see," Ethan said, raising an eyebrow.

His interest, or rather his look of distrust, in my answer made me nervous. *What is with these questions?* I thought.

Ethan looked like he was ready to ask another question when Luke jumped up. "Rebecca, Sarah, I could use your help with our project." Luke smiled, but his eyes were fiery. He picked up his plate. I was surprised to see food still left on it.

"I thought you said your project had to be finished by a deadline," Rebecca said, raising her eyebrows.

Luke lowered his eyebrows, his lips tightening into a frustrated line. I elbowed Rebecca and made a face while nodding at Luke. She nodded slightly. "We'd be happy to help you guys." She grabbed her plate and stood up. "Let's go!"

I picked up my empty plate and smiled at Ethan and Ryan. "Have a good evening."

"And you as well," Ethan replied. His crooked grin was gone.

Luke and Daniel's project only took ten minutes to finish. "Thanks for your help," Daniel said as we put everything back in order. "This would have taken much longer if it was just Luke and me."

Luke had stayed unusually quiet the whole time. "You okay?" Rebecca asked as he closed and locked the control panel.

Luke swallowed. "Just fine." He brushed dust off the panel door and refused to make eye contact.

I giggled awkwardly. "You probably shouldn't lie to an expert people-reader like Rebecca. She's practically a human lie-detector." Rebecca rolled her eyes.

There was an awkward silence. "Well, it's just that," Daniel sighed, "well, it's those new agents."

Figured, I thought.

Luke shook his head. "I probably shouldn't be so upset with them. We are supposed to be welcoming to them and all, but—but they get on my nerves!" Daniel nodded his head in agreement.

Luke ran his fingers through his hair. "I'm sorry, guys. I shouldn't have been so grumpy this evening. Thanks for your help, Rebecca and Sarah."

"You're welcome," we replied in unison.

Rebecca glanced at her watch. "Seven o'clock. What are your plans this evening?"

Daniel's jaw dropped. "Seven! Oh, man! I forgot I'm on clean up in the mess hall today. I've got to go! See you later!" He rushed out of the room.

Luke laughed. "Maybe I should help Daniel since I'm the one who dragged you all to help me. But first, I'm starving. I'm going to get a doughnut. Would either of you like one?"

Rebecca grinned. "Why not?"

After grabbing our doughnuts, we headed to our room. We stopped in the lobby of the dorms and got our mail from our box. "What are your plans tonight?" I asked, closing the mailbox.

"I have some online studies to finish tonight," Rebecca replied as we climbed the stairs.

"I have some paperwork to finish." I grabbed my key and unlocked our door. I pushed it open and walked inside. While we called the building the girls' dorms, the rooms on the second floor were more like apartments. Each apartment had a mini kitchen with a small fridge, microwave, and sink connected to a small living room area and a full bath. Some apartments had two bedrooms, like ours, while others just had one.

I turned to face Rebecca, trying to hide my grin. "Luke seemed rather jealous today, didn't he?"

Rebecca rolled her eyes and slammed the door. "Whatever."

"I think he likes you!" I teased, setting the mail down on the counter. A pillow promptly hit me in the head. "Hey!"

Rebecca shrugged. "Just trying to knock some sense into you." Her face was flushed with embarrassment.

"You never know!" I said with a wink.

"Give me the mail," Rebecca said, grabbing the stack of envelopes off the table. She sat down on the couch and started tearing them open, intensely studying each one.

I think she likes Luke, too. She just doesn't want to admit it, I thought, but decided to drop the subject. *At least she doesn't like Ethan. He's starting to give me the creeps.* I went to my computer and sat down to check my email.

"What?"

I turned around, startled by Rebecca's exclamation. "What is it?"

"This letter—it's odd," she replied. "It says, 'Better watch your back. You never know who's after you.' That's it."

I felt a shiver go up my spine. "That's creepy." I walked over to Rebecca and looked the note over. It was typed on standard printer paper, and the envelope was also typed. "Maybe it's a practical joke," I suggested, but my mind was running all the worst possibilities.

Rebecca shook her head. "Maybe, but it's rather coincidental if you ask me."

"What do you mean?"

"Mr. Zaiden used to say that all the time—those exact words."

Mr. Zaiden, Rebecca's former boss, had been an assassin and was secretly training Rebecca to become one as well. He'd trained Rebecca to be the top-notch spy she was and used her to perform undercover operations to take over a power company, steal government security information, and learn how to use an EMP. If Rebecca hadn't decided to do the right thing and blow his operation, no one knew just how elaborate or destructive his plans would have been.

Rebecca looked the letter over again. "Let's check for fingerprints in the morning."

"Do... do you think he's after you?" My heart started racing at the thought of it. Facing Mr. Zaiden again was the last thing I wanted to do.

"I don't know how he could be—he's under such high surveillance. But I don't know why someone else would send me this exact phrase. It was Code Fifteen, and he said it often when I first started working for him." She rested her chin in her hands. Her face was determined, the look she got in the heat of a mission. "We'll figure this out in the morning."

I nodded and swallowed hard. *Is an assassin out to kill my sister?*

r

Rebecca shook me awake the next morning. "Sarah, get up!" She shoved me out of bed.

I fell to the ground with a thud and groaned. "Rebecca, what was that for?" I looked up at my clock. "It's only five forty-five! Why are you up this early?"

I tried to climb back into bed, but Rebecca pulled me onto my feet. "We're going to go check that letter for fingerprints! I waited to wake you up until I was ready to go. Now go get ready, sleepyhead!"

She flipped on the lights, blinding me. I groaned again.

"I hate getting up early." I grabbed my outfit from the closet and went to change.

It was six o'clock by the time I was ready to go. "Here's some coffee," Rebecca said, handing me a to-go mug. She smirked. "I know the secret to getting you up early."

I smiled and sipped my favorite pumpkin-flavored coffee. "You know me too well."

We quietly left the dorm building and headed to the computer lab. "Why so early?" I asked quietly. Our voices seemed to carry so much farther when there were so few people up.

"We'll have the lab to ourselves, for one. And secondly, if this is a serious threat, I don't want a thousand people knowing about it. That would be too dangerous for everyone." Rebecca's game face was on, and I knew that she didn't think this was a practical joke. My heart rate started rising.

Because we were up so early, the computer lab was still locked. *I'm glad I'm a technician,* I thought as I grabbed my keys from my pocket. *Otherwise, we wouldn't be getting in.* "You thought this through, didn't you?" I said, opening the door. "Without me, you couldn't have gotten in."

"And it would've been suspicious for me to steal your keys, wouldn't it?" Rebecca said, grinning. "Besides, I enjoy waking you up early." I rolled my eyes.

We got out the fingerprint scanner and plugged it into the main computer. I logged in and ran the letter through the scanner. Two fingerprints from the database showed up—mine and Rebecca's.

"Figured," Rebecca said, nodding. "Let's try the envelope."

I ran the scanner again. This time, three fingerprints showed up—mine, Rebecca's, and the mail lady's. "Well, that helpful," I said sarcastically. I reached to turn off the scanner.

"Wait! Look!" Rebecca pointed at the screen. On the corner of the envelope, half of a fingerprint was illuminated. Rebecca zoomed in on the print and compared it with our fingerprints and the mail lady's fingerprints. "It doesn't match," she said excitedly.

"And it either isn't in our database, or there's not enough of the print for the computer to recognize it."

"Well, let's test it." Rebecca put on some plastic gloves and grabbed a sticky note from the desk. "Put half of your fingerprint on this paper. Let's see if the scanner picks it up."

I pressed half my thumb onto the note and held it for a few seconds, then Rebecca placed it on the scanner. We held our breath, waiting for the scan to load. Finally, it pulled up. The screen read: "Insufficient data. Possible match: Sarah Sanders."

I raised my eyebrows. "That is a specific answer."

"So, it should have said 'insufficient data' for that other fingerprint and given a possibility if it was one of the agents here?"

"It seems so."

Rebecca saved a picture of the unidentified half-print and sent it to herself. "You put the scanner away while I erase our tracks," Rebecca said, and began typing.

This must be serious if she's worried about not getting anyone else involved, I thought, placing the scanner in the cabinet. *I hope this note isn't from Mr. Zaiden.*

Click.

I froze. Someone was unlocking the computer lab door. I glanced at my watch. *Six-thirty.* "Rebecca, they're unlocking the lab for the day. We need to hurry," I whispered.

Rebecca signed out. "Done. Let's go." She motioned toward the back door. I followed her through the exit. I glanced behind us as we walked around the outside of the building, then ran into someone. I jumped back.

"Luke!" Rebecca cried, then sighed with relief. "What are you doing back here?"

"Uh, Matthew was unlocking the front door to the lab as I was walking past, and he asked me to check the back door because he thought he heard something. So, I guess the real question is, what are you two doing?" Luke folded his arms, but he couldn't keep a straight face.

Rebecca opened her mouth to answer when the back door to the lab opened again. "Luke, what's taking you so long?" Matthew called.

"We'll tell you later," Rebecca whispered. "Just cover for us. Please."

Luke caught the urgency in Rebecca's voice. He nodded and jogged over to the back door. "Coming!" he called. He looked back at us and winked before going inside.

"Do you think Matthew saw us inside?" I asked worriedly.

"I doubt it," Rebecca replied. "Let's just hope he doesn't check the security cameras."

CHAPTER 3

"Sarah."

I jumped at Matthew's voice. "Yes?" I asked, trying to keep my voice from shaking. My heart raced as I waited for his answer.

"We need someone to run the training room this afternoon for the Junior Squad. Are you up for that?" His voice sounded calm without a hint of suspicion. I nodded, and he continued, "Great! They're starting at 2:30."

"Okay, I'll be there." I watched him walk away, then sighed with relief.

I'd spent the whole morning looking over my shoulder, trying to avoid Matthew. I tried to tell myself that we didn't actually do anything wrong. I had access to the computer lab at any time since I was a Squad 4 technician. We didn't break in, and we didn't use any off-limits equipment. But I still couldn't keep my heart from racing every time I saw Matthew.

At lunch, Rebecca told me I looked suspicious. "Thanks a lot," I replied sarcastically.

She rolled her eyes. "You're constantly glancing around, and you jump whenever people talk to you. Just act natural."

I sighed. "Easy for you to say."

Luke sat down at our table, grinning sneakily. "So, when do you tell me what you two are up to?"

Rebecca looked over my shoulder and shook her head. I glanced behind me and saw Ethan and Ryan headed to our table. Luke rolled his eyes. "Let's meet after I finish running the junior training session," I whispered. Luke and Rebecca nodded in unison.

The moment Ethan and Ryan sat down, Rebecca launched into questions. "You guys haven't told us much about yourselves. Where did you grow up?" She raised her eyebrows and began twirling her hair around her finger.

Ethan looked surprised. "Well, uh, we both grew up in Toronto." He glanced at Ryan.

"Yeah," Ryan said, fidgeting.

"So, you knew each other growing up?" Rebecca asked.

Ryan opened his mouth, but Ethan cut in. "Yes. We went to the same school."

Ethan looked directly at Ryan. Ryan kept fidgeting. "Uh, yeah. So, um, we, like, hung out a lot in middle school and stuff." Ryan looked down at his plate, messing with his food. "We both, uh, played basketball."

"Cool! I played basketball, too. What positions did you play?" Luke asked. I was surprised to hear him contribute to a conversation.

Ryan shrugged. "I played point guard."

Luke kept asking Ryan basketball questions, and Ryan began to get into the conversation. The whole time, Ethan kept eerily silent. *Weird that they would have both played basketball, yet Ryan's the only one talking,* I thought.

Rebecca finished her food and motioned for me to follow her. We quietly left the mess hall. "Strange that Ryan didn't know much about growing up with Ethan, don't you think?" she asked.

"Maybe," I replied. "But he's not been one to talk much, so he could have just been nervous."

"True. But did you notice how eager he was to talk about basketball? That seemed odd, too." Rebecca shook her head. "There's something interesting about those two, but I can't figure out what it is. I think we need to keep an eye on them."

At 2:30 I went to the control room for the junior training. I watched through the control room window as the ten Junior Squad members entered the training room. They were so much fun to watch as they hopped up and down and talked to one another excitedly. *So much more fun than boring Squad 4 agents. We just walk in and line up,* I thought as I turned to the controls.

The training was an undercover mission, where they had to work together to retrieve the flag without being detected. I pressed play on the recorded instructions and set the program to level one. Once the teens were in place, I pressed start. The two-minute countdown began. Through the sound system I could hear the excited teens talking as they huddled together to strategize. After a minute, they broke off into two groups, one headed down the left side of the room and the other down the right. The countdown finished, and the start signal sounded.

After a few failed attempts, the Junior Squad finally retrieved the flag and successfully brought it over to the starting point. I powered off the program and turned up the lights in the training room. "Well done!" I said into the loudspeaker. "Please take off your training equipment and leave them in their proper bins." I watched as the teens slowly began leaving.

Jonathan, Hope, and Faith were still in the training room talking after the rest of the teens had left. I smiled and giggled quietly as they excitedly rehashed how the mission went, assessing what they said "went awesome" and wondering how to do even better next time.

Reluctantly, I pressed the button for the loudspeaker. "Alright, you three, it's time to head out."

Faith and Hope turned and looked up at the control window. They smiled sheepishly. "Sorry."

Suddenly, an alarm sounded. "What's that?" Faith cried.

"SECURITY LOCKDOWN," the electronic voice boomed. I heard a loud bang. I turned to see the metal security doors slammed shut.

I heard Hope scream, and Jonathan cried, "Sarah, shut down the simulator!"

I looked back through the window. The training room was running! *This isn't supposed to happen. It's supposed to shut down with the lockdown!* I thought, typing the force-stop code into the control panel. I hit enter.

"Sarah! It's not turning off, and we're trapped in here!" Jonathan cried, this time sounding panicked.

My heart was pounding. The control panel wasn't working, and the training room was out of control. All the systems were on in the training room—the floor was moving, the room was shaking with fake explosions, the heat was on full-blast. The lasers that could shock you, used only for Squad 4 agents, were firing everywhere.

What do I do? I worried. *Lord, please help me stay calm!* I closed my eyes, trying to think through the blaring alarms.

The electrical panel! I raced down the ladder to the training room door. I opened the panel outside the door and found the breaker. I pulled at the handle, but it was jammed.

"What? No, not now!" I cried, pulling as hard as possible.

"Sarah!" I heard the three teens pounding on the metal door.

"Get us out!" Faith yelled.

I looked closer at the handle. There was a metal pin stuck in the joint. *My tool kit,* I thought, and sprinted back up the ladder to the control panel. I grabbed my pliers and ran back to the breaker. *Please let this work,* I prayed, pulling at the pin. I could hear the training room shaking and the screaming teens pounding on the other side of the door. Finally, the pin pulled loose. I grabbed the handle and shoved it down. The panel sparked, then the lights turned off. The sounds in the training room died down, and Jonathan yelled, "It worked!"

I breathed a sigh of relief. With the power shut off, the security door couldn't be locked by the electronic magnets. I pulled it up and let the three teens out.

"That was insane!" Faith said as they ran through the door.

Hope had tears in her eyes as she grabbed my arm. "I was so scared," she whispered.

I hugged her. "Me too."

"What happened?" Jonathan asked seriously.

"I don't know," I replied, shaking my head. *But I'm pretty sure it wasn't an accident,* I thought grimly. *That pin kept the training room from shutting down like it was supposed to. That was intentional.*

We tried to open the door to the outside of the building, but it was locked with a regular bolt, so we had to wait for the security team to let us out. After all the excitement, the teens got the giggles and began telling jokes and laughing at everything, whether it was funny or not. Their laughter helped me calm down. Eventually, I remembered I could use my watch to contact help.

Why didn't I do that earlier? I thought, stepping back from the teens. I pressed the radio button, but nothing happened. *Strange.* I tried again. Nothing. I tried to send a typed message to Rebecca, but the screen flashed "no signal." *How is there no signal in here?* I thought, frustrated. *My watch is connected to satellite, so the lockdown has nothing to do with it.*

"Sarah." I jumped as Hope tapped my arm. "Are you okay?"

"Yes, you just startled me." I smiled.

"Are you contacting someone to open the door?" Jonathan asked, slight concern showing on his face again.

"There's no connection, so we'll just have to wait," I explained, feeling uneasy. *Why isn't there connection? This is weird,* I worried. I saw the looks of concern on the teens' faces, so I decided to worry about my watch later. "Do you guys like riddles?" I asked.

"Oh, yes! I know a great riddle!" Faith said, grinning as she rubbed her hands together.

The mood lightened again as we told riddles and more jokes. Fifteen minutes later, the security guards unlocked the door, and we walked out of the dark building into the sunlight.

"Freedom!" Jonathan yelled, charging from the building. He didn't get far before his dad stopped him with a bear hug.

"Are you okay, son?" Mr. Truth asked. I could see worry lines on his forehead.

"Yes," he replied, looking embarrassed as he tried to push out of his dad's arms.

Mr. Truth laughed. "Hey, I'm your dad. I get to embarrass

you all I want." He let him go with a friendly nudge. "I want you to go straight home, understand?"

"Yes, sir," Jonathan replied, walking away.

Mr. Truth turned to me. "Sarah, I want to see you in my office."

I swallowed hard and nodded.

🔫

"Take a seat," Mr. Truth said as he walked behind his desk.

I sat down and placed my hands in my lap, trying to calm my racing heart. *I didn't do anything wrong, so I don't need to be worried,* I told myself. But part of me wondered, *What if Mr. Truth blames me anyways?* I looked up at Mr. Truth, waiting for him to sit down. He stood behind his desk, staring out the window. He opened his mouth, closed it, ran his fingers through his hair, and then stood still again.

I couldn't stand the awkward silence anymore. "Sir," I said, my voice shaking.

"Hmm." Mr. Truth kept his gaze fixed on the window, his voice sounding far off. He finally blinked, shook his head, and looked at me. "Sarah, we take the safety of the youth at Truth Academy very seriously."

"Yes, sir."

He paused again, then threw up his hands. "What happened?"

"Sir, I don't know," I replied, shaking my head. "The kids finished the training session, and Jonathan, Hope, and Faith were still talking after the others had left. I told them to head out, and then suddenly the system went into security lockdown."

Mr. Truth paused and glanced at my watch. "Why didn't you contact help?"

"Once I got the kids out of the training room, I tried to call for help to get the door open, but there wasn't any signal."

"Isn't your watch connected to satellite?"

"Yes."

"Hmm." Mr. Truth shook his head. "That doesn't make any sense. There should always be satellite signal on our campus." Mr. Truth sighed and sat down. "Sarah, I know you, and I know you're not careless, but the security lockdown only affected the training room. Is there any possibility that you accidentally hit a button or something?"

I thought for a minute, going over everything I did. "Not that I can think of. I've run the training program so many times I could do it in my sleep. I don't know how I could have done something unusual like that."

Mr. Truth nodded. "Can you think of any other way that a lockdown could have accidentally happened?"

"Not unless a lockdown took place throughout the whole campus. But even if that had happened, it wouldn't explain why everything went haywire."

"Yeah, and that's what worries me."

I thought for a minute. "Matthew and Luke recently did some programming for the training room. Is it possible something was messed up then?"

"Could be," Mr. Truth said slowly, but he didn't look like he was buying it.

"You think someone hacked it?"

He sighed. "The training room locks down and goes haywire, and you can't get ahold of anyone from the outside to let you out? And it happens when only four people are there? It seems suspicious, but I don't know why anyone would do it. There seems to be no reason for it."

"Unless they wanted to prove they could," I said, my

eyes widening. *I wonder if this has anything to do with the threat Rebecca got.* I thought for a minute. "Maybe we should search the training building for a jamming device," I suggested. "If we can find one, it might lead us to whoever hacked us."

"*If* it was hacked," Mr. Truth replied. "Let's not get ahead of ourselves."

I nodded. "Yes, sir." My thoughts raced back through the incident, and the image of the pin stuck in the electrical panel flashed through my mind. "Sir, there's one other detail I need to mention."

Mr. Truth raised his eyebrows. "Yes?"

I took a deep breath and explained about the pin jamming the breaker handle. "I think that points to this being intentional." I swallowed nervously, noticing Mr. Truth's expression didn't change.

"Sarah, I want you to write up a report on what happened today. I'm going to look at the security camera footage and see if I can spot anything unusual. I'll have Matthew look for any evidence in the training building, see if there's any jamming devices or anything else out of place. I'll also have him check on that pin." Mr. Truth stood up and grabbed a file from his cabinet. He handed it to me. "Turn this in directly to me, and don't leave my office until it's complete."

"Yes, sir." I watched as Mr. Truth sighed and left the room. *He's really concerned about this,* I thought, opening the file and taking out the form. *So am I. It all makes no sense. Why would someone hack the system, sabotage the breaker, and block my communications while teenagers were there? Does this have anything to do with the threat Rebecca received? If so, then why am I involved in all this?* I shook my head and grabbed a pen. *It doesn't make sense.*

I signed the file, stood up, and stretched. Suddenly, the office door slammed open. "Sarah."

I jumped. "Yes, Matthew?" The sternness of his voice and the look on his face made me nervous.

"Mr. Truth and I looked at the security footage from today, and you and Rebecca sneaked into the computer lab this morning." He crossed his arms. "What do you have to say about that?"

I forgot about that, I thought. "Mr. Truth said he was going to have you check the training room for a jamming device," I said, raising my eyebrows.

"I did, and we found one in the control room. But that has nothing to do with my question. Why did you sneak into the computer lab?"

"Well, it wasn't sneaking in because I have full access to the lab as a technician." I put my hands on my hips.

Matthew's shoulders drooped for a second. "That's right," he said slowly, "but that doesn't explain Rebecca." He raised his eyebrows. "What was she doing in the lab at six in the morning?"

"That's not really that early," I replied.

"Don't avoid the question."

I sighed, not sure how to reply. "It's none of your business," I said lamely.

Matthew rolled his eyes. "Okay, I'll spell this out for you. You and Rebecca go into the computer lab at 6 a.m. this morning. At 2:30 p.m., the security cameras turned off in the training room and remained off until Mr. Truth turned them back on ten minutes ago. There was no other unusual activity in any of the footage. That makes the two of you suspects."

"What? Matthew, why would I sabotage the training center

when kids are in there? And when I was trapped inside too? That doesn't make any sense."

"Yes, but what about Rebecca? Hacking is her thing."

"She wouldn't do that either."

Matthew shrugged. "I think you all put too much faith in her. She was a hardened agent for an assassin. She's not trustworthy."

"That was two years ago. She's obviously changed. She's a believer now. People can change," I argued.

"Really?" Matthew said. "She's also an excellent actress."

"What about the pin?" I asked, raising my eyebrows. "You were supposed to be checking on that, too."

Matthew tilted his chin haughtily. "What pin?" My stomach dropped as a smug grin crossed his face. "I found no sign of a pin to keep the breaker handle from functioning."

"But it was there!" I said, my voice pitching higher than I intended.

"So, someone could have removed the evidence while you were meeting with Mr. Truth? That would be pretty easy for Rebecca to do," Matthew said, folding his arms. "I'm not removing her as a suspect just because you're her twin."

I sighed and shook my head. *Why is he so frustratingly against my sister?* I wondered. I decided to change the subject. "Did you find any footage around the placement of the jamming device?"

Matthew's eyes widened. "No." He paused awkwardly. "I didn't think to look for that."

Maybe because you're so focused on finding Rebecca guilty, I thought, but decided to keep it to myself. We stood silently for a moment, Matthew staring off into space. "So," I said slowly, "are you going to look into that?"

Matthew jerked his head up and glared at me, raising

his voice. "Yes, I will. But just remember, your sister is still a suspect."

"Just because we were in the computer lab this morning?" I said, crossing my arms.

"Not just because of that. It's also because she's—"

"...an expert hacker. Right. But she would have no motive. And to throw a wrench in your reasoning, we both were in the computer lab, so if she had been hacking the training room, I would have known." I raised my eyebrows.

Matthew tilted his chin up. "Exactly. Which is why you are also a suspect in my book."

"What?" Anger boiled up inside of me. Before I could think up a response, the office door slammed open again.

"What is going on?" Mr. Truth asked, stepping into the office. "I can hear you arguing from down the hall."

Mr. Truth's tone of voice made me feel like I was being scolded by a parent. I opened my mouth to answer, but Matthew cut in. "She's upset that Rebecca is a suspect for the training room fiasco, which she shouldn't be. It's only natural that we would..."

"Matthew." Mr. Truth's stern voice silenced Matthew's haughty one. "We haven't placed anyone as suspects as of now. We haven't even completely ruled out that this was a malfunction in the system. I don't want another word said about who is a suspect and who's not until we have looked further into the details." He raised his eyebrows at Matthew. "The rule is you are innocent until proven guilty."

"But you saw the footage of those two sneaking into the computer lab!" Matthew said, pointing at me.

"Yes, I did, but I'm not jumping to any conclusions just yet, and neither should you." Mr. Truth turned to face me. "Did you finish the report?"

"Yes, sir," I replied, picking it up off the desk and handing the file to him.

"Thank you. You are both excused from my office."

"But sir," Matthew began, but Mr. Truth shook his head. Matthew sighed, frustration written across his face. He whirled around and marched angrily out the door. I followed.

"Sarah." I turned back to face Mr. Truth. He sighed. "Matthew was far too hasty to come in here and accuse you and Rebecca. But the fact is, the footage of you two hurrying into the computer lab this morning and sneaking out the back door does appear rather odd." He raised his eyebrows.

I nodded. "Yes, sir."

He stared at me for a moment. I wasn't sure whether to explain the threat we were looking into, or to wait and let Rebecca decide when to tell him. Our decision to sneak into the computer lab so early was beginning to feel like a dumb move, especially since we didn't know whether the threat was serious or not.

Finally, Mr. Truth cleared his throat. "And that pin you mentioned? There's no evidence to prove that it was there. We couldn't find the pin, and the cameras weren't working during the incident."

I bit my lip and nodded. Mr. Truth's face was serious, almost distrusting. *Does he think I made it up to get out of trouble?* I thought, feeling nervous and concerned.

Mr. Truth paused, then nodded. "See you later."

I quickly made my way out of the building. My mind raced as I headed toward my dorm. *Why didn't I take that pin with me? And why didn't I tell Rebecca to wait until later to go to the computer lab?* I thought, mad at myself. I was surprised at Matthew's hasty judgment of Rebecca, but I was even more concerned about Mr. Truth's serious tone regarding our trip to the computer lab and the missing pin. *He wouldn't really believe Rebecca would endanger the lives of teenagers, would he?*

I ran up the stairs to our dorm and pushed the door open. Rebecca looked up from her laptop. "That took a while."

I walked over and plopped down on the chair beside her. "Matthew is convinced you are the primary suspect in the training room mishap."

Rebecca's eyes widened. "Me?"

"He saw the footage of us sneaking into the computer lab this morning and decided that made us suspects. Mr. Truth said Matthew was jumping to conclusions, but he also said that the footage did look suspicious." I shook my head. "We should have never done that. What if the threat you got is just a joke?"

Rebecca rested her chin in her hand. "Well, it could have been. I've been studying the envelope, and I think it was sent by someone here on campus because there weren't any postage or mail stamps. But what is concerning is that the phrase matches exactly what Mr. Zaiden would say, and there were no fingerprints besides ours and the mail lady's. Why would someone go to all the trouble of writing a note like that, being careful not to get their fingerprints on it, when it was all a joke?" She looked at me expectantly.

I shrugged. "Well, there was one fingerprint that the computer couldn't identify," I pointed out.

"That's true. But if the computer couldn't identify it, then I think it's even less likely that it was a joke. Someone not in the Truth Squad database has somehow been able to send me a letter as though they are from Truth Squad. I think that's unusual." She closed her laptop.

I sighed. "Matthew also thinks we're suspicious because I told them that the breaker was jammed with a pin, but when they investigated, they couldn't find any evidence of that happening."

"They think you lied about it?"

"I'm not sure." Suddenly, I remembered our conversation with Luke at lunch. "We were supposed to meet with Luke to tell him why we snuck into the lab."

Rebecca's eyes widened. "That's right! I forgot." She stood up. "I'll message him and see if he can still meet. I think it would be good to let him know what's going on. Maybe he'll have some insight we haven't thought of yet." She grabbed her phone off the counter and texted him.

I leaned back in my chair and waited, my mind whirling. *Are we being too hasty? Too jumpy?* I shivered as the memory of Mr. Zaiden holding a knife above Rebecca's face flashed through my mind. I shook my head quickly and tried to focus on something else. No matter how hard I tried to forget that memory, it kept resurfacing, filling me with anxiety. *I do not want to face that again.*

Rebecca's phone dinged. She glanced down at the screen. "He says he'll meet us at the walking paths." She slipped her phone into her back pocket. "You ready?"

I stood up and nodded. "Let's go."

We met Luke at the head of the walking path. "Wonderful day for a walk, don't you think?" he asked, grinning.

Rebecca smiled back. "Of course."

We started down the bark-chipped path that meandered through the trees on the far side of the Truth Squad campus. Luke and Rebecca kept up the small talk, I assumed so that they could fill time until Rebecca felt no one could be eavesdropping.

I let my mind drift off as I glanced around us. The walking paths were my favorite place to be on campus. The path was beautiful with the surrounding evergreen trees, rhododendron bushes, and ferns. There were also occasional patches of blackberry bushes which, when ripe, always called Luke on a snack detour.

Rebecca and Luke started slowing their pace. I glanced behind me at the buildings in the distance. No one else was on the walking paths.

"Do you think we're good?" Luke asked, nodding his head in the direction of the buildings. Rebecca and I nodded in unison. Luke rubbed his hands together, grinning. "So, ready for the interrogation?"

Rebecca rolled her eyes. "Sure."

Luke cleared his throat dramatically. "So, what were you two doing at the computer lab this morning, at approximately..." he paused, "uh, before seven?"

"We got there just after six," Rebecca corrected.

He grinned sheepishly. "I guess I wasn't totally prepared for this interrogation. I didn't even know what time you guys showed up at the lab."

"It probably wouldn't have been suspicious if it was anyone else at the lab. It's only suspicious because everyone knows I hate getting up that early," I said, frustrated.

Luke laughed. "That's so true. I remember that one time we had to leave unexpectedly at two in the morning, and you were supposed to be our pilot. Matthew thought we were for sure gonna die. You were so mad about getting up that early."

"We were just fine. No one died." I felt my face getting red. I didn't like to be reminded of that embarrassing day. "Anyways, back to the reason we're here."

Rebecca pulled the note out of her pocket. "I received a weird note in the mail yesterday. We were running it through the fingerprint scanner to find out who sent it." She handed the note to Luke.

Luke read the note aloud. "Better watch your back. You never know who's after you." He raised an eyebrow. "That's odd. Do you think it's a joke?"

Rebecca shook her head. "These are the exact words for Code Fifteen; Mr. Zaiden used to say it all the time when I first started working for him."

"Could there be any possibility that it's just a coincidence? That it's a practical joke that just sounds like something Mr. Zaiden would say?" I asked, hoping someone would say there was.

Luke shrugged. "Maybe. What did you find with the fingerprint scanner?"

"We found half a fingerprint that the database couldn't identify. The rest of the fingerprints belonged to the mail lady and us. Whoever sent this letter was careful not to leave clues behind, which is what makes me even more suspicious," Rebecca said.

"That is odd. But why did you two sneak in early in the morning?"

I shrugged. "Good question."

Rebecca sighed. "I don't know. I guess I was thinking I didn't want everyone to know about this note. If it was a real threat, it would be dangerous for everyone to know, and if it wasn't a threat, it would be embarrassing for everyone to know I was worried about it." She shook her head. "Instead, I made us look extra suspicious."

"And now Matthew thinks we snuck into the lab so that Rebecca could sabotage the training room," I told Luke, quickly filling him in on the rest of the training room incident details.

"Wow," Luke said, raising his eyebrows. He paused,

glancing at Rebecca. "Sometimes I think Matthew just has it in for you, no matter what you do. I mean, when you got that new training record, he was so upset about it he tried to say you cheated somehow, but Mr. Truth wouldn't hear it."

Rebecca rubbed her forehead. "I can't blame him, I guess. It feels like a lot of people don't trust me with my history."

I placed my hand on her shoulder. "We trust you. God has changed you. It's been evident in your actions."

Luke nodded. "And Mr. Truth believes in you, too, which is good since he's the president." He grinned. "But seriously, Rebecca, God's in the business of changing people. I mean, look at Paul, one of the greatest dudes in the New Testament. He had quite the record before Christ changed his life, but then he ended up being an unstoppable force for the spread of the gospel. That's pretty awesome, and pretty encouraging."

Rebecca smiled and nodded. We walked on a few steps in silence. "So, what do you think about this threat? Should we take it seriously? Should we show Mr. Truth? Should we ignore it?"

"Hmm." Luke pondered that for a moment. "It seems unlikely that it's a practical joke, but I also don't know if Mr. Truth would take it seriously. On the other hand, we don't want to do anything that would make you look even more suspicious."

"I think we should remain on the cautious side," I said. "It might be best to take it to Mr. Truth, even if he doesn't take it seriously."

"But what if Matthew sees this as a cover-up for the training room fiasco?" Rebecca asked.

"I think we should ignore Matthew for now. Sarah's right. We want to be cautious. Let's take it to Mr. Truth. If he thinks it's serious, great. We'll just tell him not to make the threat known to the whole campus since that could be dangerous. And if he doesn't take us seriously," Luke nodded dramatically, "we'll do our own investigation."

⚐

After dinner, Luke messaged Mr. Truth and asked if we could show him something. Mr. Truth agreed, and the three of us hurried to his office.

"Do you have the note?" I asked as we reached his office.

"In my pocket." Rebecca slipped her hand into her pocket and pulled out a piece of paper.

Luke knocked on the door, and Mr. Truth called for us to enter. "What brings you to my office?" he asked cheerfully.

Luke stood up straight. "Rebecca received an anonymous note yesterday that she was concerned about, and we thought it might be best to show it to you." He nodded at Rebecca, and she handed the paper to Mr. Truth.

Mr. Truth unfolded the paper. His eyebrows lowered in confusion. "Is it in invisible ink?"

"No," Rebecca replied slowly, raising an eyebrow. "Why?"

Mr. Truth turned the paper around. It was blank. *Oh, no, I* thought. *What happened?*

"Is this a joke?" he asked, still looking confused.

"No, sir," Rebecca replied quickly. "The real note must have fallen out of my pocket, or something. It said, 'Better watch your back. You never know who's after you.' I was concerned about it because that was a code Mr. Zaiden used to use when I worked for him."

"And the reason we were in the computer lab this morning was to run the fingerprint scanner to see who sent the note. We thought if it was a joke, then the fingerprint scanner would tell us who sent it because if it was someone here, their fingerprints would be in the database," I hurriedly explained. "But whoever sent the note was very careful not to leave fingerprints, and there wasn't a return address either..."

Mr. Truth sighed. "I'm sorry to disappoint you, but I don't see anything suspicious in any of this. You don't actually have a real note here, and just because whoever sent it didn't leave fingerprints doesn't mean it's not a joke." He shook his head. "We've had several practical jokes pulled over the years here. Many times, agents get too caught up in the serious nature of their work to see that it is just a joke. I think that's what this is, a joke." Luke tried to respond, but Mr. Truth held up a hand. He handed the blank paper back to Rebecca. "Just forget about it."

I was surprised by his answer. Mr. Truth's usually patient face looked tired and annoyed. He seemed to be eyeing Rebecca doubtfully. *Maybe Matthew's suspicions are starting to rub off on Mr. Truth,* I worried.

Luke excused us from the office, and we slowly walked out of the building. For some reason, Mr. Truth's insistence that this note was a practical joke made me even more sure that this note was serious. *Why didn't she have the real note?* I thought, feeling both confused and frustrated.

"We need to find the real note," Luke said, heading toward the dining hall.

"Are you thinking what I'm thinking?" Rebecca asked, keeping stride with Luke.

"I think the note was switched out for the blank paper," Luke replied. "Someone didn't want the threat to be read by Mr. Truth."

"Which makes this an inside job," I said, raising my eyebrows. Luke nodded as he opened the dining hall door.

We hurried inside and started looking around the room. The cleaning crew had already cleaned the tables and were in the process of sweeping the floor. We searched the whole area, but no scraps of paper could be found. Luke checked the trash can, but it had already been emptied for the night. We left the dining hall, and I suggested we go back and check the walking paths.

Rebecca shook her head. "I had the note with me when we came back for dinner. Luke was holding the note the whole time we walked until we left the walking path, and I stuck it back in my pocket."

"We could check the space between the walking path and the dining hall, though." They agreed, and we retraced our steps, but we didn't find any paper.

"Let's think," Luke said, folding his arms. "Do you remember anyone taking something out of your pocket?"

Rebecca thought for a moment. "Not really, but the best time would have been when the group from Canada walked past our table. They were teasing each other and bumping each other around, and several people bumped into us as they walked past."

"But were they switching out the note because they didn't want Mr. Truth to see it?" I asked. "If so, how did they know we were going to show it to Mr. Truth?"

"The disappearing note makes this seem more like a real threat and less like a practical joke as Mr. Truth was insisting," Luke said, shaking his head. "I think we need to do some investigating."

Rebecca and I agreed. "Luke, why don't you take the blank piece of paper and see if you can find any clues from it?" I suggested.

"Good idea. I have my own fingerprint equipment I can

use, and I'll also look for any hidden messages. Mr. Truth could have been right on that point."

We agreed to meet again in the morning before breakfast to see what Luke had found out. After saying goodnight, Rebecca and I headed to our room.

I lay down on my bed that night with a million thoughts running through my mind. *Is this threat really from Mr. Zaiden? Is someone at Truth Squad working for him? But if it's not from him, then who? Why would someone threaten my sister?* I shivered. Images of being kidnapped by Mr. Zaiden flashed through my mind. The familiar memory of my intense fear from that day resurfaced. I remembered the fear that I might never see my sister, or anyone else I loved, ever again. I remembered trying hard to pretend to be Rebecca, but Mr. Zaiden could still see my fear and knew I wasn't her. *Why do I struggle with so much fear? Why can my sister and Luke be so brave, and I'm so scared all the time?*

I shook my head and rolled over. My mind was wide awake, but I knew I needed to sleep. *Lord,* I prayed, *this threat scares me. I don't know where it's from, or why Rebecca received it. I don't know what to do. I want to ignore this threat, pretend it never happened, but that won't help anything. Give us wisdom, a lot of wisdom. And be with us, because I'm scared.* Slowly, I drifted off to sleep.

CHAPTER 4

We decided to meet Luke the next morning at a coffee shop down the road from Truth Squad. Luke beat us there.

"Good morning, sleepyheads," he said when we walked in, waving us over to a table in the corner that already had three iced coffees sitting on it. "You took so long to get here I figured I'd place three random orders and see what we'd get."

"Are you serious?" I asked, too tired to know if he was kidding.

"Totally serious." He kept a straight face, then burst out laughing. "No, I texted Rebecca, and she told me what to order."

I sighed with relief and sat down. No matter how hard I tried to be a morning person, I still took a while to fully wake up. After a few minutes of small talk and sipping my coffee, my brain began to feel more alert, ready to focus on our real reason for meeting. "So, what did you find out about the paper?" I asked.

Luke pulled a notepad from his pocket. "I ran a fingerprint scan on the paper, but no luck. Whoever switched the note must have been wearing gloves. I checked the security cameras from dinner to see who walked by our table, and to see if any of them wore gloves. I noticed several of the Canadian squad wore gloves as a part of their uniform, and so did a couple of our squad, but where we sit is barely visible in the security cameras, and you can't zoom in with enough clarity to see who switched the notes." He flipped to the next page in his notepad. "I did search the paper for a hidden message."

"Did you find one?" Rebecca asked, leaning forward.

Luke nodded, his eyes lighting up with excitement. "It's the old-fashioned lemon juice message. I wrote it down in my notepad. Here." He handed Rebecca the notepad. I glanced over her shoulder.

It read, "Your cover is only as good as your facial expression."

"That's it?" I raised an eyebrow. "Why would someone write that? It makes no sense."

Rebecca shook her head. "That's Code One."

"Code One?"

She nodded. "Mr. Zaiden always said the number one rule of a double agent is to master your facial expressions. If you can't keep every muscle of your face under control, you can't be a good liar. And you have to be a good liar to be a good double agent."

"So, this was like the first thing you had to work on? That makes sense." Luke nodded. "But why have you gotten two notes that are both codes from when you worked for Mr. Zaiden? It's weird."

"Do you think Mr. Zaiden is the one sending these to you?" I asked.

Rebecca shrugged. "If he is, then he's sending them through someone at Truth Squad."

Luke tapped his chin. "But Mr. Zaiden doesn't have a reason to send these to you, does he?"

"I don't know," Rebecca said. "The only reason I can think of is if he wants some kind of revenge."

My heart rate picked up. *Revenge? What kind of revenge could an assassin want besides to permanently get rid of my sister?* I shook my head. *No, he can't do that.*

"So, what should we do next?" Luke asked.

We sat silently, thinking. "Well," I began, "if Mr. Zaiden is behind this and he's somehow hired someone, maybe we should check that dining room footage again to see if there's anyone out of place. Maybe someone has snuck into Truth Squad who doesn't belong, doesn't check out. With all the new agents this summer, it would be easy for someone to slip in who isn't actually with them."

"Easy to slip in probably isn't true. We had a lot of security when the group first showed up, but you're right. If someone was to sneak in, that would be the best time," Rebecca said. "Let's look into that next."

Luke nodded. "I can do that. And if everyone checks out, that tells us this is an inside job."

I shivered. "Let's hope not." We were silent for a moment, each of us sipping our coffee. A thought kept nagging me. Finally, I sighed, "There's something that doesn't make sense."

"What?" Rebecca asked.

"How did this person know to switch the note just before we went to Mr. Truth?"

Luke shrugged. "It could have been a coincidence."

I shook my head. "Why else would they have done a lemon juice message? The paper looked blank when we went to Mr. Truth and made us look guilty. That seems intentional."

Luke nodded. "But we discussed the note out on the walking paths and made sure we weren't followed."

"Well, not necessarily," Rebecca corrected. "The walking

paths are surrounded by trees. It would be easy to track someone without being spotted."

"We need to be careful about when and where we talk about things," Luke said. "We'll watch our backs more carefully, and make sure we meet where we are less likely to be spied on. Like here at the coffee shop." He waved his arm. "No one else from Truth Squad is here right now."

I nodded, glancing at my watch. "If we want to get back in time for breakfast at the mess hall, we'd better head back."

Rebecca stood up. "We should. We don't want to look any more suspicious than we already do."

I noticed the hint of worry in Rebecca's eyes as she glanced around the room. I stood up, trying to smile encouragingly. *If she's worried enough to let it show in her eyes, that's bad,* I thought as we walked out of the shop.

When we got back to campus, Luke decided to go do some sleuthing while Rebecca and I went to breakfast. As we ate, I kept my eyes open for any suspicious activity. Nothing seemed out of place, except for Matthew's occasional hard glance in our direction.

The rest of the day passed slowly. Rebecca and I went about our normal routine, waiting to hear Luke's report. At lunch, I again noticed Matthew's glances. *Is he just suspicious of us,* I wondered, *or is there something more going on? He wouldn't try to frame my sister just because he doesn't like her, would he?*

The thought kept nagging me as I worked on replacing the engine of an older jet that afternoon. I'd known Matthew for a long time, and it seemed out of character for him to try and frame Rebecca, even if he disliked her so much. *Plus, he would have to be connected to Mr. Zaiden somehow. Otherwise, he wouldn't know the codes.* I shook my head, realizing I had zoned out from my work. I climbed down the ladder to grab another tool from my box.

"You're working slower than normal."

I jumped at Daniel's voice. "Oh, yeah." I smiled, trying to cover up being startled. "I've just been lost in thought, I guess."

He raised his eyebrows. "Well, Luke told me to let you know he was looking for you."

"Okay. I'll find him after I finish this." I nodded toward the jet.

"Need some help?" Daniel grinned expectantly.

"Sure." I handed him the toolbox, and he carried it up the ladder.

With Daniel's help and conversation, the time passed more quickly. Before I knew it, the engine was replaced. "Thanks," I said as we finished putting away the ladder and tools.

"No problem," Daniel replied, smiling. "I'll see you later."

I walked back to my dorm to wash up. I noticed Rebecca wasn't there. I sent her a quick text to find out where she was. I also sent Luke a text, asking where to meet.

A minute later, Luke replied. "Meet in my lab."

I waited a few minutes longer for Rebecca to reply. When no text came, I decided she must already be with Luke and headed his direction.

Luke and Matthew shared an experimental lab where they worked on inventing gadgets. I found Luke tightening some small screws on a gadget. "What's that?" I asked. It was a thin, rectangular box about the size of his palm.

He finished tightening the screws before he answered. "Well, I'm hoping this is a multipurpose-secret-agent-tool."

"Okay," I replied slowly. "So, what does that mean?"

Luke set down his screwdriver. "I haven't come up with

a good title for it yet. It needs to be super cool, because this gadget is super cool! Look at this!" He slid open the box face to the left, revealing several small tools. "These are lockpicks." He closed the box and opened it again from the short end at the bottom, revealing a microphone. "Listening device." He slid the face to the right and revealed a red button. "Taser." Then he slid the short end down to reveal the top compartment. "And a small compartment to hide things in. But get this! This is the coolest part. Are you ready?" He slid the box closed.

I smiled. "Sure."

He handed me the box. "Try to open it," he said, grinning. I pushed on the box, trying to open it. It didn't budge. I tried using two hands, but still no luck. "Yes!" Luke exclaimed, doing a fist-pump. "It works!"

"So why can't I open it?" I asked, handing the box back to him.

"It's fingerprint activated. Only I can open the box. Otherwise, it's held shut by super strong magnetic locks. Pretty neat, huh?" He grinned excitedly.

"That is neat." I glanced around the room. "Rebecca's not here?"

Luke shook his head. "I messaged her half an hour ago asking her to meet me here, and she said she was on her way, but she hasn't shown up yet."

I checked my phone. "She hasn't texted me back, either." I took a deep breath, trying to keep calm instead of thinking up worst-case scenarios. "Should we go find her and then meet somewhere else again?" I asked.

Luke paused, folding his arms. "I guess so," he finally said. He put his new invention into his safe and locked it. "Let's go."

We left the experimental lab and headed toward the

computer lab. We checked inside but didn't find Rebecca. We checked the training room, but she wasn't there, either.

"Do you want to check your room while I check the classrooms?" Luke asked. His phone dinged. He pulled it out of his pocket and read the message. "Rebecca says to meet her in classroom 203."

We hurried to the classrooms and up to the second floor. Rebecca stood behind the teacher's desk, staring off into space when we got there. Her face was set determinedly, but the lack of color in her face made my heart rate pick up. Something was wrong.

"What's up?" Luke asked, sitting down on top of the desk.

Rebecca paused before making eye contact with him. "I was just in a long interview with Matthew." Her face and voice were expressionless. "He believes his suspicions against me are well-founded and wants to open an investigation against me to prove that I hacked the training room and my parole records."

Luke tensed. "Well, that's dumb!" he exclaimed. "He's not going to find any evidence against you because you are innocent."

I sighed. "No wonder he was watching us so closely today."

Rebecca nodded. "I tried to find out if Mr. Truth was allowing his investigation, but he wouldn't tell me anything. My suspicion is that he's doing this behind Mr. Truth's back."

"Well, that's good for us," I said hopefully. "If Mr. Truth is still on our side, then we should be safe, right?"

"I hope so," Luke said, but his voice sounded doubtful. "The thing is, Matthew is the vice-president of Truth Squad. He's got power on his side, and we don't."

"We'll just have to prove his investigation wrong," I said, surprised at the confidence in my voice. My tone didn't match my racing heart. "His investigation won't lead him anywhere, but ours will. We need to discover who's behind all this."

Rebecca nodded. "That's our best bet." She turned to Luke. "So, what did you uncover in your 'sleuthing' today?"

Luke grinned. "Some pretty interesting stuff. I checked through the video footage from when the new guys showed up, and everything checked out. No one got through security without being checked. I looked through the records of everyone who checked in that day and matched them up to the list of people the Canadian base sent us two months before they showed up. Everything matched."

"And you're sure you didn't miss anything?" I asked.

"I wondered that, too, so I checked through some footage of when they came to dinner that first day. I checked the footage from the first time they trained in the training room. Everyone checks out," he said, crossing his arms. "So, you know what this means?"

"It's an inside job," Rebecca replied.

"Correct!" Luke said, using an announcer voice. "You win!"

We stood in silence for a minute. Rebecca crossed her arms, staring at the ground. "We need to be extremely careful with our investigation. We don't want to look any more suspicious to Matthew than we do right now."

Luke rolled his eyes. "Matthew's out to mistrust you no matter what. Let's just ignore him and get to work."

I nodded. *I just hope we can figure this out before Matthew gets a case together,* I worried.

Luke stood up. "Let's think for a minute. When did you start receiving creepy notes? When did the security breach happen?"

"After the new agents showed up," I said.

"Exactly!" Luke said, grinning. "I've got a hunch that one of them, or more, is up to something."

I opened my mouth to say something, then hesitated. "What?" Rebecca asked, raising an eyebrow.

"Well, I know this sounds crazy," I began, trying to word my response carefully. "I've been thinking about Matthew's strange behavior all day, and, well, doesn't it seem... weird that he would be so quick to accuse Rebecca for everything that's gone wrong?" Luke looked offended at my suggestion, so I hurried to explain. "I mean, it doesn't seem to match his character, but at the same time, his behavior has been unlike himself. Could he be trying to frame Rebecca so she has to leave?"

Rebecca shook her head. "That doesn't make sense. Why would he know Mr. Zaiden's codes? He's not the kind of guy who would contact Mr. Zaiden for them, either."

I shrugged. "I still think we should keep an eye on him. If anyone has access to the training room or your files, it's him."

Luke sighed. "As much as I hate to admit it, I think you're right. It doesn't make any sense, and I still doubt Matthew's behind this, but we can't be too careful."

"So, Luke, do you want us to do some spy work and pinpoint our suspects?" Rebecca asked. She straightened up, a light of excitement glimmering in her eyes.

There's my adventure-loving sister, I thought, but I still felt fear in my heart, knowing the risk we were taking.

"Let's make a plan!" Luke said, jumping with excitement.

I hope this isn't a bad idea, I thought.

Luke and Rebecca decided the best course of action was to spend the next couple of days looking for "lone wolves."

"If anyone spends lots of time alone, doesn't interact much with others, keeps information about themselves to a minimum, they're a suspect," Luke had explained. Luke also decided to keep an eye on Matthew since they worked together frequently. "Plus, it will be less obvious for me to keep an eye on him than you two, since he's trying to investigate you and all," he had said.

I kept my eyes open for "lone wolves" and noticed a lot of people fit this description. A couple girls from Canada tended to sit in the corner by themselves, whispering to each other in French and giggling whenever Matthew walked by. I sat near them a couple times and overheard one of them ask one of our agents if Matthew was single, and they giggled with delight when they found out he was. I decided they weren't suspects.

Another lone wolf was a short lady with purple hair that she always wore in a bun. She barely talked to anyone who sat by her, and I never saw her smile. She seemed to be very observant of everyone's comings and goings not only in the mess hall, but also in training. *She definitely fits the "Code One" Rebecca told us about,* I thought, deciding she might be a suspect.

I was asked to help serve dinner on short notice when I finished my mechanics class the next day. They needed someone to monitor the Junior Squad for their night of serving since Mary wasn't feeling well.

I stood behind the serving line and watched as people walked through the line while keeping an eye on the food. I saw Ethan and Ryan step up to the counter and pick up their plates. Ethan looked up and made eye contact. He smiled. Ryan kept his head down. Suddenly, it hit me. They hadn't sat with us for several days. In fact, I hadn't seen them in the mess hall at all for the past two days. I tried to smile back and hide my shock. I noticed the mac-and-cheese was almost empty and quickly grabbed the pan and took it to the kitchen. *I hope I didn't blow anything,* I thought, trying to control my expression as I brought out a new pan of mac-and-cheese. *I sure don't fit Code One.*

Ethan and Ryan had already gone through the line. I saw them filling cups at the soda fountain and watched as they sat down at a corner table. They leaned forward, obviously discussing something serious.

"Sarah!" I turned toward Faith. "I called your name three times." She looked annoyed.

"Sorry, I was..."

"We need more green beans," she interrupted. "Hurry, Luke's waiting."

I looked up to see Luke holding back a laugh. I felt my face turning red as I grabbed the green beans container and ran back to the kitchen. I returned in time to hear the teens laughing as Luke told them a story about an explosion he and Matthew accidentally created.

I set the green beans down on the serving counter. "Thank you, ma'am." Luke grinned and winked.

"You're welcome," I replied, knowing he waited for the green beans in order to cover for my lack of discretion. *No more spy work tonight,* I told myself.

It was eight o'clock by the time the serving crew had finished eating and cleaning the mess hall. Faith and Hope stayed behind to help me put away the leftovers. "I'm surprised by how many leftovers there are. With the amount of food Jonathan eats, I would think the only leftovers would be the Brussel sprouts." Faith giggled.

I laughed. "Teenage boys do know how to eat, that's for

sure." I closed the fridge door. "Thanks for your help putting this all away."

"No problem," Hope said, smiling. We walked out of the mess hall, and I locked the door.

"I'll walk you home," I offered.

"Sounds good," Faith said as we headed toward the campus entrance.

The twins lived with their grandparents just outside the entrance to the campus. Their parents worked for Truth Squad and did a lot of overseas work fighting for religious freedom. They were currently gone on a top-secret mission that only the higher-ups knew anything about. The twins admired their parents and worked hard at their training so they could someday make a difference in the world, too. I admired Faith and Hope's bravery, especially since they always kept a positive attitude when their parents were doing top-secret work. I couldn't imagine living with the thought that your parents might not come back from a mission, or knowing that when they are at home, they could be called away at any given moment.

"Sarah, why does Matthew not like Rebecca?" Faith asked.

I was surprised by the sudden question. "I don't know." I thought for a minute. "I think Matthew believes that she couldn't have changed, that she's just acting like a Christian but isn't really one in her heart."

"But she seems like a real Christian to me," Hope said, raising her eyebrows in concern.

"Yeah. Jesus said you will know someone by their fruit, and Rebecca seems like a genuine Christian," Faith said defensively.

"You're right. She repented of her old life and has chosen to live for Christ. That's not an easy decision to make. When she worked as a double agent, she made a lot of money and had an exciting life. The fact that she gave it up, did the right thing in turning in Mr. Zaiden and herself, and has chosen to live like Christ is a testimony to God's redemptive power and grace," I said. We walked out the front gate and turned onto the sidewalk.

Faith nodded. "But I still don't get it."

"What do you mean?" I asked. We stopped outside the door of their grandparents' house.

"We overheard Matthew talking to some of the other guys about not trusting Rebecca and looking into some stuff," Faith explained.

Hope nodded. "He was pretty angry looking. And it seemed like these guys believed him, too. What is he looking into?"

I shook my head, not wanting to get them involved. *Knowing these two, they'll probably insist on trying to help us, and that might be dangerous.* "It's nothing. You two don't need to worry about it. Matthew will get over it soon enough."

Both girls crossed their arms in unison. "You're a bad liar," Faith said, tipping her chin up.

I rolled my eyes. "And it's getting late. Your grandparents are probably waiting for you. I'll see you later."

"Okay," Faith said, sighing dramatically.

Hope smiled and waved as they walked inside. "Goodnight!"

I waved and started walking back down the sidewalk. *Why is Matthew spreading his suspicions around campus?* I wondered. *Is he trying to get help for his investigation? Whatever he's planning, this doesn't look good. He may not have any evidence right now, but neither do we.* I shook my head as I stepped through the front gate and headed to my dorm.

Lord, I don't know what's going on, I prayed, *but we need Your help. Please guide us. Help us to find out the truth behind what's going on so we can prove Rebecca is innocent. You're a God of justice; please reveal what's going on.*

🔫

We met early the next morning at the coffee shop to discuss our suspects. After ordering our coffees, we sat down at the table in the corner. "There sure are a lot of 'lone wolves,'" I said, shaking my head.

"Yeah, I never noticed how many agents stick to themselves until now," Luke said. "It makes me realize that I need to be more observant and reach out to people who are by themselves."

"Good point," I said. The barista called my name, so I went up to the counter to grab my iced caramel latte and Rebecca's iced Mexican mocha.

After sitting back down, I told Luke and Rebecca about my conversation with Hope and Faith.

"Wow, Matthew's taking this seriously!" Luke exclaimed, rolling his eyes.

"What did you learn while keeping an eye on him?" Rebecca asked.

"I don't think he's the one behind the threats. He didn't seem to know anything about us taking the note to Mr. Truth. I checked around and confirmed that he hasn't had any communications with the prison that Mr. Zaiden is at, so in my mind, that totally clears him. However, since he's trying to get people turned against you, we still need to keep our eyes on him."

"Do you know what he's basing his investigation on?" Rebecca asked.

Luke nodded. "I asked, and he said he's basing all his

theories off the surveillance of you two going to the computer lab before hours and the training room malfunction later that afternoon. It's very weak evidence, in my opinion. Matthew just has a real chip on his shoulder that he needs to deal with."

I nodded. "So, have we come up with any suspects so far?"

Rebecca nodded. "I noticed a few people who tend to sit quietly in corners and don't talk about themselves. There's that group of four who sit in the far-right corner every day, two girls and two guys. The one who stands out, though, is the girl who wears glasses and keeps her hair in a ponytail. She doesn't really interact with their group, and if you try to talk to her, she doesn't answer with more than one or two words."

"I noticed her too," Luke said, nodding.

"What about the girl with purple hair?" I asked. "The one who sits alone and watches everyone as they come and go?"

Rebecca nodded. "I would say she's also a suspect."

"I noticed a guy who tends to wear a baseball cap low on his face, and he has a scar on his left arm," Luke said. "He doesn't talk much and tends to be off by himself. He hangs out in the computer and science labs a lot."

"I didn't notice him, but that sounds more suspicious than my glasses and ponytail girl," Rebecca admitted.

"What about Ryan and Ethan?" I asked.

Rebecca looked surprised. "They're not really lone wolves."

"No, but when I was working in the mess hall yesterday I realized that they hadn't been in the dining hall for a while. They've stopped sitting at our table, and they sat in a corner quietly discussing something," I explained.

"Yeah, Sarah was staring so intently at their table, I thought lasers were going to shoot out of her eyes," Luke joked.

"But they talked about themselves when they sat with us," Rebecca argued.

"Not Ryan," I countered.

Rebecca sat silently for a minute. "Well, if I think about it, that does make some sense. Ethan seemed very interested in being able to tell us apart."

"Extremely interested," Luke replied sarcastically.

"And if you were trying to spy on someone, wouldn't it be easier to do so if you were on their good side?" I asked.

Rebecca nodded. "It's just as likely a technique as the lone wolf idea. I think you're right; they should be suspects, too."

"So, we've got five suspects?" I asked.

Luke nodded. "Glasses-ponytail, purple-hair, baseball-scar-dude, Ryan, and Ethan."

I grabbed my phone and wrote a note of the suspects.

"I say we each pick a suspect and try to follow them around for the next three days. Note everything they do, suspicious or not. And most importantly, don't let them catch you," Luke said.

"I'll take Purple-hair," I said.

"I'll keep an eye on glasses-ponytail," Rebecca said.

"I'll do Ryan and Ethan. They tend to be together." Luke leaned back in his chair. "That leaves baseball-scar-dude."

"I'll watch him, too," Rebecca said. "We reconvene in three days. Good luck."

CHAPTER 5

I glanced around at my team as I finished tightening the straps on my training vest. Purple-hair was in the corner already suited up, tapping her foot impatiently.

I was surprised at how hard tracking this girl was. When I agreed to keep an eye on Purple-hair, I thought I had the easier job of watching one person. Instead, I could barely keep up with her. The day before, I sat at the table in front of where Purple-hair sat. She was joined by a few other people but never talked to anyone. I turned for a minute to visit with Mary as she walked past my table, and when I turned back to face Purple-hair, she was gone. Somehow, she'd managed to be in and out of the dining room in ten minutes. During my free time, I wandered around different parts of the campus to see if I could find where she liked to hang out. I never found her. She didn't show up to dinner, either. The fact that she disappeared for half the day sent alarms through my mind.

After checking all my gear, I made my way toward Purple-hair. *Act natural,* I told myself as I wove between my other teammates. Luke and Rebecca were always getting after me for being too obvious about my suspicions.

I took a deep breath and smiled at Purple-hair as I stepped

next to her. "Are you ready?" I asked, hoping I wasn't overdoing my excitement.

She shrugged. "Sure." Her voice was monotone, and she didn't make eye contact.

I paused, unsure of what to say next. *What would be natural?* I thought frantically. Finally, I said the first thing that came to mind. "So, I don't think we've formally met."

"Yes, we have. You're Rebecca." She still didn't make eye contact.

I giggled, inwardly cringing at how nervous my giggle sounded. "No, I'm Sarah."

Purple-hair jerked her face towards me. "What?" She lowered her eyebrows. "Don't play jokes with me."

"I'm not, honest!" I said, trying to keep a straight face. "Rebecca's my twin."

She glared at me without saying anything. I shrugged, trying hard not to break eye contact. Finally, she rolled her eyes and looked away. "If you say so."

I hesitated. I still didn't know her name. *But if I ask, will that make her suspicious? Oh, how do I act natural when I'm second-guessing everything?* I was glad she was looking away, because I was sure my frustration was showing on my face.

"My name's Carrie in case you want to know."

I looked back at her, surprised she spoke to me without being asked a question. I quickly smiled, hoping my surprise didn't show too much. "It's nice to meet you, Carrie. I hope you're enjoying your time here."

Carrie didn't have time to reply because the training room doors slid open, and we were ushered inside.

The training course was intense, and no matter how hard I tried, I couldn't keep an eye on Carrie. After a close call with the opposing team, I decided to give up on keeping an eye on

Carrie during the training. I turned my attention to helping my team, knowing I needed to step up my game.

Time ran out twenty minutes later, the training ending in a draw. Since we were the defending team, the draw counted as our win. Our team high-fived as we left the training room. I took off my vest and put all my gadgets back in their containers. As I walked out of the equipment room, I saw Matthew glaring at me, his arms crossed.

I smiled at him and tried to walk past.

"Sarah."

I rolled my eyes before turning to face him. "Yes, Matthew?"

He raised an eyebrow. "What's up with your performance today?"

"What do you mean?" I asked, knowing exactly what he meant.

"The first half of the game, you lost several points for your team, and then suddenly, you picked up a ton of points in the last half. You're normally steady in training."

"Yeah, well, I guess I was kind of distracted when we first started," I said, shrugging.

"No kidding." He rolled his eyes.

"Why do you care?" I asked, annoyed.

He paused, then shrugged. "I've noticed you've been distracted lately." He tipped his chin up. "I hope it doesn't have anything to do with your sister's trouble."

I started. "What?" I tried to fake being weirded out by his suggestion. I shook my head. "Just drop it, Matthew. You're getting yourself nowhere by obsessing over your suspicions." I turned around and marched away.

What is with him? I fumed, keeping my gaze fixed on the ground and ignoring everything around me. *No matter what happens, Matthew finds fault with us. Luke may not think he's guilty, but he sure is causing a lot of trouble.* I could feel my heart racing and my face flushing. I was angry. Really angry. I normally didn't get angry like this. I took a deep breath. *I need to calm down.* I tried to imagine myself in Matthew's shoes and tried to sympathize with his point of view, but I couldn't. I was too annoyed with him. I shook my head. *I need to think about something else,* I told myself, forcing my mind to change gears.

I'm supposed to be keeping an eye on Purple-hair, on Carrie. The thought made me look up and realize that I had walked all the way to the back of the campus and had started down the walking paths. I turned around and looked back toward the way I came. I could see some people walking from building to building. A group of teens sat at a picnic table outside the dorms. Nothing purple was catching my eye.

I slowly made my way back toward the main complex of buildings. *I probably won't find her, considering my record from yesterday.* I thought about going to my dorm room, but I decided I should look around for Carrie first. *It is my job to keep an eye on her,* I told myself.

I walked through the science lab, which was relatively empty. After wandering through and finding no purple-haired girl, I stepped out the back door. I started toward the computer lab when I noticed some movement out of the corner of my eye. Turning, I saw someone quietly step behind a tree. A second later, the person quietly darted to a tree farther back.

Purple hair, I noticed. I glanced around, and after being sure no one was following me, I decided to see where Carrie was headed. Keeping my distance far enough away so that I couldn't be heard, I followed behind Carrie, mimicking her pattern of darting behind trees, pausing, and darting again.

Carrie went farther and farther into the forest behind

the labs. Eventually she stopped hiding behind trees and picked up her pace. I glanced behind me. *The labs are hardly visible anymore with all these trees.* I picked up my pace, trying to keep up with Carrie while remaining hidden. She continued farther back. I knew she would eventually run into the wall that separated the main complex from the acres of protected rainforest land.

As the concrete wall came into view, Carrie stopped, glanced around, and pulled her phone out of her pocket. She typed around on the screen, paused, typed some more, and then held the phone up to her ear.

Did she come all the way out here to make a secret phone call? I wondered.

A second later, she started talking. She was too far away for me to make out what she was saying.

I wish I had some gadgets on me right now, I thought, looking down and realizing the only gadget on me was my watch. It didn't have any remote listening capabilities. *Should I risk getting closer to find out what she's saying?* I wondered, biting my lip nervously. *But what if she discovers she's been followed? That will ruin everything. But what if this phone conversation is an important clue?* The internal battle raged within me as I watched her continue talking. *I have to know if this is important,* I decided, ignoring the fearful doubts within me.

I quietly stepped toward a tree to my left so that I could sneak closer from behind Carrie instead of being visible in her peripheral vision. After glancing around my cover and being sure that Carrie's back was toward me, I slowly stepped out from behind the tree and moved forward toward the next one. As I moved closer, I could hear Carrie's voice, but I couldn't make out her words.

I paused a few trees away from Carrie and turned my

watch to record audio. I still couldn't quite make out Carrie's quiet voice, but I knew that if I were a few steps closer I would be able to hear. I also knew the closer I got, the more I risked her hearing me.

I took a long, slow breath, trying to calm my racing heart and quiet my breathing. *It's probably not as loud as it sounds in my head*, I told myself.

I carefully picked my way over to the next closest tree, avoiding stepping on any twigs or branches. I could finally make out some of Carrie's words. It sounded like she was talking about today's training. My ear picked up on Rebecca's name. I strained to hear the rest of the sentence, but she stopped talking. *I need to get closer*, I thought, stepping toward the next tree.

As I got behind my new cover, I planted my foot down and heard a loud snap. Carrie inhaled sharply. I leaned back against the tree, wishing it were larger around, so I didn't have to position myself so still. I breathed as shallowly and quietly as I could. I heard Carrie take a few steps in my direction, then stop.

"I just realized the time. I need to go before someone comes looking for me," Carrie said. There was a long pause. "Mm-hmm. I'll call you back when I can. Feel free to message me if you need. But use the other number." She paused again. "Okay. Bye."

Carrie ran right by me as I darted to the other side of the tree. I glanced out from my hiding spot to see her dashing away, not looking back.

I clicked off the audio recorder and saved the recording to my watch. As it loaded, I looked at the time. Forty-five minutes till dinner. *If she still has free time, why was she worried about getting back soon?* I wondered.

Seeing that Carrie was completely out of sight, I stepped out of hiding and started back in the direction of the science lab.

Why was she telling that person to message using another number? That is rather unusual.

As I got closer to the science lab, I decided to go around through the woods and come out on the walking paths. *That will look less weird than walking out of the woods behind the lab,* I decided.

I came to the walking path and stepped on with determined speed toward the path entrance, hoping to appear like I'd been out for some exercise.

"Sarah!"

I jumped and whirled around. Matthew and Daniel were walking toward me. I knew from the look on Matthew's face that they'd seen me walk out from the woods.

"What are you doing?" Matthew asked, the tone of his question more condemning than curious.

"Walking. What are you doing?" I hoped my smile and tone of voice sounded sweeter than I felt.

Matthew raised an eyebrow. "Walking in the woods where there's no path?"

I shrugged. "Why not? It's beautiful and more challenging for exercising than a walking path due to the uneven ground." I surprised myself with my quick answer.

Daniel looked intrigued. "I never thought of that before. I mean, we do have miles of walking paths, but there's plenty of new routes to be taken in all this property." He waved his arm in the direction I'd come from.

Matthew glared at Daniel, but Daniel didn't seem to notice. Finally, he cleared his throat. "I've got work to get back to. See you later." He pushed past me with a glare and left.

Daniel raised an eyebrow. "What was that about?"

I shrugged. "Matthew's just been on my case all day."

"Weird," Daniel said. We started walking down the path. "But really, why were you walking through the woods?"

I felt my shoulders tense. *Should I trust Daniel?* I thought back to our investigation of Mr. Zaiden and Daniel's help. *This is a serious threat Rebecca's facing. I don't think we should tell too many people. It might cause more danger.* I looked up at Daniel. *I trust him, but I can't tell him everything,* I decided. "Just looking into something."

Daniel stared at me for a minute. "Okay." He shrugged.

Daniel headed toward the dining hall, and I rushed to my room. I found Rebecca sitting at the table, scribbling notes. She glanced up when I walked in but didn't say anything. I could tell she was laser-focused, so I didn't interrupt her. Interrupting Rebecca when she was in the zone like that was always a bad move; she could get pretty annoyed.

I sat down at my computer and took off my watch. After syncing my watch to the computer, I downloaded the audio I'd recorded. As it downloaded, I synced a pair of earbuds to the computer so I could listen to the audio without distracting Rebecca.

"Download complete" flashed on the screen. I opened the link and played the recording.

I heard my footsteps as I moved closer to where Carrie stood. I could also hear my breathing loud and clear. I rubbed my forehead in frustration as I listened to the recording of myself breathing with faint words in the background that I couldn't make out. The only words that came through were the few sentences I heard while I was there in person. The audio ended, and I sighed. I took out my earbuds and put them away.

Now what? I wondered.

"What was that sigh for?" Rebecca asked.

I turned around to see her putting her notepad in her purse. "I was following Carrie, you know, with the purple hair, and she snuck off back into the woods and made a phone call. It seemed rather suspicious, so I was going to record her conversation. Instead, I got a wonderful recording of my breathing, which drowns out anything she's saying." I ran my fingers through my hair in frustration. "I'm not sure what to do."

Rebecca was smirking. I could tell she was trying not to laugh. I glared at her. "It's not that funny," I said.

She raised her eyebrows and started laughing out loud. "Yes, it is. It's funny because it's relatable. I've taken excellent recordings of my breathing before, too." She took a deep breath to control her giggles. "I bet we could run the recording through a program that can separate out the conversation from the breathing."

"Oh. I didn't think of that. Would it work?"

"It's worth a shot."

The dinner bell started ringing. I put my watch back on and shut off the computer. "I'll ask Luke if he knows how to do that."

We hurried out the door and met up with Luke outside the dining hall. I told him about the audio.

"I know of a program that can do that. If you send me the audio, I can separate it for you," he said.

"That would be great!" I said. I found the file on my watch and forwarded it to Luke's watch.

I kept an eye open for Carrie as I ate dinner. I finally spotted her come in as people were getting up for seconds. She slipped into the food line, not looking around at anyone. I noticed her hair was wet and she had changed clothes. *Is that something odd, or not?* I wondered as I watched her sit down at an empty table. *I'm probably overthinking this. I mean, it's not that weird to shower and change before dinner if you were going to something fancy or had gotten sweaty, I guess.* It still seemed odd, though.

Later that evening, I got an email from Luke saying he'd divided the audio. I opened the link and listened.

The beginning of the audio was too muffled to make anything out. After a moment, the words became clearer.

"...met in the training center. I didn't know she had a twin." Pause. "Seemed nice enough." Pause. "Not really. I'm ready to get this over with and get out of here." Pause. Carrie inhaled sharply. "I just realized the time. I need to go before someone comes looking for me." Pause. "Mm-hmm. I'll call you back when I can. Feel free to message me if you need. But use the other number." Pause. "Okay. Bye."

So, she mentioned us to whoever she was talking to, I thought, resting my chin in my hand. *Interesting.*

I opened my eyes and glanced at the clock. 6:30 am. *I can't believe I beat my alarm clock,* I thought. I considered rolling over and trying to fall back asleep until my alarm went off at seven, but remembering that it was the last day to do more sleuthing before Luke, Rebecca, and I reconvened to go over our notes pushed me to stay awake.

I sat up and leaned against my headboard. *I need a plan to somehow keep track of Carrie today without losing her this time,* I thought. *The only problem is I'm teaching this morning. How do I keep tabs on her and still teach mechanics?* I ran several ideas through my mind. There was only one option. *I've got to enlist some help.*

I slowly swung my legs over the edge of the bed and stood up. *Who could I trust, and who would be inconspicuous?* I wondered, stretching. Daniel came to mind, but I decided he would be too out-of-place. Besides, he was a free-lance detective, so he might be gone anyways. Another idea kept coming to mind, but I kept shoving it away. *I can't ask them,* I told myself, but every other name that surfaced was either a name I couldn't trust because of their close ties to Matthew, or a name of someone who would be too conspicuous.

I got dressed, still trying to come up with other names. Finally, I had to face it. *Faith and Hope are the least conspicuous people I can ask,* I told myself. *I don't think there's another option. It'll only be for an hour and a half while I teach. They can do it.*

After brushing my hair and putting it in a side braid, I walked out to our kitchen to get some coffee.

Rebecca sat at the table, reading her Bible. She looked up at me, her eyes wide. "You're up before seven. It's a miracle!"

I rolled my eyes without responding. After pouring myself a cup of coffee and adding creamer, I sat down next to my sister. I tapped my fingernails on the coffee mug. "So, it's our last day of sleuthing."

Rebecca looked up from her reading again. "Yup."

"With that recording, I really want to keep close tabs on Carrie, but the problem is, I'm teaching this morning," I said slowly.

"Okay," Rebecca replied expectantly.

I paused. "Well," I took a deep breath, "what do you think about me asking Faith and Hope to keep an eye on Carrie while I'm in class?"

Rebecca's eyes widened. "Faith and Hope?"

I shrugged. "I ran through all the possible people I could ask. Matthew's caused so many people to be suspicious of us, and a lot of other people I thought of would be too conspicuous," I explained. "I wouldn't tell them anything about the threats or anything like that, and I wouldn't tell them to follow her, just to keep their eyes open." Rebecca looked doubtful. "At least they believe in us," I said.

Rebecca sighed. "It just makes me a little nervous after the training room incident. I mean, if that incident is connected to the person sending threats, then they obviously don't care that much about the safety of the Junior Squad." She shook her head. "It does seem like the best option, though."

The email notification dinged on the computer. Rebecca got up to read it. I stood up and walked back to my room to grab my Bible. When I walked back out, my heart rate picked up as I noticed Rebecca's wide eyes and stern face.

"What is it?" I asked.

"Come read this," she said, nodding me over.

I set my Bible down on the table and read the email. The sending email address was a bunch of random numbers and letters. The message read, "Rebecca, I know you know exactly what my messages have meant. You have information that I need, and I will get it one way or another. Don't think you can hide forever."

I looked at Rebecca. "That's super creepy."

She shook her head. "It doesn't make sense. 'Don't think you can hide forever?' I'm not hiding."

I tilted my head. "Good point." I reread the message. "What information do you have that this person needs?"

She shrugged. "I don't know. That doesn't make sense, either. If these threats are somehow coming from Mr. Zaiden, he would know everything I know. And I told everything I know to the police. There wouldn't be any information that I have that he could possibly need."

I raised an eyebrow. "Then, do you think... do you think this threat isn't from Mr. Zaiden?"

"I... I'm not sure," she replied, lowering her eyebrows. "I don't know who else it could be."

I glanced back at the screen. "Rebecca!" I exclaimed, pointing. The screen was blinking rapidly. "Did this email have a virus?" I asked.

Rebecca didn't reply. She whipped her phone from her pocket and snapped several pictures of the blinking screen. She put her phone back and pressed the escape key on the keyboard several times. She tried moving the mouse and tried using the touchscreen. Nothing was working. "I'll just power it down," she said, and held down the power button. A second later, the screen went dark.

"That was weird." I shivered.

"I'll let it sit for a minute," Rebecca said. She walked back over to her coffee and Bible and sat down.

I sat down next to her and sipped my coffee. My heart was still racing. I pulled my Bible over to me, but I didn't open it. I knew I was too nervous to pay attention to the words.

Lord, I don't know what's going on, I prayed, staring at the gold lettering on my Bible. *But I know You do. My heart is racing, and I'm feeling overwhelmed. Please give me peace and a clear mind. We need Your help to figure this all out.* I glanced at my sister. She was rubbing her forehead as she read her Bible. I could tell she was worried. *Lord, I don't want to lose my sister because of Matthew's suspicions or because of these threats from this unknown person. And now, Rebecca's not even sure whether her theory that these threats might be coming from Mr. Zaiden is right. Please help us, Lord. We need You.*

When Rebecca turned the computer back on, the email threat was gone. It wasn't in the inbox or anywhere else to be found. Rebecca figured the virus in the email was intended to delete the message so that we couldn't track the sender. Luckily, she'd taken pictures of the message.

At breakfast, Rebecca filled Luke in on what happened and showed him the picture of the message. "Wow," he said, shaking his head. "That's serious."

"I think we need to look into this address. I'll work on it tonight," Rebecca said, putting her phone in her pocket.

I glanced across the room at Carrie. She looked like she was hyper-focused again today. She glanced around her frequently and watched closely when people entered and exited the building.

Rebecca elbowed me. I looked away from Carrie and turned to face her. "What?"

"When are you teaching?" Her tone told me she'd asked me several times.

"Oh. At nine-thirty."

Rebecca nodded toward the door. I turned and saw Faith and Hope leaving. "You should probably finish eating and catch up with them," she said.

I shoved a few more bites of food into my mouth and then threw the rest away. After putting my dishes into their bins for washing, I hurried outside. I soon found Faith and Hope sitting at a picnic table playing cards.

"Hi, girls." I waved as I walked up. "Can I join you?"

Faith smiled. "Sure. We're playing Kings-in-the-Corner. I'll deal you in next round."

"Thanks," I said, smiling back. I watched them play a few turns. "So," I began, "can I ask you two a favor?"

Hope cocked her head toward me. "What is it?"

"You know the girl with purple hair?" I asked.

"From the Canada group?" Faith said.

I nodded. "Well, I'm supposed to be keeping an eye on her, but I'm teaching mechanics from nine-thirty to eleven. Would you girls be willing to keep your eyes open for her and let me know if you see her?"

Faith's eyes lit up. "You mean you want us to spy?" She grinned. "I am totally in."

"Wait a minute," I cautioned. "You're not spying. You're just keeping your eyes open. I don't want you to be following Carrie around or anything, understand?"

"So, you don't want her to know she's being watched," Faith said, nodding her head.

I sighed. I'd forgotten how much Faith loved adventure. "That's true. But I also don't want you getting into trouble."

Hope smiled at me. "Don't worry. I'll make sure Faith doesn't get herself into trouble."

Faith rolled her eyes and said in a nasal voice, "You underestimate me."

"Okay. So, you know the plan, then?" I asked.

Faith nodded. "Keep our eyes peeled for purple hair, and report to you at eleven with any intel we might possibly gather." She grinned and flipped her hair. "See, I even know the right spy words."

I smiled. "Thanks so much for your willingness to help." I played a few rounds of their game until I saw Carrie leave the dining hall. "I need to get going," I said as Hope shuffled the deck. "Thanks for letting me play."

"Bye!" Hope waved.

I hurried off after Carrie, being sure to keep my distance and act nonchalant. She was headed in the direction of the walking paths. I noticed a grey satchel at her side that I'd never seen her carry before. As Carrie passed the girls' dorm building, a dark-haired girl pushed the door open hurriedly and ran to Carrie. Carrie turned around, and I saw her smile for the first time as the girl gave her a bear hug. They were instantly immersed in conversation. The dark-haired girl waved toward the dorms, and the two walked inside. *I've never seen that other girl before,* I thought, curious. *I'll have to find out who she is.*

I decided to sit in the comfy leather armchairs in the dorm lobby and wait to see if Carrie would return before I had to go teach.

As I waited, I sent Luke a text. "Can you find out if any new recruits came in today or last night?" A few minutes later, my phone dinged.

Luke replied, "Matthew confirmed we had two late comers fly in last night, siblings Alex and Alethia Jeffries. Apparently, they had a virus that we didn't want to spread here at the base. Their doctor finally confirmed that they are no longer contagious and released them yesterday morning."

"Thanks," I typed back with a smiley face and sent the message. *That must be Alethia,* I assumed, leaning back in the leather chair. After a few minutes, I was starting to feel bored, so I grabbed the notepad and pen sitting on the lamp table and began doodling flowers.

Fifteen minutes later, the alarm on my watch went off. *I'd better head to my classroom,* I thought with a sigh. There was no sign of Carrie that whole time.

I pushed open the door and stepped outside. I noticed Faith and Hope sitting at the same table I'd left them at. Faith was waving frantically for me to come over. I jogged over to their table and sat down. "What's up?" I asked.

"We saw the girl with purple hair leave the dorms

with another girl and head back to the dining room," Faith whispered excitedly. "They left through the door on the end of the building closest to us." She pointed.

Oh, duh! I thought, mentally scolding myself. *Of course they'd leave by the door closest to Carrie's room.* "Thanks for the info," I said, standing up.

"You're welcome," Faith replied.

"Are you headed to teach your class now?" Hope asked.

I nodded. "If you could keep your eyes open for Carrie until I'm done at eleven, I'd greatly appreciate it."

Hope gave me a thumbs-up. "We'll do that."

I waved and hurried off to my classroom.

***

It was eleven twenty by the time I finished answering questions from students who'd stayed after class. After logging out of the computer system, I hurried back to the table Hope and Faith had been sitting at, anxious to hear if they'd seen Carrie go anywhere while I was gone. When I got to the table, the twins were gone.

Where are they? I wondered, looking around me. No one was outside at the tables. I noticed it had warmed up quite a bit during the time I was teaching. *Maybe they found a cooler spot to sit at,* I thought, walking slowly through the area.

I searched every spot outside I thought they might be. No luck. I sighed. *I was twenty minutes late,* I told myself, wishing I hadn't had to answer so many questions. *Why today, of all days, did my students have to ask so many questions?*

"Pst! Sarah!"

I jerked my head toward the sound of my name. I saw

Faith's head, sticking out from behind a tree. "What are you doing?" I whispered, joining Faith and Hope behind the tree.

"We saw Carrie leave the dining room about half an hour after you went to teach your class," Hope began.

"She went to her dorm for a while," Faith continued, "and then we saw her walk behind the science building, so we came over here to get a better vantage point."

I put my hands on my hips. "I thought I told you not to follow Carrie."

"We didn't follow Carrie. We just found a better spot to keep an eye on things," Faith argued, grinning sneakily.

"Anyways, she went back into the woods and was gone for a while. She came back not too long ago, and we had to hide quickly behind this tree so she wouldn't see us. Then she went back to her dorm room." Faith grinned. "So, what do you want this info for?"

I shook my head. "I can't tell you that, but thanks so much for your help."

Faith pouted. "I want to know why you're spying!" she whined.

I shook my head. "I'll see you later. Thanks again!"

Hope smiled and waved, but Faith just rolled her eyes and said, "Sure."

I hurried to my room and took some notes on what Faith and Hope told me. *So, she went back to her spot in the woods again, I'm assuming to make another call. I wonder if this is a daily thing. And I wonder who she's calling*, I thought as I finished my notes.

🔫

"So, who wants to go first?" Luke asked, setting down a notepad on the table.

Rebecca set down her coffee and pulled a notepad from her purse. "I can go first. I didn't learn anything interesting." She sounded disappointed.

We were meeting in the coffee shop again to go over the last three days of spying. I was surprisingly awake this morning, excited to hear what Luke and Rebecca had found out and to share what I'd learned about Carrie.

"So, the girl with the glasses and ponytail is definitely not a suspect," Rebecca said, shaking her head. "Her name's Anna. Mary told me that her mom died recently, and it's been tough on her. That's why she's been so quiet. Mary has been spending some time with her, mentoring her. Anna's been opening up more and has started interacting more since finding someone to confide in."

I nodded. "What about the baseball-scar-dude?"

"Well, I had a few conversations with him. His name's Paul. He has a degree in chemistry, so he enjoys hanging out in the science labs. He says the scar on his arm was from a mission he did overseas. Actually, he was originally from Holland and moved to Canada a few years ago. He has a thick accent, so people have a hard time understanding him despite being fluent in English," Rebecca explained.

"Which could explain why he doesn't talk much and tends to hang out by himself," Luke said, nodding.

"Exactly. It's a convincing story, at least," Rebecca said, resting her chin in her hand. "But a convincing story doesn't necessarily let him off the hook." She sipped her coffee. "What did you guys find?"

"I found some pretty interesting information about Carrie, our purple-hair person," I said, pushing my notes into the middle of the table. "I noticed her sneaking off into the woods behind the science lab, so I followed her. She walked all the way out to the wall and then made a phone call. I wasn't able to hear all of it, but she mentioned Rebecca and me in the call, and she talked about getting something over with. Then she said she needed to hang up before someone came looking for her and went back. Yesterday she went back to the woods behind the science lab again. I didn't get to follow her because I was teaching, but Hope and Faith said they saw her head out there." I leaned back and folded my arms. "That seems suspicious to me."

Rebecca nodded. "It is weird that someone would hide to make a phone call." She turned to Luke. "What did you find?"

Luke rolled his eyes. "Tracking Ryan and Ethan turned out to be harder than I expected. I tried to hang out with them casually, but Ethan always had some reason to exit our conversation or not meet to hang out." He sighed, running his fingers through his hair. "Honestly, it was hard to be friendly and objective in my spying because Ethan just rubs me the wrong way."

"Did you talk to Ryan at all?" I asked.

"I tried!" Luke exclaimed, throwing his hands up. "Any time I tried to talk to Ryan, Ethan would answer for him. And if I caught Ryan alone, we'd maybe get a few sentences in before Ethan would show up and talk for him again, or Ryan would get a message from Ethan and have to leave. It's like Ethan was deliberately keeping me from talking to Ryan."

"See, that seems odd," I said, raising an eyebrow.

"The question is, why would Ethan work so hard to keep you from talking to Ryan? Does Ryan know something Ethan doesn't want to get out?" Rebecca cocked her head thoughtfully.

"I also noticed they missed most meals in the dining hall. For the past three days, they only showed up at dinner. Out of those three days, only once did they sit with other people. That's very different in comparison to their first few days here," Luke said.

"Well, if Ethan is trying to keep Ryan silent, sitting by themselves and skipping mealtimes would help," I suggested.

We sat silently for a minute. "I think Carrie, Ethan, and Ryan are our most likely suspects," Rebecca said, leaning forward. Her face was serious and her eyes determined. "I think we need to focus our efforts on those three."

Luke nodded. "I think you're right." He sipped his coffee, then tipped his head toward Rebecca. "What did you learn from the email address of the threat you got?"

Rebecca shook her head. "Not much. I tracked the address, but whoever created it has already deleted this address. I did some scans on my computer and found some unusual codes in my email, and I figured they were leftover from the virus. After some work, I found out where the email was sent from. The computer lab."

"At Truth Squad?" I asked, raising my eyebrows.

"Yup. I couldn't figure out which device it came from, but its location was definitely from the computer lab."

"So, we need to look at the time stamp from the pictures you took and then check security cameras to see who was in the computer lab at the time," Luke said.

Rebecca nodded. "I think that should give us a lead." She pulled out her phone and looked through her pictures of the email. "It looks like the email was sent at 6:57am."

"So, we need to check the security cameras from before 6:57," Luke said.

"But can't you send emails that are set to show up at a certain time?" I asked. "Like, I can write an email, and when

I send it, I can choose to delay sending the email for a few hours."

"Good point." Luke nodded. "We can start with checking 6:57, and go back from there."

"Let's meet after dinner to look at the footage. Where do you want to meet?" Rebecca asked.

"The science lab," Luke said. "We can access the camera footage from there."

"Are we allowed to just access the footage?" I asked, raising an eyebrow. *Well, Luke already has been,* I thought, remembering his looking into the footage from the threats being switched.

Luke nodded confidently. "I've accessed footage before. We're Squad 4, so we both have access." He raised an eyebrow at me. "Why, are you worried about it?"

"I'm just thinking of Matthew catching us looking at security footage and saying it's proof that we've been up to something." I shook my head, nervousness flooding me. I sipped my coffee, trying to ignore my nervousness.

"I think we'll be fine," Luke said, his voice sounding reassuring, but his eyes hinted nervousness.

I walked briskly to the science lab, glancing around as I walked. I didn't see Matthew anywhere, but it didn't calm my nerves. I pulled the science lab door open and stepped inside. Luke and Rebecca were the only ones there.

"Hi, Sarah!" Luke smiled and waved me over to the computer by the back door.

"What took you so long?" Rebecca teased, elbowing me as I joined them.

I shook my head but didn't answer. I had taken my time

finishing eating, trying to pay attention to what was going on around me. I noticed Ethan and Ryan sat alone again during dinner. Matthew seemed to be keeping his eye on us. I was surprised to see Carrie laughing with her friend, Alethia. She didn't seem to be so absorbed with watching her surroundings now that Alethia was here. I had also waited until Matthew left before heading to the science lab. I didn't want him trailing any of us.

Luke logged into the computer. "Okay, let's get to the security system."

Rebecca tapped me. "Let's do some experimenting," she said, nodding toward the center table.

I shrugged. "Sure." *She probably wants us to look less conspicuous on camera,* I thought. *It's probably a good idea. I'm sure Matthew's been watching the security cameras extra closely.*

I got some tools out while Rebecca grabbed some scrap metal from the box under the table labeled "free scraps." We started putting the scraps together in different ways, trying to decide what to make with it.

"We could make metal art," I suggested. "We could spray paint it and hang it in our room."

Rebecca agreed, and we got the pieces laid out in a fun pattern.

"Got it!" Luke exclaimed.

We joined Luke back at the computer. He had the security camera footage up from the time Rebecca received the email. We watched the footage.

"There's no one there." I shook my head. "Maybe they were there the night before and timed the email to send in the morning," I suggested. I glanced over at Rebecca. She was studying the footage intensely.

"What are you thinking?" Luke asked her.

Rebecca pointed to the time in the corner of the footage. "Back the video up a couple minutes and watch the time." Luke pulled the video back and pressed play. I stared at the time. *6:53. 6:54. It's staying on 6:54 for quite a while,* I noticed.

"It still hasn't changed," Luke said.

"Exactly," Rebecca said, nodding. "Classic trick, and rookie mistake."

"What do you mean?" I asked.

"Oh," Luke said, his eyes widening with understanding. "You mean the trick you pulled on me when I went undercover at the PBPC."

Rebecca nodded. "You freeze the frame to a picture of an empty room so that when you walk in, you can't be seen. It's a good trick because most people won't check the time stamp, but professionals know that a good security run-through includes checking the time stamp. It's a rookie mistake to not leave the time running while you freeze the frame."

"I'm guessing it's challenging to keep the time running," I said.

"Yeah, it took me a while to figure it out." Rebecca pointed to the screen. "Look, the time just changed from 6:54 to 6:59. The screen was frozen for five minutes."

"So, our culprit was in the computer lab for five minutes and, during that time, was able to send you an email with an encrypted virus?" Luke said, shaking his head. "That's fast work."

Rebecca crossed her arms. "You're right. Whoever did this may have made a rookie mistake on the camera clock, but to have gotten their email encrypted that quickly is pro work."

"Could they create the email on a personal device and then sent it from a computer in the lab?" I asked.

Rebecca shrugged. "That's a good point. They probably

could have." She paused. "No matter what, they're still good at what they're doing. The virus made it extremely difficult to track where anything came from. I worked on it for several hours."

Luke closed out the security footage and signed out of the computer. "So, is there anything else we can do to figure out who sent you the email?"

We thought silently. *I have no clue. This is not my specialty,* I thought, frustrated.

Rebecca sighed. "I can't think of anything."

Luke ran his fingers through his hair, obviously frustrated. "Me neither."

We walked out of the science lab in heavy silence. "Hey!" Luke said, turning towards us with a huge grin. "You know what I think we need?"

"What?" Rebecca asked, raising an eyebrow.

"Doughnuts!" Luke grinned, double-raising his eyebrows. "Doughnuts are my de-stressor," he said, placing his hand on his heart.

We laughed. "Sounds good!" Rebecca said.

CHAPTER 6

I was startled awake by the emergency alarm on my watch. *What is going on?* I wondered, looking at the time on my clock. 5:30. I grabbed my watch from the lamp table and read the alert.

"All Squad 4 agents to conference room 100. Urgent."

That's vague, I thought. I jumped out of bed and quickly got into uniform. I brushed my hair and put it in a quick bun, then hurried out of my room.

"What's going on?" Rebecca asked, stepping out of her own room, looking confused.

"Squad 4 meeting," I said, hurrying to get my boots on. I felt guilty for making so much noise so early in the morning.

"Is there an emergency?" Rebecca asked, plopping down on the couch.

I shrugged. "Must be since they're calling a meeting at 5:30. I'll see you later!" I rushed out the door, trying to be quiet as I made my way down the stairs.

Once I got outside, I picked up my pace, no longer needing to worry about being quiet. I saw other Squad 4 agents hurrying toward the conference building.

"Do you know what's going on?" I asked Luke, catching up to him as we entered the building.

He shook his head. "No clue."

We filed into the conference room and took our seats. Despite meeting in a different room than usual, we all sat in our usual pattern. Mr. Truth and Matthew stood at the head of the table, and everyone else sat together based on their training and roles at Truth Squad. I sat with two other flight technicians. Luke sat on the opposite side of the table with others trained in special operations with a focus on spy work and acting. I noticed everyone at the table looked just as confused as I felt.

Maybe this is a drill, I thought, looking to the head of the table. Matthew and Mr. Truth were the only ones who didn't look confused, but Mr. Truth's calm expression was unreadable.

"Welcome, agents. Thank you, all, for getting here so quickly," Mr. Truth stated.

I don't think this is a drill, I thought, noticing him pause and take a deep breath.

"This morning, we received an unusual, anonymous message to our mainframe system," Mr. Truth said, looking around the table. "It appeared long enough for our security officer to read it before disappearing."

Just like the email Rebecca got, I thought. I glanced at Luke. He made eye contact and raised his eyebrows. I figured he was thinking the same thing.

Luke raised a hand. "What was the message?"

A security officer standing at the opposite end of the table stepped forward. "I didn't have time to copy it before it disappeared," he explained, "but I wrote down what I remembered, and I think I have it all." He unfolded a piece of paper in his hand. "It said, 'Get ready. 3:00. An adventure awaits. Amidst the excitement, oh, do take the bait. There is only one thing I want, you must know. Don't try to run. You have nowhere to go.'"

"It rhymes? That's creepy," Luke said, his eyes wide.

Matthew cleared his throat. Luke straightened up, acting like he'd never interrupted.

"After the rhyming part, at the bottom of the email, it said, 'Don't track me. You won't find me.' And then the email destroyed itself." The security officer folded the paper back up and walked over to Mr. Truth.

"Thank you," Mr. Truth said, taking the paper. "I've called Squad 4 together because we don't take threats lightly."

Don't take threats lightly? I thought, raising an eyebrow.

"Security, Matthew, and I believe that this note constitutes a threat." Mr. Truth glanced around the room.

So, the threat Rebecca received is a joke, and this one is for real? I thought, anger boiling up in me.

"We've called everyone here because we need to look into this threat. We need to prepare for the worst but hope for the best." Matthew nodded, standing tall with his hands behind his back.

"I want to get some techs looking into the email," Mr. Truth said. "Officer Scott can show you to the device he was using, although the message was sent to the mainframe, so it probably doesn't matter where you look for it."

Hannah, one of the computer techs, raised her hand. "Actually, it will be helpful to use the same device. I bet we can look for unusual codes and trace back to the source."

But they won't be able to, I thought, leaning back in my chair, my heart rate picking up. *If this is the same person, they'll track back to the computer lab and find no evidence.*

"Sounds good. Hannah, Paul, and Matthias, when can you get to work on that?" Mr. Truth asked.

Hannah stood up. "Now."

"Good. But make sure you eat breakfast, too," Mr. Truth said, raising his eyebrows. Mr. Truth was particular about making sure his agents stayed healthy, and he believed eating breakfast was an essential aspect of that. Agents could only perform their best when they were well-fueled, he would say, just as any jet can only perform at all when fueled up. It made me smile.

The techs excused themselves and followed Officer Scott out of the room.

"Let's do some brainstorming. Is there anything in the note that someone heard that seemed important?" Matthew asked.

"The time. Three o'clock," Mary said, looking up at her husband.

Mr. Truth nodded at his wife. "Whatever this 'adventure' is, we need to be ready for it at three."

"And what's with taking the 'bait?' Is it just for rhyming purposes, or does our mysterious sender want us to respond in a particular fashion?" Gideon, one of the special operations agents, asked.

Matthew shrugged. "We don't know. This message is so vague."

I raised my hand. "Were there any hidden messages? I mean, things like italicized letters or changes in font that we need to focus on?"

"I don't know," Mr. Truth replied. "Let me message Officer Scott and ask if he remembers."

"Wait a minute!" Luke exclaimed, jumping to his feet. "Why are we relying solely on Officer Scott's memory? I mean, not that he has a bad memory," Luke corrected, waving his hand. "But what I'm thinking is, the security cameras are designed to see every angle in a room, which means we have to be able to see the mainframe computer from a camera, right?"

Matthew leaned his head back and sighed in frustration. "Why didn't I think of that? Of course, we can!" He gave Luke a slap on the back. "Good thinking! We can look at the footage and zoom in on the message before it disappeared."

"And then we can see if there are any special letters or words we need to pay attention to!" Luke said excitedly.

Matthew signed into the big screen computer on the wall. He quickly pulled up the security footage and found the message. He zoomed in and adjusted the clarity so we could read the words.

I noticed the sender of this message didn't have any address or time stamp on the message. *They learned from their mistakes on the last threat,* I thought.

"The letters 're' in 'adventure' and 'b' in 'bait' are italicized," Luke noted.

"Look, some of the letters are capitalized," I said, standing up and walking over to the screen. I used my finger on the touch screen to circle the letters. Inside the words "await," "amidst," "excitement," "there," "one," "you," and "must" were the capitalized letters W-A-T-C-H-O-U-T.

"Watch out?" Luke said, looking at me with raised eyebrows.

Mr. Truth shook his head. "That doesn't offer any clarity to the threat. It just makes it seem more... sinister."

"What does this mean?" I asked, pointing to some numbers and letters in the bottom corner of the message. CA1214PS25262728.

"It could be part of the code used to self-destruct the message," Gideon suggested.

That answer didn't satisfy me. *Everything else in this message is significant. That has to be significant, too.*

I glanced at Luke and noticed he was discretely taking a picture of the screen with his phone. He slipped his phone back into his pocket before anyone seemed to notice.

After a few more minutes of unsuccessful brainstorming, Mr. Truth decided to end the meeting. "I want everyone to stay in uniform and stay on alert, especially as it gets closer to three," Mr. Truth said. "Watch out for unusual activity and be prepared for action. Report anything remotely suspicious to me, Matthew, or security. I'd like to station Squad 4 teams on patrol every hour. I'll get a schedule posted by eight. Until then, Gideon, can you and your squad take the morning patrol?"

Gideon nodded. "Do you want full-grounds patrol or just the main campus?"

"Full-grounds."

"Yes, sir. We'll get on it." Gideon stood, and the rest of his squad joined him.

Mr. Truth looked around the table. "The rest of you stay alert for the posting of your squad's time. This meeting is adjourned."

We filed out of the meeting room. I followed Luke, and once we were outside, I tapped his shoulder. "What are you going to do with those pictures?" I whispered.

"Show them to Rebecca," he replied. "The italicized 'REB?' While everyone else said it made no sense, I'm pretty sure that's short for 'Rebecca.' This threat is really meant for her."

I sighed. "I was thinking the same thing."

"Is Rebecca up? Should I message her to meet us somewhere?" Luke asked.

I nodded. "She'll be up."

Luke messaged Rebecca, and we decided to meet at the walking paths. When Rebecca joined us, Luke showed her the threat.

Rebecca raised her eyebrows. "Am I supposed to see this? I'm not a Squad 4 agent."

Luke rolled his eyes. "Technically, no, but I'm positive this message was meant for you. Did you notice the italicized letters?"

"The 'REB'?" she said, looking at the pictures again. "Yeah. I also noticed the capital letters that spell 'watch out.'"

"What's up with the numbers at the end?" I asked, pointing out the CA1214PS25262728. "No one paid much attention to them during the meeting, but since everything is so purposeful in this note, I feel like they must mean something."

We stared at the sequence. "It seems like some kind of code," Luke said, shaking his head. "But what are we supposed to unlock with it? Do the numbers correspond to letters?"

I shook my head. "I don't think so. Look at how many twos there are. It wouldn't spell anything. And if you were to match them with the other numbers, it would be twenty-five through twenty-eight, and there aren't twenty-eight letters in the alphabet."

Luke shrugged. "Good point. What else could it be?" We stared at the numbers longer. "Are the letters significant?" Luke asked.

"C-A-P-S," I read. "Caps."

"The capital letters spelled 'watch out,' so we already found those," Rebecca said. Suddenly, her eyes widened. "What if the numbers correspond to words in the note?"

"That's an idea," Luke said. "Should we count out one, two, one, four? Or should we assume it's twelve, fourteen, twenty-five, and so on?"

We looked closer at the words. "It doesn't make sense to do one, two, one, four," I said. "It has to be the other."

Rebecca ran her finger along the words, counting. "Twelve is take... fourteen is bait."

"Twenty-five through twenty-eight is 'don't try to run,'" Luke finished.

"'Take bait, don't try to run'? That doesn't make much sense." I shook my head.

Rebecca raised an eyebrow. "Maybe..."

"What?" Luke asked excitedly.

Rebecca paused. "I'm not sure, but... it kind of reminds me of Code Forty-Five."

"What's Code Forty-Five?" I asked.

"Don't take the bait and don't try to run; use your brains," Rebecca explained. "Code Forty-Five was all about staying alert to what's going on around you and thinking one step ahead of your opponent."

Luke nodded. "That makes sense. I really think this threat is from the same person the other ones were from. But what's with these codes? What does this person want?"

I glanced at my watch. "It's almost eight. The patrol list should be up by the time we get back to the conference room."

"Yeah, we should probably go check that," Luke said, heading back.

I fell behind Luke and Rebecca, lost in thought. *Why are all these threats codes? They don't even seem to go together. And why is there an "adventure" at three? What does this person have planned?*

I looked up from watching the ground when I heard some giggling. Carrie and her friend were walking from the dorms to the mess hall. *Is Carrie the one sending these threats? Or is it Ethan, or Ryan? I wonder if any of them have backgrounds in coding?* I thought.

Luke had already gone inside to read the patrol list and was leaving the conference room when I reached the door. "Matthew, you, and I are on patrol from two to three."

I raised my eyebrows. "Interesting."

"What?"

I shrugged. "It's interesting that our shift ends at three, and that we're with Matthew. It seems like he's intentionally making sure he can keep an eye on us."

"Or separate us from Rebecca," Luke said. He turned to Rebecca. "Do you have anything going on during that time?"

Rebecca shook her head. "Just studying for classes."

Luke nodded. "Maybe you should study outside where people can see you. That way, if something happens at three, there can be witnesses to say you were studying, not creating whatever 'adventure' is supposed to happen."

"Okay."

The breakfast bell rang, and we hurried off.

I snapped my utility belt into place and pulled on my blue Truth Squad baseball cap.

"Three minutes till two!" Rebecca called. "I'm headed outside." I heard the door open and close.

After making sure my uniform was pristine, I hurried out of our room and headed toward the front gate where Matthew said we'd trade posts. I waved at Rebecca as I hurried past her sitting at a picnic table in the shade. She smiled as she opened her textbook and mouthed "good luck."

As I neared the front gate, I saw Matthew and Luke already there. The ordinarily talkative friends were unusually quiet, not even facing each other. Luke was bouncing on his toes, thumbs in his pockets. Matthew stood at attention with his arms folded. The tension was awkward.

I forced a smile as I walked up. "How's it going? You two ready?"

Luke grinned. "Always ready!" He gave a thumbs-up.

"Yes," Matthew answered, eyeing me suspiciously.

We stood in awkward silence. I glanced around me, noticing the group we were supposed to be replacing wasn't in sight. I checked my watch, noting it was already 2:01. "Should we just get started even though the other group isn't here? Were they supposed to meet us to switch off?" I asked.

Matthew glanced at his watch. "Oh, it's two. Hmm." He scanned the area. "I'll call their leader." Matthew pushed a button on his watch. "James?"

James's voice sounded through Matthew's watch. "Yes, Matthew. James, here."

"We are in position to start our patrol," Matthew said. He paused for a minute, looking thoughtful. "You know, your group doesn't need to worry about meeting up with us. Just let us know where you left off and anything unusual you've noticed."

"Okay. We had half our group take the path around the perimeter fence while the other half patrolled the main campus area. We didn't quite finish going around the perimeter. Stopped about halfway through quadrant three. No unusual activity has been identified."

"Sounds good. Thanks. Out." Matthew turned off the communications.

"I think we should finish up the perimeter search and then head to the main campus area after that," Luke suggested.

Matthew glared at Luke. "I'll make the decisions." I widened my eyes. Matthew was not normally this way.

Luke raised his hands in surrender. "Okay. Whatever."

Matthew pressed his lips together and sighed. "You're right, though. We need to be in the main area as it gets closer to three so that we can prevent this threat from happening. Let's head to quadrant three."

Luke glanced at me and shrugged. We followed behind Matthew. "I do not know what's up with him," Luke muttered.

I shook my head. "He's so focused on trying to prove Rebecca guilty. I'm worried he's going to hinder us from finding the real culprit."

Luke rolled his eyes. "He already is. If he wasn't so suspicious of us, we probably could have convinced Mr. Truth of the seriousness of the other threats Rebecca's gotten."

"What are you two doing?" Matthew's harsh voice cut into our conversation.

"Talking," Luke replied sarcastically.

"Quit talking and do your job," Matthew snapped.

We completed the perimeter walk with minimal communication. We didn't find anything unusual, so we headed to the main campus. As we walked, I waited for Matthew to give us instructions for this part of our patrol, afraid to say anything that would make him angry.

We walked past the science building, still silent. Luke finally spoke up. "So..." he paused, then grinned. "Hast thou any plan, Sir Matthew?"

Matthew turned to face us, rolling his eyes. "We need to be thorough. Three o'clock will be here in thirty-five minutes. I think we should follow a grid pattern. One of us will go east to west, one of us will go north to south, and the other will go north-west to south-east. Whenever we cross paths, we'll update each other."

"I can take north-south," I offered.

Matthew nodded his approval. "I'll do east-west and leave Luke the challenge of north-west to south-east."

Luke rubbed his hands together, grinning. "I'm always up for a challenge!"

We parted ways, and I headed back to the science building. Once there, I faced north and began walking that direction. I tried not to walk too fast so I could watch closely for any unusual activity. I made my way through three passes heading north, south, and north again. Nothing was unusual. As I turned south again, I walked through the open space between the buildings. I glanced at the picnic table Rebecca had been studying at. My eyes widened. She wasn't there.

Where did Rebecca go? I wondered, looking around me. I took a deep breath, realizing I was panicking. *She probably found somewhere else to sit since that table isn't in the shade anymore,* I reasoned. I continued walking south. *Why would she move out of this main area, though? The whole point was for her to be sitting where people could see her and vouch for her if she got blamed for the threat.*

"Hi, Sarah!"

I jumped at the voice and whirled around. I saw Faith, Hope, and Rebecca headed toward me from the mess hall. Seeing Rebecca was with the twins flooded me with relief, but I could also feel my cheeks turn red. *You shouldn't jump to suspicious conclusions so fast like Matthew,* I scolded myself.

I forced a smile. "What are you three up to?" I asked.

Hope held up a popsicle. "They're giving out popsicles in the mess hall right now. Do you want one?"

I shook my head, pointing to my cap. "I'm on duty right now, but thanks for the offer. Maybe there will be some left when I'm finished."

"I doubt it," Rebecca said, grinning. "I saw Daniel take three."

I laughed. "Of course, he would!"

The twins and Rebecca waved and headed to a picnic table in the shade. I continued my march south, looking around me as I walked. *Nothing,* I sighed, reaching the end of the main space. I walked a couple yards over and turned north again. As I walked, I began to wonder whether we were doing the right kind of patrol. *Should we be monitoring the airspace above us? Should we be watching our computer systems, or patrolling the buildings instead of the grounds?*

I found myself yawning as I turned south again. I crossed paths with Luke a few yards later. "Nothing?" I asked.

He shook his head. "Nope. Not a trace." He glanced at his watch. "It's 2:54, so six minutes until the 'adventure' is supposed to take place."

I nodded and continued walking. After crossing paths with Matthew a couple minutes later and hearing the same negative report, my suspicion escalated. "Matthew, what if we're on the wrong track? Is anyone monitoring the computer systems or the airspace?" I asked.

Matthew rolled his eyes. "We have to be ready for any kind of danger, whether physical or cybernetic. We can't stop patrolling the grounds just because we received the threat electronically." With that, he pivoted and marched on.

"That didn't answer my question," I muttered. I sighed and glanced at my watch. *2:59.* My heart rate sped up. *One minute left.* I picked up my pace as I neared the edge of the perimeter and turned around, hurrying back to the buildings. *If something's gonna happen, it's got to be in one of the main buildings,* I thought.

Suddenly, a deafening boom came through the loud-speakers. I covered my ears as an obnoxiously loud, robotic voice rang out, "Three... two... one." A bright flash came from between the science lab and computer lab, and then a smoke bomb exploded. I pressed a button on my watch. "Matthew, Luke, smoke bomb between science and computer labs!"

I ran toward the smoke as other Squad Four agents directed people away from the smoke and toward the safety shelter.

"Sarah, look!" Rebecca called, running up beside me, pointing to the control center. We saw two people duck inside.

"Let's go!" Luke said from behind us. He ran toward the door. We followed behind him.

Luke shoved the door open. "Hey, what's going on?" he called as we rushed in. The control center was filled with smoke. I heard footsteps running up the stairs. We hurried after them.

The intruders lead us to the mainframe computer room. The light from the main computer reflected off the smoke, concealing the two intruders.

"You need to exit the building and head to the safety shelter." My order ended with a cough from the thick smoke. I walked toward the two people.

"Okay, well, take this!" The taller intruder shoved me to the ground, forcing a metal object into my hands.

"Stop!" Luke yelled. He lunged at the intruders. I heard a scuffle and then footsteps running back down the stairs.

Rebecca helped me up. "What is that?" she asked, pointing to the object.

"I can't see with this smoke," I said. "Let's go."

We ran back downstairs and out the back door, following the sound of the intruders' and Luke's footsteps. As we stepped outside, I noticed more smoke throughout the campus. I could

CHAPTER 7

"Well?" Matthew yelled, stepping closer.

I shook my head, staring at the metal object. "I... I don't..." Suddenly, it clicked. "Wait, is that a detonator?"

Matthew cocked his head. "Is it? It was in your hands, so you should know."

My jaw dropped as I realized what he thought. "Wait, Matthew, let me explain. We were following these two people into the computer lab—"

Matthew shook his head. "Likely story. You have a story for everything, don't you? I have work to do, and so do you. But we are not done with this." He shook the detonator, then pointed it at Rebecca. "And don't think for a moment that you can place all the blame on your sister. I know what you're doing."

I watched him march off, horrified. "What have we done?"

"It's not what we've done, it's what those two intruders did. This was a brilliant plot to frame us," Rebecca said. I glanced at her, noticing how calm she was. "Let's just focus on what we need to do. I need to be in the safety shelter, and you need to help Squad 4."

I nodded. "You're right." I headed back to the main grassy area to help the team with the smoke bombs. *Get your head in the game. Don't think about Matthew right now,* I told myself as I joined my squad. Daniel filled Luke and me in on our job. "We're assigned to scanning the mess hall for smoke bombs," Daniel said, starting toward the building.

"Are we waiting for Matthew?" Luke asked.

Daniel shook his head. "I don't know where he is, and time is of the essence."

I stepped into the mess hall behind Daniel and Luke and took a deep breath of the smoke-free air. I regretted such a deep breath as I started coughing again. "That smoke is terrible," I choked out, shaking my head.

Daniel coughed. "Yeah. I'm glad we're working in here instead of out there," he said, pointing his thumb behind him. "Anyways, I'll search the kitchen, and you two can search this main area. Sound good?"

I nodded, and Luke saluted him. "Sir, yes sir!" he said.

We scoured the building but found no evidence of a smoke bomb. "I'd say that's mission accomplished!" Daniel said.

Luke pointed to the closet. "Did anyone check the janitor's closet?"

"Oh, I forgot about that," Daniel said, swinging open the door. I noticed a black dot on the outside of the door as Daniel opened it. The two guys looked inside the closet, Luke checking the top shelf while Daniel rummaged through the cleaning supplies.

I walked over to the front of the door and looked at the black dot. It looked like a peep-hole. I checked the other side of the door, but the wood was smooth. I pulled the black dot off the door. It had been stuck on with a glue dot. "Guys, I think I found something."

"What is it?" Daniel asked, walking over.

"I don't know."

He grabbed the object and turned it over in his hand. "That's odd."

"What?" Luke asked, joining us.

"Isn't this a remote video camera?" Daniel asked, showing Luke the button. "I've used these before during some detective work."

Luke looked it over. "I think you're right."

"How does it work?" I asked.

"It only works if it's connected wirelessly to a computer," Daniel explained. "As long as it's connected to a computer, you can record endless footage, at least until your computer runs out of storage. This one is rounded on the top, see? That means it's meant to see 180-degrees of footage. It won't be as clear as a flat one that has a more focused view, but it would still be clear enough to see what's happening."

"Why is this in the mess hall?" Luke tapped his chin. "I mean, it could come in handy to see what people are eating in case something looks tasty and I want to get some."

Daniel laughed. "True, but I doubt that's the point. Most people use these for spying on other people, not food."

"So, the question is, who put it here?" I asked, folding my arms.

Daniel shrugged. "I don't know, but we'd better take this to Mr. Truth. We should also check for other hidden devices like this if there's any possibility it's connected with the threat and smoke bombs."

We decided to do another check of the mess hall for more hidden cameras but didn't find any. Daniel volunteered to run the camera to Mr. Truth.

We walked out of the mess hall. The thick smoke had cleared, and now the air just smelled like smoke. After watching Daniel jog off, I turned to Luke. "So, where did the intruders go?"

Luke sighed and shrugged. "I lost them in the crowd headed to the safety shelter. I didn't get a good glimpse at either of them, but the taller guy had a baseball cap on backward."

"We should tell Rebecca to keep an eye out for someone with a baseball cap," I said, typing a quick message into my watch.

"What held you and Rebecca up?" Luke asked.

I looked up from my watch and rolled my eyes. "Matthew."

Luke crossed his arms. "What was it this time?"

"One of the intruders shoved something into my hands before they left. When we got outside to where we could see, which is when Matthew showed up, we found out it was a detonator. I tried to tell him about the intruders, but he wouldn't listen. He's convinced Rebecca is trying to frame me."

Luke took a deep breath. "Or the intruders were trying to frame you."

"That's what Rebecca thought."

We stopped our conversation as Daniel ran back to join us. "Mr. Truth wants us to search the conference building and the training building for more of these mini cameras." He waved for us to follow him.

We spent two hours searching every inch of the training and conference buildings. We found three cameras in the training building but none in the conference rooms. After turning in the cameras to the security team, we headed back to report to Mr. Truth.

I thought through the locations of the cameras we'd found so far. *One in the dining hall, one in the training room itself, one in the equipment room outside the training room, and one by the stairs leading up to the control room. All places anyone can be. No cameras in the kitchen where only cooking staff can be, or in the conference room where only Squad Four can be, unless there's an unusual circumstance. So, it's most likely not a Squad Four member planting these cameras.*

We reached Mr. Truth's office to find another group giving their report. My heart rate doubled as I noticed Matthew sitting next to Mr. Truth, taking notes.

Luke nudged me. "You look tense," he mouthed, winking. I rolled my eyes, and he grinned. "Relax."

I rolled my shoulders and stood up straight, forcing a smile. *Lord, please help me to stay calm,* I prayed.

We stepped forward as the other team finished their report and left. Mr. Truth nodded. "What did you find?"

"Three more cameras in the training center," Daniel replied. He filled him in on the location of each camera. "We gave them to security to investigate further."

"But no cameras in the conference room?" Mr. Truth asked, raising an eyebrow.

"No, sir." Daniel shook his head.

"My question is, why would someone put all these cameras in public places and not somewhere where they could listen in on important conversations or get access to important stuff?" Luke said, crossing his arms.

Matthew looked up from his notetaking and glared at me. "Maybe they already have access to 'important stuff.'"

I opened my mouth to defend myself, but Luke jumped in. "Maybe this person doesn't have access to those locations, or maybe that's not the kind of information they're looking for."

"What kind of information would anyone want that's not the top-notch stuff?" Daniel asked, raising an eyebrow.

Information on where my sister is at, I thought. *This is all a part of trying to get her, I just know it. But why?*

🔫

"Did you see anyone with a baseball cap?" I whispered to Rebecca as we walked to our room.

Once we were sure all the smoke bombs were taken care of, and there were no other threats, everyone was allowed to leave the safety shelter. It looked like everyone was headed to the dorms to clean up before dinner.

Rebecca shook her head. "No one. But I did notice three people missing."

"Carrie, Ethan, and Ryan?" I guessed.

She nodded. "Pretty suspicious."

We hurried up the stairs to our room. "I feel like I reek of smoke," I said, longing to shower and change clothes.

"You do." Rebecca grinned.

I rolled my eyes. "I wasn't wanting you to confirm it."

She laughed as she pushed the door to our room open. "What's this?" She pulled a sticky note off from underneath the door handle. I watched her face grow serious as she closed the door behind her. "Read it."

I grabbed the note and read it aloud. "No one will believe you, so give up while you have the chance. Don't let your teammates get in the line of fire." I looked up at Rebecca. "Another threat."

"This was probably placed here while everyone was supposed to be in the safety shelter."

"So, one of our three suspects placed it." I crossed my arms. "Do you think there would be camera evidence?"

Rebecca shrugged. "I doubt it, but it wouldn't hurt to

check. I doubt there would be fingerprints either, but we can check the note for those, too."

Rebecca messaged Luke to meet us at the computer lab, and we headed back out the door. I glanced at Rebecca as we hurried down the stairs. "Is that another code?"

She shook her head. "I think this note was a true threat."

That's odd, I thought as we stepped back outside. *Why wouldn't this threat also contain one of Mr. Zaiden's codes? All the other threats did.*

We got to the computer lab and found it blocked off with an investigation team still inside. "Well, there goes that plan," I said, shrugging.

We turned around and saw Luke jogging toward us. "Hey, guys!" He waved. He stopped next to Rebecca. "Looks like we can't get in."

Rebecca shook her head and handed the sticky note to him. "Read this."

Luke scanned the note. His eyebrows went up. "Wow."

"We were hoping to scan for fingerprints and also check the security footage to see who placed the note there," Rebecca said.

Luke nodded. "We can check the security from one of the classroom computers."

"Let's go." Rebecca spun around and headed toward the classroom building.

We hurried to the nearest classroom, and I logged in to the computer as a teacher. Luke quickly found the security footage for the hallways in the girls' dorms. He backed up the footage to three o'clock. We saw a few people hurry out of their rooms when the alarm went off. After those people left, the hallway was empty. *They probably froze the camera,* I thought, as we continued to watch an empty hallway.

After five minutes, I was starting to feel bored. "I don't think we're going to see anything."

"Wait a minute!" Rebecca pointed to another camera screen that was focused on the stairs. "Look, it's Carrie."

Carrie was running up the stairs, glancing over her shoulder. A second later, she appeared in the hallway. She ran to our door, stuck the note under the handle, and ran back down the stairs.

"She didn't have any gloves on," Rebecca noted.

"She was also careless about touching the door handle, and she didn't freeze the camera," Luke said. "This work doesn't seem to match the rest of the work we've been looking into."

I raised an eyebrow. "Do you think she's not the one behind this? Even though she's the one in the video?"

Rebecca shrugged. "I can't say for sure, but it does seem odd that this work is so sloppy compared to the rest of the threats we've gotten."

As Luke and Rebecca discussed the details of the video, I thought back to the events at three o'clock. *The bombs went off, everything was chaotic, then Rebecca pointed out the people heading into the control center. By the time we chased the intruders out of the control center, five minutes would have gone by. So, neither of the intruders could have been Carrie.* "I bet Carrie is a diversion for Ethan and Ryan," I said.

Luke raised an eyebrow. "What do you mean?"

"There's no way Carrie could have been one of the intruders in the control center and have planted this note. And you both said that the work seemed too sloppy compared to the other threats. I'll bet that Ethan and Ryan asked her to put the sticky note on the door, and they intentionally made sure she was in the cameras so that we would start tracking her instead of them."

"That makes sense," Luke said, folding his arms. "They're trying to throw us off their trail by having us track down Carrie."

"So, we need to figure out what Ethan and Ryan were doing in the control room, right?" I asked, excitedly.

"Hold on a second," Rebecca said, waving her hand. "We don't know for sure that Ethan and Ryan were the ones in the control center, although it is a good guess."

I sighed. "So, what do we do then?"

We stood silently for a minute. Luke shook his head. "I don't have any ideas. Why don't we pray about it?"

Rebecca and I nodded in unison. *We should be praying about this more. God knows what's going on,* I thought. We joined hands and bowed our heads.

Luke started us off. "Lord, we have ourselves in a predicament. I confess, we should have been coming to You with this more than we have. Forgive me for thinking that I could solve this problem in my own strength. God, we ask for Your wisdom to guide us in our next step. We're stuck, not sure how to find the evidence we need to prove who's behind these threats, and we have no idea what the purpose is behind them. We've also done a good job making ourselves look guilty to Matthew. Please show us the next step and keep us safe."

Rebecca and I each took a turn praying. As Rebecca finished, Mr. Truth's voice came over the intercom. "Luke, Rebecca, Sarah, please come to my office. Now."

❧

My heart was pounding as we stepped into Mr. Truth's office. Matthew stood next to him with a grim but satisfied look on his face. *What is going on?* I worried, not liking his expression.

"What's up?" Luke asked, his voice amazingly upbeat and his mannerisms calm, considering the looks on Mr. Truth's and Matthew's faces.

Mr. Truth silently motioned for us to sit. I glanced nervously at Rebecca, but she looked calm. I sat down, shivering at Matthew's cold glare. *This doesn't look good.*

"I'll get straight to the point," Mr. Truth said, sighing. "Rebecca, your parole file has been wiped from our system. There is no evidence, no tracks leading anywhere. Whoever did this knew what they were doing."

"What are you saying?" Luke asked, crossing his arms.

"I don't know of anyone else here who has skills so good as yours, Rebecca," Mr. Truth said.

"But you have no proof," I said, my voice coming out more anxious than I intended.

Mr. Truth turned to face me. "Matthew informed me that he ran into the two of you leaving the control center with a detonator in your hands, and the security cameras in that building were disabled before the smoke bombs went off."

My stomach dropped. The evidence stacked against us was mounting. *But it wasn't our fault!* I inwardly screamed.

Mr. Truth turned back to Rebecca. "I have given you the benefit of the doubt, I've given you second chances, but this—this is the last straw." He shook his head.

Rebecca leaned forward. "Mr. Truth, I don't mean to be disrespectful, but you said there weren't any clues, and running into Matthew outside the control center is hardly proof. What makes you so sure it was me?" Rebecca was amazingly calm.

Mr. Truth paused. "That's a good point. However, there

has been a lot of suspicious activity lately, and you have been connected to it—all three of you have been, in fact. You're right that there isn't proof, but there seems to be a strong connection." He stood up and shook his head. "I'm sorry, but I will have to report this to your parole officer. He will be the one to decide what our next step will be."

My heart sank. "But Mr. Truth, that's not fair—"

"Sarah, Luke, I wouldn't try arguing. You two are also in hot water."

I closed my mouth, gritting my teeth. *How can he do this? We aren't the guilty ones! Why is this happening?* Anger started to build up inside me. I glanced over at Matthew and saw a cocky smirk on his face. *Is he happy about this?* I felt a sudden urge to punch him.

"Luke, Sarah, I am temporarily suspending your access to the control center, training center, and Squad Four activities until we can investigate this matter further," Mr. Truth said, opening his office door. "Rebecca, you are also suspended from access to the training room." His face softened a little. "I'm sorry, but it's protocol. We'll contact you when we've finished conducting our investigation."

The three of us slowly walked out of the building. I kept my eyes glued to the ground, not wanting to make eye-contact for fear I would cry.

Luke growled and kicked a pinecone in the grass. "I can't believe those two!" I looked up to see his eyes fiery and his fists doubled. "We've got to figure this out before the parole officer shows up again."

"Is it even possible?" I asked, blinking back tears.

"It has to be!" Luke replied, hitting a fist against his hand. He shook his head and ran his fingers through his hair. "We have to at least try," he said softly.

Rebecca rested a hand on his shoulder. "It'll be okay. God will bring the truth to light."

We stood silently for a minute. *Lord, please help us. Things just went from bad to worse.*

Suddenly, Rebecca's eyes lit up. "I have an idea!"

🔫

I sat in the shadow of a rhododendron bush next to the side door of the dorm. I glanced up at the darkening sky. *I think I've been sitting here for almost an hour,* I thought, frustrated. *This was a bad idea.*

My mind wandered back to Mr. Truth's meeting. *Why would someone wipe Rebecca's parole file? Why would this benefit them?* I ran my hand over my hair, pulling at a strand that was caught in the rhododendron bush. *We still don't know what is behind the threats. All our leads have been dead ends, and we don't have a clue about the motivation behind any of it.* I could feel the tension building in my chest. I sighed, praying silently, *God, I don't know what to do. I've been sitting here for an hour, and nothing has happened. If we don't find a lead, my sister could be going back to jail.* An unexpected tear slipped down my cheek, and I quickly wiped it away. I let out a shaky breath, trying to keep myself from sobbing. *I'm supposed to be on the alert, and here I am crying. I'm not brave or strong,* I thought angrily. *I'm so afraid of losing my sister again after having her back for these two years. Lord, please give me strength.*

I jumped at the sound of the side door creaking open. I pushed myself back farther in the shadows and held my breath. I watched as Carrie quietly pressed the door closed. She turned around, looked over each shoulder, and then walked past me and around the corner behind the building.

I let out my breath and stood up quietly, pressing a finger to my earpiece. "She just exited the building. I'm following."

Rebecca's voice sounded in my ear. "Got it."

"Where's she headed?" Luke asked.

I slipped around the corner of the building and hurried to catch up to Carrie. It was dark enough I needed to follow closely to see where she was headed. Carrie stayed in the shadows, taking precise, quiet steps until she reached the walking trails. I dashed behind the nearest tree just before she looked over her shoulder. She stared behind her, squinting her eyes. I held my breath. *Did she hear me?* I worried.

She slowly turned toward the trail and started down it, taking a few quiet steps before shoving her hands in her pockets and picking up her pace.

I put my finger back on my earpiece. "Luke, she's headed your way."

"Got it!" Luke replied cheerfully.

I picked up my pace to stay close behind Carrie, staying off the walking trail near the trees so she wouldn't see me. *I hope there's no poison oak,* I thought, wishing I wasn't trailing Carrie in the dark.

"FYI, Sarah, I'm trailing Carrie on the other side of the path."

I looked to my left and spotted Rebecca's silhouette opposite me. We continued following Carrie in silence as she wound her way down the trail at a brisk pace. She glanced over her shoulder occasionally, but never stopped walking. I noticed the one-mile marker as we passed it, Carrie's pace not slowing. I stepped on a large branch, and it cracked, the sound echoing in the night air.

I froze. I felt like I had set off a bomb. I watched as Carrie stopped and whirled around. I was standing in the open, but

I didn't dare move to hide behind a tree because that would give me away for sure. I held perfectly still, holding my breath and hoping she didn't see me.

"Hello?" Carrie's voice shook.

I stood silently, hoping she would turn back around and keep walking.

"Hello."

Rebecca's voice made Carrie scream, and I jumped. I turned and saw her step out onto the path, turning on a small flashlight as she did. She motioned for me to step out.

What are you doing? I wanted to say, but Rebecca seemed confident, so I decided to follow her lead.

"Who are you?" Carrie asked, her voice shaking and her eyes wide. She held a smartphone in her hand.

"It's Rebecca and Sarah," Rebecca replied, shining the light at me and then herself before pointing it back on Carrie.

Carrie let out a shaky breath. "Why are you following me?" She lowered her eyebrows. "Are you spying on me because I'm out late?"

"No," I replied, shaking my head.

"Because I was just coming out here to make a private phone call," she continued as if I hadn't spoken.

"Private phone call? To whom?" Rebecca asked.

Carrie rolled her eyes. "None of your business."

"Is it the same person you call when you sneak out to the fence during the day?" I asked.

Carrie's eyes widened. "So, you have been spying on me!"

"I only saw you sneak out there once," I said, trying to keep her from getting upset.

Rebecca placed a hand on my arm and shook her head. "We have a question you need to answer," Rebecca said, changing the subject. "And it's not about your phone calls... hopefully."

She pulled the sticky note from her pocket. She shone the light on it. "Does this look familiar?"

I turned on my flashlight and pointed it at Carrie. Her eyes widened and her face grew pale, but she shook her head.

"Would it help jog your memory if I read it aloud?" Rebecca's voice was firm.

"I don't know what that is," Carrie replied, defensively.

"It's a sticky note," Rebecca replied sarcastically. "It showed up on our door this afternoon during the emergency."

"Are you suggesting I put it there?" Carrie asked, raising her voice.

"Well, now that you mention it—"

"I didn't do it!" Carrie shook her head, her face turning red.

"We have video evidence," I said.

Carrie sucked in a breath, pulling her hand to her mouth. She shook her head, her eyes moistening. "Wait, wait, wait. I... I didn't write that note." She stepped forward. "Please believe me. Someone handed it to me and asked me to put it on your door when the smoke bombs went off—"

"You knew the smoke bombs were going to go off?" Rebecca asked, sounding surprised.

Carrie gasped, clamping a hand over her mouth. "I didn't mean—"

Rebecca stepped forward. "You did know."

Carrie sighed, her shoulders sagging. "Please let me explain."

Rebecca nodded and folded her arms. "We're listening."

"Uh, well, these two guys caught me sneaking off one night to... to call my brother," Carrie explained, slowly.

"You don't need to sneak off to call your brother," I said, raising an eyebrow.

Carrie glared at me. "I just like privacy when I'm on the phone, okay?" I wasn't sure I was buying it, but I didn't reply.

Carrie continued, "The two guys threatened to tell Mr. Truth I was sneaking off at night. They said they wouldn't if I put the sticky note on your door when the smoke bombs went off. They said if I told anyone about the smoke bombs, they would be sure I got sent home." Carrie shrugged.

Something felt off about her story, but I wasn't sure what. "Who were these two guys?"

She shrugged. "They had masks on, okay?" She put her hands on her hips. "So, what are you going to do about it?"

Rebecca cocked her head. "We could report the incident..."

The color drained from Carrie's face again. "Please don't!"

"Or you could help us by telling us more about those two masked men." Rebecca raised an eyebrow. "I can tell you know more than what you're sharing." She stepped toward Carrie. "Look, you give us more information, and we'll keep your secret."

Carrie stood silently, looking at Rebecca, then me, and back at Rebecca.

Lord, we need a lead. Please let her decide to tell us more info, I prayed silently.

After a tense moment of silence, Carrie sighed. "Fine. I'll give you more info."

Rebecca smiled. "Great!" She put a finger to her ear. "Okay, Luke, come join us."

Luke stepped out of the shadows. Carrie whirled around, looking at Luke, then turned back to Rebecca, her eyes flaming. "I knew you were spying on me."

Rebecca's eyes softened, and she replied quietly, "Carrie, this note is a serious threat. We need to know that you're not a part of it, and we need to know who is behind it."

Carrie crossed her arms, shaking her head. She stared at the ground for a minute, then looked back up, her eyes glistening with tears. "I know it's serious." She sniffed. "I lied about the guys wearing masks."

"I think there's a bench around the corner next to the trail. Why don't we sit down while we talk?" Rebecca suggested, taking the lead.

Carrie followed, and Luke and I took the rear. I glanced at Luke, noticing a hint of pride in his eyes. *He's definitely got his eye on my sister.* I smiled at the thought.

We found the bench, and the three of us girls sat down while Luke leaned against a tree across from us. Rebecca turned to Carrie, who sat in between us. "So, what's the real story?"

Carrie shook her head. She took a shaky breath, keeping her eyes on the ground. "I haven't been calling my brother on the phone. I've been calling someone who's holding my brother hostage."

I jumped. "What?"

"He was supposed to be coming here for training with me, but these two guys needed another man to take his place so they could get some information, so they're holding him hostage until the end of training." Carrie was crying now. "I don't know who their man is. But this guy wants updates on what's going on, and I'm supposed to call him each day." She shook her head and stood up. "I shouldn't have told you. He said they'd kill him if I told anyone!" Her eyes were filled with terror.

I jumped up and put a hand on her shoulder. "No, it's a good thing you told us. We can help you."

Carrie wiped the tears from her cheeks. "How?"

"We've been trying to catch these guys for a while. With your information, hopefully, we'll be able to do that," I said.

"Yes," Rebecca agreed. "So, the guy you've been calling isn't here?"

Carrie sat back down and shook her head. "There's a guy in Canada holding my brother hostage, and the other guy is in the area, and he's the one I'm supposed to call. He's not on campus, but he said they have a man on campus. I don't know who that is, but it creeps me out." She shivered.

"Did the guy in the area tell you to put the note on our door?" Rebecca asked.

Carrie nodded. "He told me exactly what to write, told me when the smoke bombs were going to go off, and told me to put it on your door." She started crying again. "I didn't want to write that horrible note, but I had no choice. They have my brother!"

I sat back down and gave her a hug. Rebecca stood up and started pacing. "Have you ever seen the guy you call in person?" Carrie nodded. "Can you describe what he looks like?"

Carrie sniffed. "Kinda short and chubby. He has dark, curly hair and a goatee. And he always wears sunglasses."

Rebecca nodded and continued pacing. "Did he have an accent?"

"Yeah, a little. Maybe a faint New York accent?"

Rebecca stopped pacing, her eyes lighting up. "That's helpful information."

"Will you be able to catch them?" Carrie asked, her voice shaking.

"We will do everything we can to stop them," I assured her, although inside I wasn't so sure. *This mess just got a whole lot bigger.*

CHAPTER 8

After praying with Carrie, we walked back to the head of the trail and waited to talk until she had gone inside the dorms. Luke turned to face Rebecca. "Okay, so who's the guy Carrie described?"

Rebecca raised an eyebrow. "What makes you think I know the guy?"

Luke smirked. "Your emotionless agent skills are wearing down, my friend. Your eyes lit up like a lightbulb when she said the guy had a New York accent."

Rebecca rolled her eyes, but a smile still sneaked onto her face. "You're right."

"So, who is he?" I asked.

"If we are talking about the same person, then she might be describing Agent Braxton Niles," Rebecca said, tilting her head thoughtfully. "I did some training missions with him for a while when I first started working for Mr. Zaiden, but then he ended up moving to a new location. He showed up randomly a few other times when Mr. Zaiden needed him."

"What was his area of expertise?" Luke asked.

"Intimidation. He may have been short, but he had a commanding presence. He also would never take his sunglasses off, which added to the intimidation." Rebecca shook her head, smiling. "He was terrible with electronics, and his martial arts skills were poor, but he was a good messenger, and he was good at teaching new agents."

"Do you think he's the one behind the threats?" Luke asked, crossing his arms.

Rebecca shook her head. "He's a messenger, not a mastermind."

"Why would Carrie contact an agent off campus instead of the guy on campus?" I asked. "Wouldn't it be easier for her to talk to the guy who's here?"

Rebecca shrugged. "I would assume it keeps their undercover man better hidden to have her contact someone off-campus. If she were giving information to their undercover man, it would make him stand out more. Plus, if she gets caught and doesn't know who the undercover guy is, she won't be able to give him away."

I nodded, thinking back over Carrie's words. "She kept saying she didn't know who their man was on campus," I said, raising an eyebrow. "But two guys were in the computer room, most likely Ryan and Ethan. Why did she say, 'their man' instead of 'their men'?"

"Good point," Luke said, nodding. "I've been wondering what's up with Ryan. Like I told you before, anytime I tried to talk to just him, Ethan would cut me off."

We stood silently for a minute. I stared at the ground, trying to think of what to do. *Lord, what next? This operation just got more complicated. Show us what to do.*

"I think we have two options." I looked up to see Rebecca straighten, pulling her shoulders back, her face in a serious expression. "We can try and talk to Agent Braxton, or we can try and get Ryan alone to give us answers."

"I think that's only one option. Remember, Carrie said

they would kill her brother if she told anyone what was going on, and if we talk to Agent Braxton, her brother is dead." I shook my head. "That means we have to get Ryan to talk."

"That's probably the easier option, anyways," Luke said. "We know where he is, whereas we have no clue where this Braxton dude is." He stretched his arms and yawned. "I think we need to call it a night and reconvene in the morning. Coffee shop at seven? We can plan then."

Rebecca nodded. "Sounds good. See you then."

With a wave, Luke headed off to his dorm. Rebecca and I walked to our dorm in silence.

I walked into our living room and sat down on the couch, not feeling tired. My mind was racing through the day's events. I watched Rebecca walk into her room and softly close the door. I couldn't imagine the stress she must be under. *But she always keeps her cool,* I thought, frustrated that I could look so much like her on the outside but be so opposite on the inside. I sighed. *God, why didn't You give me more of those fearless, calm genes? Why do I have to be the scaredy-cat?* I felt a pang of guilt for complaining. *Sorry, God. It just doesn't seem fair that my identical twin can face threats against herself with such calm strength, and I feel like I'm falling apart when the threats aren't even toward me.*

Rebecca stepped back out of her room, dressed in her pajamas. She raised her eyebrows at me. "You know we have to get up early to meet Luke at the coffee shop, right?"

I nodded and gave a half-smile. "Yeah."

"But you're still up." Rebecca shook her head and came and sat down next to me. "What's up?"

I shrugged, staring at the wall. "My mind is racing, too awake for me to go to bed."

We sat in silence for a minute. Rebecca stood back up and walked over to the kitchen, grabbing two mugs. "Why is your mind racing?" she asked, grabbing a box of chamomile tea from the counter and tearing open the paper bags.

I stood up, grabbed one of the mugs with the teabag in it, filled it with water, and placed it in the microwave. "I've just been thinking about what Carrie told us." Rebecca filled the other mug and placed it next to my mug, then closed the microwave door and pressed start. I stared at the mugs as they went around on the glass plate. I took a deep breath, not wanting to admit to my sister that I was so afraid. *She's my sister, but would she really understand my fears?* I glanced at my sister, noticing her tired stare and serious eyes. *Maybe this is harder for her than she lets on.*

The microwave timer went off, and Rebecca pulled the two steaming mugs out, handing one to me. We sat back down on the couch, and I took a sip of my tea. I swallowed, took a deep breath, and looked at Rebecca. "I guess I can't sleep because I'm scared. Carrie just filled us in on a whole new level of danger to worry about. And with Mr. Truth taking Matthew's side, I... I'm really feeling anxious." I let out my breath, and stared into my tea mug, feeling slightly better after saying something.

Rebecca chuckled softly. "I think we're all in the same boat."

I raised an eyebrow at her. "What? I mean, Luke has seemed a little ruffled, but you've stayed pretty calm."

Rebecca shrugged. "I guess I feel like I need to stay calm. If I don't stay calm, it will be hard to focus. And I need to focus." She shook her head, biting her lip.

"You're worried about being sent back to jail?"

Rebecca nodded.

I set down my mug and put an arm around my sister. "Me, too," I whispered. "I've been so grateful to have you back in my life, and to have you leave again for something you didn't do... I don't know how I would handle it."

I felt Rebecca's shoulders quiver and looked up to see a tear slide down her cheek. "I know I don't tell you guys enough, but I am so grateful to be here, too." She took a shaky breath. "To have you and Luke in my life, people I can trust, has been amazing." She wiped the tears off her face. "But the best thing that has happened these past two years was accepting Christ as my Lord and Savior. Sarah, I don't know how I could keep staying calm if it wasn't for Him. I just keep telling myself that He is my hope, and even if everything doesn't turn out, He will still be my hope." She shook her head as another tear fell. "But it's hard."

I hugged my sister tighter as the tears I was trying to hold back spilled out. We sat there for a minute and just cried. I felt a little amazed that Rebecca, my strong sister, was crying with me. As I wiped the tears from my face and took a deep breath, a verse came to mind. "And we know that God causes all things to work together for good to those who love God, to those who are called according to His purpose."

"Romans 8:28?" Rebecca asked.

I nodded. "It's a promise I need to hear often."

Rebecca stood up and smiled. "Me, too."

⚓

I stepped into the coffee shop and rubbed my eyes, trying to hold back a yawn. Rebecca elbowed me. "Told you," she smirked. "You shouldn't have stayed up so late."

I rolled my eyes. *I don't mind being tired,* I thought, smiling to myself. *My conversation with my sister last night was worth it.*

Luke was already sitting at our usual table. "What do you

want today?" Luke asked as we sat down, flipping open an imaginary notepad.

"The usual," Rebecca said.

"Iced caramel mocha," I said.

Luke saluted and walked up to the front counter.

Luke returned moments later with three coffees and three slices of banana bread. "I thought we could use an extra treat this morning. We need to fuel our creativity!" He winked as he passed out the coffee and banana bread.

"Thanks! I love banana bread," I said, taking a bite.

Rebecca nodded. "Me, too."

I ate slowly, trying to savor every bite of the addicting bread. As I ate, I watched out the window as people walked past, enjoying the peaceful moment. All too soon, I had finished my treat, as had Luke and Rebecca.

Luke cleared his throat and leaned his elbows on the table. "Alright, snack time is over. Let's get down to business."

"How are we planning to talk to Ryan without Ethan being there?" I asked. "Ethan almost hovers over Ryan."

Luke nodded. "Anytime I try to talk to Ryan, Ethan answers for him."

Rebecca leaned back and folded her arms. "We need to get Ethan distracted, then."

"How?" I asked, raising an eyebrow.

She smiled sneakily. "Easy. You and I distract him while Luke talks to Ryan."

Luke frowned. "I don't like that plan."

Rebecca tilted her head. "Do you have a better one?" Luke shrugged. "Look," Rebecca said, leaning forward, "Ethan has been obsessed with trying to get information from Sarah and me. If we play into his hand, he won't pay attention to whatever Ryan is doing. That gives you an open door to try and get information from him."

Luke pressed his lips together, shaking his head. He sighed. "You're probably right. I just don't like it."

"What if we accidentally give him information he needs?" I asked.

Rebecca shrugged. "We'll just have to try not to. We'll avoid personal questions and only share information that is common knowledge. It won't be that hard."

"I hope not," I said, shaking my head. "I'm not as good at this acting stuff as you are."

Rebecca smiled. "You'll do great."

"I still don't like it." Luke was serious. "If he's the one behind the threats, he's probably dangerous. What if he tries something?"

Rebecca shook her head. "He won't hurt us."

"What makes you so sure?"

"I think he wants information. That's obvious from the threats he's been leaving – they're all codes from Mr. Zaiden. He won't do anything that will jeopardize getting whatever info he's after."

Rebecca's face was confident, but Luke looked skeptical. *Who's right?* I thought, feeling nervous. *I mean, Rebecca has experience in this kind of stuff, but Luke is not usually skeptical.* I watched as the two stared each other down. Neither said anything, but their gazes seemed to be doing the fighting. *Do you have any other option?* I asked myself. After a moment of brainstorming, I knew I didn't. *We've got to go for it.*

"Let's pray," I said, interrupting their silent battle. "Whatever we do will be risky. We're already on thin ice as it is. Let's pray for God's protection and wisdom."

Luke nodded, grinning sheepishly. "You're right." We

bowed our heads. "Lord, I pray for Your protection and wisdom as we continue trying to solve this case. You know what's going on, and we know You love us and will be with us. Guide us to the truth, keep us safe, and help us find an answer before..." Luke's voice choked up, and he didn't finish.

Before Rebecca gets sent back to prison, I finished silently.

We weren't exactly sure how to catch Ethan and Ryan apart. After a lot of debating, we decided we would "just wing it," as Luke said. Throughout the day, we kept our eyes on Ethan and Ryan, watching to see if they were ever apart. I noticed as we watched them, several other Squad 4 members were watching us. It made me nervous to know my teammates were keeping an eye on us like we were some dangerous threat. Even Daniel seemed to be avoiding us, which bothered me more than I thought it would.

By the end of the day, we never caught Ethan and Ryan apart. "We need a different plan," I whispered to Rebecca as we left dinner. "If we keep 'winging it' like this, we'll never get anywhere."

Rebecca sighed. "I know." She turned to look at me. "But what else should we do? I don't know how to make them separate..."

"Watch out!" I said, but it was too late. Rebecca collided with another agent. My eyes widened when I realized who she'd run into. *Ethan! And Ryan's not with him!* I quickly sent a message to Luke on my watch: *Got him.*

Rebecca stepped back, her face red. "I'm so sorry, I should have watched where I was going." She glanced at me and raised her eyebrows. I raised my eyebrows back. *Our plan is now in motion.*

"Don't worry about it," Ethan said, grinning as he ran his hand through his hair. The way he flirted with my sister, knowing he was trying to manipulate her, made me sick. *Don't let it show,* I warned myself as I tried to force a smile.

"What were you talking about?" he asked, raising an eyebrow.

My heart rate picked up. *Does he know we were talking about him?*

Rebecca rolled her eyes. "A friend of ours, but it's nothing." She grinned at him and tucked her hair behind her ear. "And what are you up to?"

I glanced down at my watch and saw Luke had replied: *Ok. Trying to find Ryan. Keep Ethan stalled.*

"Enjoying the evening air," Ethan replied.

"How's training going?" Rebecca asked.

Ethan stood up a little straighter. "Great! Although I noticed you two weren't there this morning." He raised an eyebrow.

"We were busy," I said, shrugging.

We stood in awkward silence for a moment. *Think of something to say!* I told myself. I felt my watch vibrate and glanced down at Luke's message: *Still can't find Ryan.* Suddenly, I had an idea. I glanced around us, then looked back at Ethan. "Where's Ryan?" Rebecca glanced at me but didn't say anything.

Ethan sighed. "He was supposed to be meeting me outside. He's probably still in the bathroom." He rolled his eyes.

Rebecca quickly jumped in with another training question, so I shot Luke a quick message: *Check the bathroom.*

Ethan and Rebecca kept up a banter about training, and

I added a comment here and there. Finally, my watch buzzed again. *Found him. Keep talking.*

"So, I heard from Matthew that you're actually on probation, and you're not a real Truth Squad member," Ethan said suddenly.

I gasped, but Rebecca just laughed casually. "Yeah. I did some illegal stuff as a minor, but I'm grateful for the opportunity Truth Squad has provided for me to get a fresh start."

"So, Sarah was the angel, and you were the troublemaker?" Ethan leaned closer to Rebecca.

I felt my face flush as Rebecca laughed playfully and took a small step backward. *This guy is so annoying!* I thought, hoping this awkwardness would be worth it in the end.

Suddenly, Ethan's facial expression froze, his gaze focused behind us. A second later, he looked at Rebecca and smiled. "I'd better go find Ryan. It was nice talking with you." He waved and walked away.

I quickly messaged Luke: *He's headed your way.*

Rebecca nodded toward the walking paths. "Let's go." We walked in silence for a minute before Rebecca burst out laughing.

"What?" I asked.

"That was so awkward!" she said, shaking her head.

I giggled. "Well, you seemed like a natural to me."

"I meant Ethan was awkward. He didn't switch well from pleasantries to trying to get information, and did you notice his face at the end of our conversation? I think he was listening to a com." Rebecca shook her head, chuckling.

"It seemed like he was trying to bait you to talk about working for Mr. Zaiden," I said, glancing at Rebecca.

She nodded. "I don't understand why, though."

"Hey!" Luke called from behind us. I glanced over my shoulder to see him jogging up to us.

"Any luck?" Rebecca asked.

He slowed down and started walking next to her, sighing. "Not really. I tried to ease into a conversation, but he didn't want to talk. Finally, I decided to directly ask him if everything was okay. His eyes got wide, and he started fidgeting with his watch, saying everything was fine. I asked if he was sure, and he got defensive and told me to leave him alone. That's when you messaged and said Ethan was coming."

"Ethan seemed to be listing to a com, so Ryan must have been turning his coms on when he was fidgeting with his watch," Rebecca said, tilting her head.

"So, all that awkward conversation for nothing?" I said, my shoulders sagging.

We walked a few paces silently. "Maybe not," Luke said slowly.

"What do you mean?" I asked.

"We now know that Ethan and Ryan are using some sort of coms, which means if we can discover the frequency they're on, we can listen in!" Luke's eyes brightened with excitement. "We might be able to get proof that they're the ones behind everything this way!"

Rebecca nodded, grinning. "That's a brilliant idea."

"How do we figure out the frequency?" I asked.

Luke grinned, double-raising his eyebrows. "I may have a gadget for that."

"Nice!" Rebecca said, looking impressed.

Luke's shoulders fell. "But it's in Matthew's experimental lab, and he's barred me from getting in."

"We could get in through the window. Matthew always leaves it open," I suggested.

"True, but if he catches us, we're dead meat."

"Well, if we can't use the gadget, I have some tricks up my sleeve," Rebecca said, grinning sneakily. "I've listened in on people's coms once or twice."

"Then that's the plan! Let's try and find the frequency and listen in!" Luke said, clapping his hands. "It's perfect!"

I smiled. For the first time, I didn't feel nervous about our plan.

"Got anything?" I glanced over my shoulder at Rebecca. She sat in the grass with her laptop in front of her, holding one hand on her headphone and punching numbers with the other. She shook her head and continued typing, staring at the laptop with remarkable intensity considering she had been working for over an hour.

I turned back toward the campus, watching a game of ultimate frisbee taking place at one end of the open grassy area, and a game of ninja at the other end. The weather was beautiful, sunny with a cool breeze, and everyone seemed to be outside enjoying it. *Why did it have to be so nice outside today?* I thought. Normally, I would enjoy such a day, but not when I had to keep watch for anyone who might get nosy and wonder what we were doing.

I saw movement out of the corner of my eye and swiveled my head toward it, my heart pounding. It was Luke. I sighed with relief, feeling silly for being so jumpy.

"Here you go," he said, walking up with three water bottles.

"Thanks." I grabbed one and quickly opened it, taking a sip of the cold water. Rebecca just nodded as Luke set one beside her.

Luke plopped down next to Rebecca and glanced at her screen. "Still nothing?" he asked. She shook her head. Luke gulped down half his water bottle, then let out a satisfied "Ahh." He grinned. "There's nothing better than cool water on a warm day." He paused. "Except maybe orange juice. Or an Italian soda. Or iced coffee. Or—"

"Or just about any cold drink with sugar?" I finished.

Luke nodded. "Pretty much." Rebecca slapped Luke's arm. "What?" he said, raising an eyebrow. "You're not a fan of sugary goodness?"

Rebecca shook her head. "Not that. I found it!" Her eyes were bright with excitement. She pulled off her headphones and handed them to Luke, turning up the volume on her laptop.

Luke was silent for a minute, then he looked up and grinned. "You did it!" He gave the headphones back to Rebecca. "We found Ethan and Ryan's frequency!"

"Yes!" I exclaimed, high-fiving Luke.

"It sounds like they're visiting with people, so we won't get any good info right now. I'll keep checking in to see what I can find out," Rebecca said.

"Heads up. Matthew's headed our way," Luke said, not the least bit thrilled.

Rebecca changed her laptop screen. I glanced up at Matthew, seeing his disapproving glare as he came closer. He came to a stop next to Luke, his arms folded. "What are you troublemakers up to?"

If he's trying to come across funny, he's failing, I thought, noticing the lack of humor in his tone. "Just hanging out," I said, trying to smile. "It's a beautiful day."

Matthew opened his mouth, but Luke cut in before he could say anything. "Yeah, we were discussing favorite drinks for warm days, like sweet iced tea or orange juice. What's your favorite?"

Matthew raised an eyebrow. "I like vanilla Italian sodas with cream."

"Oh, those are so good!" Luke said, grinning. "We should get some."

Matthew's face had relaxed for a moment, a smile almost peeking through, but suddenly his face became stern again. "No, thanks." He sighed. "Look, I don't know what you all are up to, but it seems rather unusual for you three to be over here by yourselves when we've got ninja and ultimate frisbee going on." He shook his head. "I know that you never skip ultimate frisbee for anything, Luke. And, Sarah, I know you love ninja. Don't think you can fool me."

I felt frozen. *What do we do?* I thought, panicking. *How do we keep someone who knows us so well from ruining everything?*

Luke rolled his eyes and let out an exasperated sigh. "Matthew, we're just working on a project. You know, you're seriously starting to get on my nerves."

"Well, you've been getting on mine a lot lately, too." Matthew straightened, taking on a commanding presence. "I will be blunt and tell you that I am keeping an eye on all three of you, and especially you." He pointed at Rebecca. "We have a report to give when your parole officer shows up, and I will make sure that it is accurate." With that, Matthew spun on his heel and stomped away.

I took a deep breath, trying to calm my emotions. I wasn't sure if I was mad, upset, or worried. Luke jumped up with a grunt and started pacing. "I don't even feel like playing ultimate frisbee, I'm so frustrated."

Rebecca shrugged. "Maybe we should go join in so that Matthew can't get after us. I can work on this tonight." She closed her laptop and stood up, nodding her head toward the games. "I'll put my laptop away, and then let's join in."

"I'll come with you," I offered, falling into step with my twin.

"I'll go punch something in the gym and be back," Luke replied, half-jokingly.

Rebecca and I walked silently to our room, put the laptop away, and headed back out the door. "You know, we have got to get some hard proof soon, or Matthew is going to make sure you get the blame for all the weird stuff that's happened," I whispered.

"I know." Rebecca smiled as we passed another agent, then continued, "But we can't risk letting him find even more reason to prove us guilty. We're listening in on people's coms. That's suspicious." She raised her eyebrows.

I sighed, knowing she was right. *I just wish someone would believe us,* I thought as we stepped outside. All the Squad 4 agents knew Luke and I had been suspended from activities, and it felt like everywhere we went, people's stares followed us. Everyone seemed to avoid us, and even though none of the lower ranks knew what was going on, there still seemed to be rumors going around. We even got interesting looks from the Junior Squad.

"Ninja or ultimate frisbee?" Rebecca asked.

"Neither." I felt like running back to our room and hiding under the covers in my bed, reading a book to escape the awkward tension surrounding us.

"Okay, ninja it is." Rebecca grabbed my arm and pulled me forward.

I noticed the round was down to five people left with the rest of the players sitting on the ground around the action. I smiled, noticing Faith and Jonathan were in the top five. Hope waved to us from where she sat in the grass, and we walked over to join her.

"Gonna play?" she asked as we sat down.

"Yup," Rebecca replied.

"How far did you make it?" I asked.

She shrugged. "Just to the top twelve. Faith got me out. She and Jonathan are ganging up on people." She rolled her eyes.

I nodded. "That seems to be their strategy every time."

"But now it's predictable," Rebecca said, looking at Hope. "If they play the same strategy every time, then you can know their next move and outsmart them."

Hope nodded slowly, watching Faith and Jonathan play the game. "You're right. I've noticed they both like to go for the same hand so that the person forgets to guard their opposite hand. Then they get their other hand out when the opponents aren't paying attention."

"Good observation," Rebecca said, smiling in approval.

I watched as the game continued, appearing to be at a stalemate with these top five. Each player went in turn, having one motion for their turn to try and slap another player's hand to get it out. The person being lunged at also had one move to try and keep their hand from being hit. When someone's hand was hit, they would hide it behind their back and not use it for the rest of the game. Some players would use their one move to retreat from the fight and try to stay alive throughout the game by avoiding the competition. That seemed to defeat the point of the game in my mind, but there was almost always that one player who would make it to the top five using that strategy.

It looked like four of the players were trying to get the "scaredy-cat" player out. They were all trying to chase him down as he used each turn to try and move away from the group.

"Don't step out of bounds, or you're out!" Jonathan called. The other player was getting close to the edge of the circle, the boundaries being marked by the circle of players who were out.

Eventually, he stepped out of bounds, and the game was down to four. Faith and Jonathan got another player out using the tactic Hope had pointed out.

"We'll have to watch out for that move when we join in," I said.

"We'll have to find a way to separate those two," Rebecca agreed.

Faith and Jonathan moved in on the third competitor and quickly got him out.

"Isn't there a rule against tag-teaming?" I heard someone grumble next to me.

The two kept going back and forth, swinging and pulling back. Finally, Jonathan got out one of Faith's hands. Now they were even. Someone blew a whistle for the ultimate frisbee game, and the two friends jumped, turning toward the sound. Jonathan pulled himself back to the game before Faith did and quickly slapped her hand, getting her out.

Everyone clapped as the two shook hands like good competitors, then Jonathan took a bow. "Oh, thank you. You're too kind!" he said, dramatically. Faith rolled her eyes and walked over to us.

"Let's take a water break before we start the next round!" someone yelled.

As people scattered, Faith sat down beside Rebecca, sighing. "I was so close."

"Good job!" Hope said, smiling at her twin.

Jonathan joined us a second later. "Ready to be beat again?" he asked, sitting cross-legged in front of us.

"Not a chance. I'm not gonna let you win this time," Faith retorted.

"Let me win?" he said, raising his eyebrows. "Sure, sure." He looked at Rebecca and me. "You two joining?" I nodded. "So," Jonathan said, scooting closer. He lowered his voice, "what's up?"

"Nothing," Rebecca replied, grinning. "We just plan to beat you in the next round of ninja."

He rolled his eyes. "Not that. I mean, what's up with you two and Luke? I've heard some theories going around. I've also heard some arguments between my dad and Matthew..."

"Wait, have you been eavesdropping on your dad again?" Hope asked, raising an eyebrow.

Jonathan's eyes widened, and he glanced around. "Uh, why would I do that?"

Hope put her hands on her hips. "Jonathan, you don't fool me. I know you eavesdrop all the time."

Jonathan pressed his lips together and glared at her. Obviously, this was something he did not want other people to know. "Forget that I said anything about that. Besides, Matthew was yelling loud enough for people in New York to hear. How can that be called eavesdropping?" He shook his head. "We're getting off-topic. Okay, Sanders twins. Spill the beans." He looked at us expectantly.

"I don't have any beans," Rebecca replied sarcastically.

"You know, I am kind of curious. I've heard some rumors that you guys are in trouble," Faith said, crossing her arms. "Is that true?"

I glanced at Rebecca. Her look told me to change the subject. "You know," I began slowly, trying to remember how Mr. Truth always worded his response when I asked questions about Squad 4 as a teen, "Squad 4 happenings are confidential and are not to be discussed unless the information is necessary." *That wasn't quite how Mr. Truth would say it, but it's close enough.*

"So, something is going on?" Faith said, not letting the conversation drop.

"Hey, rules are rules," Rebecca cut in, her voice stern. "I'm not Squad 4. I don't get to know everything that's going on either, even though I'm Sarah's sister. Confidentiality is important, both for the security of missions and the agents involved, and for the protection of people who should not be involved."

Hope, always the peacemaker, jumped in, changing the topic. "What did you all have for lunch?"

After a few minutes of talking about food, everyone was ready to play ninja again. As we joined the circle, Rebecca gave me a wink, and I knew what that meant. *Get Faith and Jonathan separated.*

Several players got out in the first round. I kept my eye on Rebecca, waiting for her signal. Once the group shrunk to about half of the starting size, Rebecca winked again. On my next move, I took a step back from the circle. On Rebecca's turn, she stepped closer to Jonathan. Each turn, I kept stepping closer to the two tag-teamers, hoping to end up behind them without their notice. Hope seemed to notice what we were up to, and soon she was closing in on Faith and Jonathan, too.

I glanced around the circle and noticed that we had ended up with several smaller groups battling it out. *Perfect. Let the other players get each other out while we take on last round's champions,* I thought, trying to hide my grin.

Rebecca and Hope were now each focused on a target, Hope against Faith and Rebecca against Jonathan. Neither group seemed to be paying me any attention. I took a step closer to the two battles, then waited for my next turn. Rebecca swung for Jonathan's hand, and he pulled it behind himself out of her reach, but it was totally unprotected from mine. My next turn, I lightly tapped his hand.

"What?" Jonathan yelled, bending his arm behind his back to signify that it was out.

Faith turned her head, and her jaw dropped. "Jonathan, we're being attacked from behind!"

"Like I didn't figure that out already!" he replied, frustrated.

Rebecca laughed. "We're getting you off your rhythm."

The two had gotten so used to their plan of attack, and now that it was messed up, they were flustered. Rebecca quickly got Jonathan's other hand, and he was out. Hope got one of Faith's hands. I jumped and barely reached Faith's other hand. She was out. But now my hand was stretched far in front of me, wide open for Hope to get out. I looked at Hope's face and saw her determination. *Oh, boy. I'd better have fast reflexes.*

Hope swung for my hand, and I pulled back quickly, losing my balance and falling over. Hope had missed my hand, but now it would be hard to dodge from the ground.

Rebecca lunged for my hand, and I rolled away. "Great, now you two have teamed up against me?" I said, smiling. Hope shrugged in return.

Hope made it to the top six, and I made it to the top three before getting out. I left the circle to sit by Faith, Hope, and Jonathan as Rebecca battled for first place.

"Great job! You made it to the top three!" Hope said, high-fiving me.

"Thanks," I said, grinning. "And great job to you, too. Our plan worked."

"Whatever," Jonathan said, obviously sore about getting out so soon.

Faith smiled. "I have to admit, it was well played." She scooched closer to me and lowered her voice. "And just so you know, I don't believe the rumors people are saying, and neither does Hope. We trust you."

I smiled. "I appreciate that." I looked away quickly to hide the watering in my eyes. It felt comforting to hear those words. I looked up and noticed Matthew standing a few yards away, watching our game with his arms crossed. The comforting feeling vanished.

🔫

Because Matthew was keeping such a close eye on us, we didn't go back to our room until after dinner.

"Hopefully, we'll hear something good tonight," Rebecca said, grabbing her laptop and plopping down on the couch.

I decided to pick up our dorm while Rebecca worked. *I can't help that much anyways*, I thought, picking up a pile of papers off the floor. *Plus, we've been so focused on finding our culprit, we've let this place become cluttered.*

I got all the clutter put away and organized, and I was contemplating vacuuming when Rebecca waved me over. "Got something?" I asked, sitting down.

She nodded and turned the sound on her laptop on. "I think that should work," I heard Ryan say.

Ethan laughed eerily. "If it doesn't, I don't know what will."

"How do you plan on getting out of here when we're done?"

"I'll just fake an emergency, like grandma's dying and needs me to come say goodbye or something."

"So, I have to come up with my own excuse?" Ryan sounded nervous.

"Yup. Honestly, it won't be that hard. These people are softhearted. If it pulls at their heartstrings, they'll let you go."

Rebecca snorted. "Can you imagine Matthew overhearing this conversation? He would be so offended."

I grinned. "No kidding."

I heard what sounded like a text message notification. "Okay, looks like our man is ready," Ethan said. "So, it's all systems go."

"I can't believe how long this has taken. I thought you told me this was going to be a quick job, like just a couple weeks," Ryan whined.

"This is a quick job," Ethan replied haughtily. "Most jobs that I take require months of stalking and planning before attack. This—"

"But this isn't one of those jobs." I couldn't tell if Ryan was making a statement or asking a question. He almost sounded like he was pleading with Ethan. *What does Ethan normally do?* I wondered.

"Don't you worry about that." Suddenly, a beeping sound went off.

"Oh, no," Rebecca said.

"Is that from our laptop?" I asked.

Rebecca shook her head, typing furiously.

"We've got a security breach!" I heard Ryan say.

"You can't be serious!" Ethan yelled.

"I am serious. We've been hacked."

"Well, track the hacker down!" Ethan screamed.

The sound shut off. "What happened?" I asked.

Rebecca continued working. "They must have an excellent security system, or we stayed on too long, or something."

"Will they be able to track back to us?" I asked, feeling nervous.

Rebecca was silent for a minute, concentrating on her codes. Finally, she hit her last number with force and closed her laptop. "Hopefully, I have properly erased our tracks, and they will have no clue what happened." She shrugged. "Don't worry about it."

"Okay," I said, sounding more skeptical than I intended.

Rebecca rolled her eyes. "I've done this a lot more than you'd think, Sarah. Trust me."

"I know. I'm sorry, I just can't help but worry," I said, resting my chin in my hands.

Rebecca was silent for a minute. "Honestly, they will probably assume that we were the ones who hacked them. No one else would have reason to."

"Except Carrie."

"She doesn't know who they are, though," Rebecca countered. Her face got serious. "But still, I hope we didn't put her or her brother in danger." She shook her head. "I've got to remember that we've got someone's life in the balance!" She sounded like she was scolding herself.

I sighed. "Did you get the conversation recorded?"

She nodded. "I'll send it to Luke."

"We didn't really get any hard proof from the conversation, but it's obvious they're up to something big. It sounds like they're about to do whatever they came to do," I said, crossing my arms. "But what is that? We still have no clue what they are trying to do!"

"The weird notes, the training room and smoke bombs, and then framing us... it's all connected, but I don't see the purpose behind it." Rebecca leaned back, her arms crossed and her face serious. "What do they want?"

The next day was supposed to be a training day, but because we were suspended from Squad 4 activities, Luke, Rebecca, and I sat outside at a picnic table, watching as other agents filed into the training room.

"This is dumb," Luke said, shaking his head. "They would be better able to keep an eye on us if we were in the training room than having us out here."

"But if something goes wrong, it's easier to point the finger at us now," Rebecca replied sarcastically.

Luke shrugged. "True." We sat silently for a minute, and once the last agent entered the training room, Luke turned toward us, a sneaky grin on his face. "I heard there are doughnuts in the dining hall." He double-raised his eyebrows. "Do you want to go get some?"

"Sounds delicious," I said, standing. "Let's go!"

We hurried to the dining hall and found the chef frying doughnuts. "How do you get in on this info?" I asked as the chef handed me a fresh maple bar.

Luke grinned. "You have to have the right connections."

The chef grinned. "I may send him notifications when I'm frying doughnuts."

Rebecca took a bite and smiled. "Mmm. I want in on these notifications! This is amazing!"

"Thanks, Joe!" Luke said as we headed back outside. With the agents in training and the Junior Squad in a summer class, the open grassy area was empty. We sat at a table in the shade and finished our doughnuts before discussing what to do next.

"Have you tried the coms again?" Luke asked.

Rebecca nodded. "This morning, but they must have changed frequencies. I would have to search again."

"Could we plant a listening device?" I asked. "That way, their security couldn't pick up on it."

"Well, I don't know about you, Sarah, but I don't have access to any of my Squad 4 gear, and Matthew won't let me into our lab." Luke looked frustrated. "I could search my room and see if I have any, but I usually keep all my stuff in our experimental lab." He shook his head. "It's not right for Matthew to keep me out when half the stuff in there is mine!"

Rebecca smiled sadly. "Normally, I rely on you for our gadgets, but I can see if I have anything."

"Well, if Luke doesn't have access to his gear, I probably can't get to mine either, so we'll have to see if you have some," I said.

Rebecca nodded. "I'll go check."

As she jogged away, I turned back to Luke. "Like I said before, Matthew always keeps the window open to your lab. If she doesn't have one, we could always sneak in."

Luke shook his head. "That seems like a bad idea."

Rebecca returned a few minutes later, shaking her head. "Nope. I've got a box of random gadgets, but no listening devices." She sat back down and folded her hands. "Now what?"

"We could break into the lab—"

"No!" Luke and Rebecca replied in unison.

"Hey, are we twinning?" Luke said, grinning. "I thought you two were supposed to do that."

Rebecca rolled her eyes, but a small grin still escaped. I turned my head to try and hide my smile. *He totally likes her.*

Just then, the door to the training room opened, and a flood of agents poured out, filling the quiet morning with loud talking and laughter.

As people dispersed, Rebecca suddenly sat up straight. "I left my backpack at the other table over there. I'm going to go get that." She got up and hurried through the crowd, then returned with her bag.

Luke glanced at his watch. "Fifteen minutes till lunch."

"I'll put my backpack in our room and meet you at the dining hall."

"Sounds good," I said, standing.

"I'm going to see if I can find a listening device in my room. I'll see you later," Luke said.

I guess I'll see if I can help with anything in the dining hall, I thought, watching Luke and Rebecca walk away.

Luke and Rebecca were both late for lunch. Luke showed up first, looking disappointed. "No luck?" I asked as he walked past my table toward the lunch line. He shook his head.

Rebecca joined us right after Luke sat down with his plate, her eyes wide. She leaned in close, glancing around before she whispered, "I found another threat in my backpack. Someone must have put it there when I left it at the other table." She slid a piece of paper onto the table and then walked over to the lunch line.

I picked it up and read the note. "Meet me outside building 204 at 11:25pm tonight. Don't be late or someone gets hurt. Timing is everything for an agent, remember?"

I shook my head and passed the note to Luke. His eyes quickly scanned the note, then he folded it and put it in his pocket.

Rebecca joined us a minute later. "I think this must have something to do with the conversation we overheard."

"You're probably right," I said, then shook my head. "But, Rebecca, this is too far. You shouldn't go."

Rebecca paused, waiting for someone to walk by before replying, "But it says someone will get hurt if I don't." She leaned in closer. "I'm going."

"It's too dangerous. You've been threatened and framed. What if they try to kill you?" I felt panic rising in me.

"And what if they hurt some of the Junior Squad because I don't go, or kill Carrie's brother? They hacked the training room while teenagers were inside, so I don't think they would be afraid of doing it again." She shook her head. "I'm not taking that risk."

"You're right," Luke said, looking back and forth between us. "Both of you are right. There's danger if you go and danger if you don't show up." He took a deep breath and sat up straight. "I'll go."

CHAPTER 9

"This is a bad idea." Rebecca crossed her arms and glared at Luke.

Luke put his hands on his hips and glared back. "It will work," he replied slowly, over enunciating every word.

The two had been going back and forth between all the possible scenarios of how things could turn out depending on what we did. It was almost humorous to watch the two most stubborn people I knew trying to battle for the number one spot. *It would be funny if this didn't involve people's lives being in danger,* I told myself, shaking my head. This stalemate had lasted for almost an hour. *We can't keep arguing like this. We won't be ready to do anything.*

I stood up and stepped in between the two glares. I cleared my throat, preparing my teacher voice. "Excuse me." I glanced at my watch. "It is 2:30. If we don't put some sort of plan into motion, it will be 11:25 before we know it, and we will have no plan whatsoever." I looked at Rebecca, then at Luke. "Neither of you want the other person to go to the meeting, but you both believe having no one go is a bad plan, right?"

Rebecca nodded, and Luke replied, "Yup."

"Have we ruled out telling Mr. Truth about this threat?" I asked.

"I tried to get to his office, and Matthew tailed me the whole way," Luke said, shaking his head. "We would have to find a way to talk to Mr. Truth without Matthew, or we won't get anywhere."

"What about stationing some reinforcements?" I suggested. "Like, what if we ask Daniel to be back-up?"

Luke shook his head. "Daniel is out of town for the day and won't be back until tomorrow morning."

Rebecca shook her head. "I don't see any other option than having me or Luke meet with them."

"And I'm going," Luke said, standing up straight.

"No—"

I held up a hand before the argument could start again. "Forget who's going and who's not. Let's work on the plan for security. We can fight out who's going later."

Rebecca nodded. "Okay."

"Sounds good!" Luke said, giving a thumbs-up.

The two stared at me, and suddenly I realized they were waiting for me to say what to do. *Oh, man. I didn't want to be in charge,* I thought, frustrated. *I hate being in charge.*

I thought for a moment, trying to decide what we should do. "Okay," I said slowly. "I think we should... let's check the security cameras for building 204."

Rebecca nodded. "On it." She pulled her laptop out of her backpack and sat down at the table.

"Luke, what kind of equipment do we still have access to?" I asked.

He shrugged. "Not much. We have our watches and coms. I have a taser in my room, but that's about it."

Rebecca looked up from her computer, her eyes lighting up. "I just remembered I have a box of a few gadgets from Luke back when we were working to catch Zaiden. It's somewhere in my closet." She turned back to her work.

"Perfect. So, we have gadgets, we're checking the security," I paused. *What else?*

"Here's the video footage," Rebecca said, waving us over. Building 204 was the farthest building on the main campus grounds and was used to store yard work equipment.

Luke pointed to the dumpster. "It looks like we have a blind spot in the cameras."

Rebecca nodded. "And there doesn't appear to be any kind of camera on the other side of the dumpster."

"That must be where they plan to meet, then," I said.

Rebecca nodded. "So, we need to be extra careful. Whoever's watching the video won't be able to see if our agent is in trouble."

"There's an SOS button on our watches," Luke said.

I raised an eyebrow. "There is? I didn't know that."

Luke grinned. "Of course, there is. I mean, it doesn't call the cops or anything, it just signals the other watches that someone is in trouble. Here." He pointed to a small black button on the right of the watch's face. "If I hit this button, it will make your watches flash red until I hit the button again." He pushed the button, and Rebecca and my watches started flashing red. "See? Pretty neat, huh?" He pressed the button again, and they stopped flashing.

Rebecca nodded. "That's great, actually. The red light is dim so it wouldn't be too visible in the dark, and it doesn't make a sound, so if you signaled someone else on a spy mission, it wouldn't signal everyone else."

Luke nodded. "That's the hope. I've thought about changing the feature to vibrate instead of flash red so that it would be even less visible, but I haven't tried it out yet."

"So, what do we do now?" I asked. "Should we check around the dumpster for any traps or anything?"

Rebecca tilted her head. "I'm not sure. We don't want to be caught on camera if they're monitoring right now. They would know we were up to something."

Luke's eyes lit up. "I have an idea! I'll take the garbage to the dumpster today for the kitchen. I do it all the time, so it wouldn't be weird."

"Perfect!" Rebecca and I replied in unison.

Luke took the trash to the dumpster around five o'clock. He came back and reported that there was nothing unusual in or around the dumpster. "I didn't stay for too long because I didn't want to look suspicious," he said. "Hopefully I didn't miss anything obvious."

"So, where are we meeting tonight?" Rebecca asked.

"The game room," I suggested. "We still have access to it, it's close by, and it wouldn't be too suspicious a place in case Matthew notices we're out so late."

Luke nodded. "I think that's a good plan."

"Okay, then. We meet there at 10:45, but don't all show up at once," Rebecca warned.

"I'll just hang out there this evening, that way if someone locks the doors, I can let you two in," Luke suggested.

"Sounds good," I said. "We'll bring Rebecca's old gear and see if any of it is useful."

"And my laptop to watch the security cameras," Rebecca said.

"Right." Luke nodded. "Because you two will be watching, and I'm going." His tone of voice implied no arguing.

Rebecca stared him down for a long minute. Neither of the two said anything, but their eyes appeared to be arguing. Rebecca's gaze was firm but searching. Luke's gaze was stubborn, but behind his firm stare was a depth of care, and eventually, Rebecca's face softened. "Okay," she whispered.

🌠

"Found it!" I pulled a box down from the top shelf in Rebecca's closet and handed it to her. I stepped down from the stepstool. "What do we have?"

Rebecca opened the box and pulled out a purse, giggling. "I don't think this will be helpful," she said, setting it down on the bed.

I remembered that purse, an invention of Luke's designed to disable security cameras as you walked by. "That does exactly the opposite of what we need."

Rebecca pulled out some earrings. "Coms, but we already have those." She set those down on the bed.

I looked into the box. There were a few trinkets, some of which I recognized, like the taser sunglasses, and a few small items that I was unsure of their purpose. "We could just bring the whole box."

"Yeah." Rebecca picked the purse back up and dumped the trinkets from the box into it.

I raised an eyebrow. "You're still bringing the purse?"

She shrugged. "If there are cameras in the game room, we don't want Matthew spying on us and using this mission against us."

I nodded. "True."

Rebecca glanced at her watch. "10:35. We'd better head out."

I grabbed Rebecca's backpack with her laptop inside and slung it over my shoulder. After sticking my taser in my concealed carrier holster, we hurried out the door.

We stuck to the shadows and quietly made our way to the multipurpose building. There was a workout room on the bottom floor and a game room on the top floor, along with a few study rooms along the left side of the building.

Luke met us at the door, opening it for us and making a grand sweep with his arm. "Welcome, ladies." He wore all black and had a holster with his taser on his hip.

Rebecca faked a curtsy, and we hurried inside. We set up Rebecca's laptop on the game table and dumped the gadgets out of the purse onto the table.

Luke rummaged through the gadgets. He grabbed the sunglasses and put them on. "Now I'll have two tasers." He pulled down the corner of the sunglasses so you could see just one squinting eye. "Do I look intimidating?"

"Let's check our coms," Rebecca said, ignoring Luke's goofing off.

Luke tapped his earpiece. "Check."

"I read you," I replied.

Rebecca typed for a second on her laptop. "I think we are good to go."

"Hey, I remember this!" Luke said, grabbing a pen off the table. "It's got a video camera in it." He stuck it in his shirt pocket. "I'll turn it on to record when I leave, that way we can get a good video of these guys."

"Good plan," Rebecca said. "Is it possible to connect that camera to my computer? That would be even better."

Luke shook his head. "Unfortunately, no. There's no Bluetooth or anything, and it would take too long to modify right now."

"Anything else you need?" I asked Luke. We still had about fifteen minutes before he had to meet with our threat writer.

He shook his head. "I've got all the tools I'll need." He took a deep breath. "But I could use some prayer."

I nodded, and Rebecca stood up to join us. We held hands and bowed our heads. Rebecca started, "Lord, we have a dangerous mission. It seems like no matter how we respond, there's danger. But we know that You are our fortress, our rock, and our deliverer. We ask You for wisdom and guidance, and we ask for protection."

"Lord, I ask for peace and clear minds to think quickly," I continued. "I admit, sometimes it feels like everything is against us, and everything seems impossible. But I know You can do impossible things, so I ask for your help." My throat started to choke up from tears, so I stopped praying aloud. *Lord, I'm scared,* I prayed silently. *Please be with us.*

"God, I want to take a minute to thank You," Luke said, surprising me.

He's about to go on a dangerous mission, and he's taking time to thank God? I thought, surprised at his bold faith compared to my fearful heart.

"You have blessed me with so much, most importantly with salvation through Christ and the promise of eternity," Luke continued. "I thank You for that promise, that even in scary times, I can have hope." He paused, then said softly, "And thank You for these friends You've blessed me with, friends who will pray with and for me, who encourage me." He took a shaky breath. "Thank You, Lord. I pray now for this mission. God, we don't really know what is going on, what is motivating these threats and attacks, but You do. Bring the truth to light and straighten everything out, because we sure can't do it ourselves."

That's true, I agreed silently.

"Lord, be with us. Thank You for promising to always be with us. We love You, Lord. In Jesus' name we pray, Amen."

I looked up to see Luke grinning. "You two ready?" he asked.

Rebecca nodded. "Yup."

Luke glanced at his watch. "Let's do this!"

"Luke." Rebecca suddenly gave him a hug. My jaw almost dropped. "Be careful," she said, then pulled away.

Luke's eyes were wide with surprise. He smiled, then saluted. "Yes, ma'am." With that, he turned and walked confidently out the door.

I looked at Rebecca and started laughing uncontrollably. I knew the laughter was mostly from pent up nerves, but I couldn't help myself.

Rebecca rolled her eyes, her cheeks flushing. "Whatever. Let's get to work."

Rebecca had the security cameras pulled up on her laptop. We'd decided I was in charge of watching the cameras, and she was Luke's back-up.

Luke's voice came through the coms, "I have left the building, and I am staying in the shadows."

"Copy that," Rebecca replied.

I glanced at my watch. "You still have five minutes till 11:25. Don't rush."

"Got it."

Three minutes passed. We sat tensely, watching the security cameras.

"I'm at building 204. Going silent," Luke whispered.

"Copy that," I replied. I heard the sound cut from his earpiece. I glanced at Rebecca, wide-eyed. "Wait, why did he cut the sound?"

Rebecca shook her head. "I don't know. Normally going

silent just means he would stop talking to us." I could tell by her tense shoulders she was worried.

She studied the footage of the building. "I don't see anyone. They must know about the camera's blind spot."

"Well, they've known just about everything else," I said, biting my lip.

Luke appeared on the screen for building 204. I could hear Rebecca hold her breath the same moment I did. Luke slowly rounded the corner of the dumpster and disappeared from view. There was no movement. *I wish we could see the camera in Luke's pen. And how I wish he hadn't cut sound!* I thought nervously. We sat in silence, waiting.

Suddenly a red light began flashing on Rebecca's watch.

"The SOS alarm! Luke needs help!" Rebecca jumped up and grabbed her taser. "Watch my back." She raced out the door.

Lord, please keep Luke and Rebecca safe... and alive, I prayed, my heart pounding.

Moments later, I saw Rebecca dash into view of the camera for building 204. I saw movement near the corner of the building. "Someone's coming around the corner on the other side of the building," I warned.

"Got it." Rebecca ran to the right side of the building. "No one's here."

"Are you sure?" I asked, but I couldn't see anyone on the screen anymore, either. "You're right. They must have snuck inside or something. Go check on Luke. I'll watch your back."

Rebecca ran behind the dumpster and out of view. She gasped. "Sarah, call 9-1-1. Luke is badly injured!"

"What?" I cried, fumbling for my cellphone. My heart pounded as my hand shakily tapped the numbers. "Rebecca, give me more info."

"Just let me talk through the coms," she replied, her voice steadying.

I connected my com's Bluetooth to my cellphone just as the operator replied, "9-1-1. What's your emergency?"

"Hello, my friend was attacked and is in critical condition. He has a knife wound and needs an ambulance. Here's the address." I heard Rebecca rattle off the Truth Squad campus address and told them the building number, but it wasn't in focus. My heart pounded, and my chest ached. The game room became blurry and seemed to spin as tears filled my eyes. I put my head in my hands. *Just breathe,* I told myself. I forced myself to take three long, slow breaths.

Once the lightheadedness left me, I turned back to what Rebecca was saying. The operator was asking questions about Luke's condition, like where was the knife wound and were there any other injuries. Rebecca's voice remained calm as she quickly told the information.

I felt like throwing up as Rebecca talked. Luke was out cold with a bruise on his forehead. He was stabbed in his side. The operator told Rebecca not to remove the knife so that he wouldn't bleed out and to pack her jacket around the knife so it wouldn't do further damage. Rebecca couldn't tell if he had any broken bones, and the operator told her to leave him alone so that she wouldn't make his injuries worse.

I'm supposed to be watching the cameras, I told myself, turning to the laptop. *I can't let Rebecca be hit, too. God, give me strength to do my job without falling apart.* I watched the screen with more vigilance than I thought possible, and soon I heard sirens coming. I listened as they entered campus, and activity began to buzz with people wondering why an ambulance and the police had arrived. I listened through my coms and watched the cameras as the paramedics loaded Luke onto the ambulance.

As the ambulance drove away, I heard through my coms the police ask Rebecca to fill them in on what she knew. As Rebecca talked, the full force of the situation hit me like a knockout punch, my head pounding with an instant headache. *Luke is going to the ER, we don't know what happened, and Rebecca was the first one on the scene.* An image of Matthew's angry face flashed into my mind. *This is bad.*

🔫

Rebecca burst into the game room, her face pale. "It was gone," she said, sinking down onto the floor next to my chair.

"What was?" I asked, not sure what she meant. *Does she mean... he's dead?*

"The pen," she said, shaking her head.

I breathed a sigh of relief. "What do you mean?"

"The pen videoing the situation. It was gone from his pocket."

"You mean... the attacker took it?" I asked.

Rebecca nodded. "I think so."

"But how would they know to take it?"

Rebecca looked me in the eye. "The only way they could have known was if they were listening in on us."

My eyes widened. "Then they're listening in right now."

Rebecca nodded. I pointed at the laptop and raised an eyebrow, wondering if they hacked her laptop. Rebecca shrugged and stood up, whispering, "I'll run a security scan. Check my bag."

I picked up her backpack and began rummaging through it. A minute later, Rebecca tapped my shoulder. I glanced over to see her pointing at her laptop screen. The security scan read, "ALL CLEAR." I nodded and continued rummaging through her bag. I pulled out her drafts from Bible papers, a Bible, and a few water bottles. At the bottom of the bag, I found a small, plastic jewelry bag. Inside were two round objects I recognized from my own Truth Squad gear. I pointed to the bag.

Rebecca nodded, mouthing, "That's it."

I felt anger boil up in me, an anger greater than I'd ever felt before. I threw the bag on the ground and stomped on the listening devices until I was sure they were both destroyed.

Rebecca stared at me, wide-eyed. Silently, she picked up the bag and threw it in the trash. "Let's go."

"Where?"

"To the hospital," she replied, sticking her papers and laptop in her bag, along with the purse and gadgets.

I followed her silently to the parking garage and located my car. I was glad Rebecca had her backpack with her license and car keys, because mine were back in our room. Rebecca hopped into the driver's seat and started the car as I climbed into the passenger side.

We rode silently the whole way to the hospital. I tried hard to suppress my tears, praying the entire time, *Lord, let Luke be okay. Don't let him die.*

Rebecca practically ran into the hospital, and I struggled to keep up. She got to the desk and asked about Luke.

"He's in surgery right now," the lady told us. "Are you relatives?"

Rebecca shook her head. "Friends."

"I'm sorry, but I can't give further information since you're not related." She smiled sympathetically. "I can let you know when visitors are allowed."

Rebecca nodded and stepped away from the desk slowly. I put my hand on her shoulder. "Let's sit in the waiting room." She nodded and followed me to sit down.

Not long after, Mr. Truth walked through the front doors. He walked up to the front desk and started talking to the lady, pulling out his badge. "Does he get to know what's going on because he has a badge?" Rebecca whispered, angrily rolling her eyes.

I shook my head. "No, Luke probably has Mr. Truth recorded as someone who can know his medical information if something were to happen since he doesn't have family around."

"Oh." Rebecca looked sheepish.

I watched as they continued talking for a minute, then he nodded and headed toward the waiting room. My heart rate picked up when he looked up and made eye contact.

"So, you're here?" he asked, sitting across from us in the plastic chairs. I couldn't tell if the tiredness in his voice was from stress or disappointment in us.

"Did they tell you anything?" I asked quietly.

He nodded, sighing. "They're fixing up the knife wound right now. Sounds like they went straight to surgery because of how deep the wound is. He has several broken ribs and, most likely, a concussion considering that bruise on his forehead. Whatever happened was quite a fight." He shook his head sadly. "What were you three doing?"

I couldn't hold back my tears anymore. "We were trying to find out who was sending these threats." I felt like I had a tsunami of tears flowing straight from my heart. My throat tightened, so I stopped talking, knowing my voice would come out in squeaks.

We sat in silence for a few minutes, Mr. Truth clearing

his voice awkwardly every few seconds and blinking rapidly, Rebecca tapping her fingers together and occasionally wiping a tear from her eye, and me crying so hard I wasn't sure how I had so many tears. I took a few deep breaths and tried to slow my tears.

Rebecca cleared her throat. "Sir, we have been receiving some strange threats," Rebecca paused. "Actually, I have been receiving some strange threats. We don't know why we've been getting them, and we tried to talk to you about it, and you wouldn't believe us. So, we've been doing our own investigation."

Mr. Truth raised an eyebrow. "If you're the one receiving threats, why is Luke in the hospital?" His voice sounded accusatory.

Rebecca took a deep breath. "Today, I got a note saying to meet the writer behind building 204 at 11:25pm or someone would get hurt. By the way, there is a blind spot in your cameras, which is where Luke was attacked. You need to fix that."

I shook my head at Rebecca, wiping the tears from my eyes. *Don't accuse Mr. Truth when we're trying to win his opinion!*

"Anyways, Luke didn't want me to meet the guys, so he went instead."

The sliding doors opened again, and I heard the loud clicks of decisive boot steps headed our way. I looked up to see the man whose gate I recognized all too well. *Matthew.* His face was flushed, and he looked angry.

"Of all the nerve," Matthew said, stomping up to us. "What are you two doing here? What, are you trying to make yourselves seem innocent? Of all the nerve!"

"Matthew!" Mr. Truth scolded. "Stop yelling."

"Stop yelling?" Matthew cried, not obeying his commander.

"Don't tell me for a minute that you don't believe these two were behind this."

"I don't." Mr. Truth's face was calm, and he shrugged nonchalantly. I felt a little better hearing those words.

"What?" Matthew yelled. Other people in the waiting room were now staring at us. "Let me guess, they had a good alibi? Well, I won't buy it. Who was the first one on the scene, huh? And who called 9-1-1, huh?" He pointed at Rebecca. "That girl. She is not trustworthy. I've said it since she first arrived, and now we have proof."

"Matthew, sit down and stop making a scene," Mr. Truth replied sternly.

Matthew sat with a thud. "Fine. But just wait for what else I tell you." His voice was slightly quieter.

Mr. Truth sighed. "What?"

"Luke let someone into the multipurpose building at 10:45, but we were never able to see who he let in. At 11:20, Luke left the game room by himself, and at 11:28, Rebecca ran down the stairs from the game room that we never saw her enter." Matthew leaned back and crossed his arms defiantly.

Mr. Truth raised his eyebrows and looked at us. "Well?"

I nodded, and Rebecca replied seriously, "That's true."

"See? I told you!" Matthew yelled, waving his arm.

Mr. Truth ignored him. "Why were you there?"

"It was close to the meeting point and seemed like a good spot for our base," Rebecca answered. "I was Luke's back-up, and Sarah was monitoring the video footage."

"You hacked our security?" Matthew asked, shaking his head with a victorious look on his face. "I knew it." He turned to Mr. Truth. "Proof."

Before Mr. Truth could reply, a nurse walked up. "John Truth?" she asked, looking between Matthew and Mr. Truth.

"That me." Mr. Truth stood.

"Luke Mason is out of surgery. He is stable, but he's still unconscious. We still need to run a few scans to check for internal bleeding and head injuries." She nodded toward the hallway. "You're welcome to come back, but no one else."

"Thank you," Mr. Truth said with a nod. He turned back toward us. "We'll finish this conversation later. We have more important things to focus on." He followed the nurse down the hall.

Matthew cleared his throat. I turned toward him. He glared at us. "Mr. Truth may have a soft spot for you two, but I don't. I know it was you," he pointed at Rebecca, "and I will prove it." He swiveled toward me. "And don't think I forgot about you. As second-in-command, I have the authority to revoke your Truth Squad membership."

I swallowed nervously. "What are you saying?"

"That as of today, your membership is revoked until Mr. Truth or myself reinstates it, and you better believe I will not be reinstating it." He turned on his heel and marched out of the hospital.

I felt like he had just punched me. Rebecca tapped my elbow and whispered, "We should go." She nodded toward the staring people in the waiting room.

I stood and slowly followed Rebecca out of the building, feeling like I was in a haze. My world was falling apart in the very last place I expected it.

"Sarah, wake up."

I opened my eyes and slowly realized that Rebecca was shaking my shoulder. *I thought that was a part of my dream, I* thought, as I slowly remembered bits of a nightmare full of natural disasters and knife attacks. *A dream where my world fell apart. The only problem is my world really is falling apart.*

I glanced at the clock. "Why are you waking me up at five?" I groaned, pulling my covers over my head. *I don't want to face today.*

Rebecca yanked the covers off my bed and switched on the light. I groaned, but Rebecca showed no sympathy. "Get up. I have breakfast ready to go. You can eat in the car."

"Where are we going?" I asked, sitting up and blinking hard.

"The hospital. I want to know how Luke is doing, and I figure Matthew wouldn't be there this early. But we won't be either if you don't get out of bed." She walked out of the room, calling, "I already got your outfit ready. Hurry up."

I glanced at my nightstand and realized she had placed jeans and a t-shirt on top. I wanted to take my time, but she had mentioned getting to the hospital before Matthew, and suddenly I felt the need to get ready quickly.

I was dressed and ready to go in five minutes. "Record timing," Rebecca said sarcastically as she handed me a to-go coffee mug and a pop-tart.

"We have pop-tarts?" I asked as we walked out of the building toward the parking garage.

Rebecca nodded, grinning sheepishly. "I kind of like them. I bought a box a while ago just to have for snacks every now and then."

I almost fell asleep in the car on the way to the hospital, but I managed to finish my pop-tart and kind of keep my eyes open. Rebecca told me I should drink the coffee first so that the caffeine would kick in by the time we got to the hospital, but I preferred not to eat a pop-tart in public, even if it did taste pretty good.

We walked through the front doors of the hospital and didn't see any Truth Squad members present. Rebecca walked to the front desk to ask a question but was informed that it was not visiting hours. She walked back to me and whispered hopefully, "Maybe they will allow visitors later this morning."

I shrugged, not feeling like talking so early in the morning. We sat down in the waiting room. I drank my coffee while Rebecca watched the morning news. The TV was playing a local station. I tuned it out since the local commercials made me cringe. But then I heard a familiar name—Luke Mason. I looked up to see the early news reporting on Luke's attack at Truth Squad. The reporter shared the details of his attack and that he was stable, then said the police were investigating the attack. "No suspects have at this time been identified," she said.

"Looks like Matthew's theory hasn't caught on," Rebecca whispered. I nodded, feeling thankful but also confused. "Wouldn't there be clues at the scene of the crime? You know, footprints or something?"

Rebecca shrugged. "I don't know. Knowing how careful they've been with the threats, I doubt they would leave any clues behind."

At six o'clock, the sliding doors opened, and Daniel walked into the hospital. He saw us and jogged over to the waiting room, his eyes filled with worry. "I got here as soon as I could. What happened?"

We quickly filled him in on the details. "Oh, man. That's serious. Who do you think did it?"

"Well, we don't have proof, but we have a pretty strong

suspicion who did it," Rebecca said. She took a deep breath and opened her mouth to say more.

Just then, the door slid open again, and Matthew's determined steps headed our way. "You're here again?" His eyes seemed like they might burst into flames.

"We're waiting to hear an update on Luke's condition," Rebecca replied, her own eyes flaming but her voice smooth.

Matthew snapped his head toward Daniel. "I'm glad you're here." His tone did not match his words. "You shouldn't be spending time with these two, though. Sarah's Squad 4 membership is currently revoked." Matthew glanced at his watch, then turned back to us. "Visiting hours begin at seven, but you will not be allowed to visit Luke. Not when you're suspects."

"We're not suspects." Rebecca's voice was firm.

"Maybe not to the police or Mr. Truth, but in my book you are. I won't let you." Matthew crossed his arms.

"I don't believe that is your jurisdiction to say. Are you a doctor? A relative?" Rebecca stood and placed her hands on her hips. When Matthew didn't reply, she raised her eyebrows defiantly. "I didn't think so."

Matthew spun on his heel and stomped out. Rebecca sat back down, shaking her head.

We sat in awkward silence. Daniel cleared his throat. "Well, you might be interested to know that Luke hired me to do a quick job."

I raised an eyebrow. "Is that why you were out of town yesterday?"

Daniel nodded. "He asked me to check on Zaiden and find out if he was able to send and receive messages. I found out that he is not able to do so. He's under high security, so he can hardly receive visitors." He shrugged. "Actually, he's currently in solitary confinement because he was attacking other prisoners, so no one can visit him right now."

"Wow." Rebecca shook her head. "That's crazy."

"That's helpful to know," I said. "Thanks."

"Why..." Daniel began, but he was interrupted by Matthew re-entering the room.

"Mr. Truth agrees that you two are not allowed access to visit Luke until the situation is sorted out." He tipped his chin up and looked at us condescendingly.

"But can't we at least receive updates on how he's doing?" I asked, my voice revealing more frustration than I meant to.

Matthew replied mockingly, "Are you a doctor? A relative?"

Rebecca rolled her eyes. She stood up and nodded toward the door, keeping her steely gaze fixed on Matthew. "Let's go."

As I stood up, Daniel stood up beside me and whispered, "I'll text you updates."

I smiled. "Thanks."

As we walked out the door, I glanced back over my shoulder and saw Matthew talking to Daniel with great expression. Daniel was paying close attention to his words, glancing back over his shoulder at us occasionally with a questioning look in his eyes. *Does he believe Matthew's story?* I worried.

"Daniel's investigation proves Zaiden didn't hire Ethan and Ryan," Rebecca said as we climbed into my car.

"Then who did?" I asked, buckling my seatbelt. *I thought the meeting yesterday would give more clarity into what's going on, but it didn't. Instead, we ended up with more questions,* I thought. *And now we're down one man and have even less time to figure things out.*

⚔

We got back to our room, and Rebecca noticed she had a new email. "It has no address," she said, sitting down in front of her laptop. She opened the message and quickly took a screenshot before reading it aloud. "Let's stop playing games. Meet me at the corner of 7th and 8th street tonight at 11:25pm." Right after finishing reading it, the message disappeared.

"What's with 11:25?" I asked.

"What do you mean?"

"Both meeting times were 11:25. Is that some kind of code? I mean, all the other messages had codes related to your work with Zaiden. It seems odd that these two messages wouldn't have a code."

Rebecca crossed her arms and stared at the ceiling. "Um," she replied slowly, "I think that was the passcode to a safe?" She shook her head. "There was nothing important in that safe, just extra keys to things, but the building exploded, so why would that code be helpful?"

"And you don't remember it being a part of anything else important?" I asked.

Rebecca started to shake her head, then stopped. "Well, I guess in the early days, we had several lunch meetings at 11:25am."

"So, the time is important, but why?" I ran my fingers through my hair. "This is so confusing."

Rebecca placed her head in her hands and sighed. "We need to come up with a plan."

I nodded, feeling a knot forming in my stomach. "It's got to be flawless," I said. The memory of the listening bug in Rebecca's backpack flashed into my mind. I lowered my voice. "Do you think it's safe to discuss our plan here? Should we go somewhere else?"

Rebecca shrugged. "I don't know." She looked around the

room. "Maybe we should go to our usual meeting place, just in case."

I nodded, and we headed out the door.

The walk to the coffee shop was silent, and I didn't mind. I allowed myself to get lost in thought as we walked the familiar route that felt so odd knowing that Luke wouldn't be meeting us there. *Lord, please heal Luke quickly,* I prayed silently, swallowing hard to keep my throat from tightening with tears. As we walked down the street, I thought about the information we learned from Daniel. *If Zaiden isn't behind this, who is?* I wondered. *And why have all the clues been connected to him? All the notes have been codes, except for the last two that both used the time 11:25. What information does Rebecca have that someone needs? And who is this someone? Lord, we need Your help,* I prayed again.

Rebecca elbowed me. "Are you going to order?"

I looked up and realized we were already in the coffee shop, and Rebecca had just placed her coffee order. The barista stared at me with a fake smile plastered on her face.

"Sorry," I said, my face growing warm as I quickly ordered. I stepped back from the counter as Rebecca paid for our drinks, embarrassed that I had been so lost in thought.

Seeing our usual table in the corner was empty, I quickly walked over and sat down. Rebecca joined me a couple minutes later with our coffees. She sat down, and we sipped our coffees silently, neither of us wanting to start our conversation.

Rebecca sighed. "I could sure use Luke's enthusiasm right now." She shook her head, muttering, "I should have never let him take my place."

"Rebecca, it's not your fault." I put a hand on her shoulder. "We didn't know we were bugged."

"There were so many other ways it could have been

avoided. We could have been more forceful about talking to Mr. Truth—"

"Do you really think he would have taken us seriously?" I asked, raising an eyebrow.

She shrugged. "I don't know."

I took a deep breath, trying to think of what to say. I couldn't think of anything profound. "Rebecca, we can't change what's happened. We just have to focus on the problem in front of us." *Wow, that was uninspiring,* I thought.

Rebecca straightened. "You're right." She looked me in the eye. "So, I'm supposed to meet our man at 11:25pm tonight at 7th and 8th street."

I nodded. "What should we do? You can't just show up without a plan."

Rebecca crossed her arms. We sat in silence.

I stared down at my coffee, thinking. I had an idea, but I didn't like it. *Rebecca probably wouldn't like it either,* I told myself as my heart rate picked up speed. *But what other choice do you have?* I argued with myself. I glanced up at my sister. She was still concentrating and didn't seem to have any ideas yet. *Could I really do it? I don't know that I'm strong enough.* I studied my sister's face. *She works so hard to be strong for everyone else. You can be strong for her,* I told myself, trying to muster up the courage to voice my idea. *Just say it already!*

I cleared my throat, took a deep breath, and then spoke quickly so that I wouldn't change my mind. "Um, what if we switched places?"

Rebecca raised an eyebrow at me. "What?"

"What if I went as you?" My voice came out timid, betraying my fear.

Rebecca shook her head. "No way. I'm not letting another person get hurt because of me."

"They wouldn't know. We're meeting at night, and I can fake being you. I did it before."

"And Mr. Zaiden figured it out."

"It took him a while. Plus, he knew you really well. Ethan and Ryan don't." I crossed my arms, trying to act confident.

"Even if we did switch places, what would we do then?" She shook her head. "We've got to have a rock-solid plan."

I thought for a minute. "So, we switch places. You'll be able to track me with my watch and listen in through our coms so you can know what's happening. If they kidnap me, you will have evidence to turn into the police."

"And what if they try to attack you like they did Luke?" Rebecca asked, concerned. She blinked rapidly, her eyes filling with tears. "I can't let that happen."

"Rebecca, I think they want information from you. Why else would their messages be full of codes? I don't think they would attack me if they thought I was you." I hoped I sounded more convincing than I felt.

Rebecca sat silently for a minute. She sighed. "You're probably right. But why would we need to switch places, then?"

"Because we don't want them to get whatever information they want. I wouldn't know it, so I could keep them stalled long enough for you to get help."

Rebecca opened her mouth to reply then paused, her eyes growing wide at something over my shoulder.

I turned around. Faith and Hope were sitting at the table next to us. They stared at us with wide eyes, and Faith's jaw was wide open.

"Hi," I said awkwardly, faking a smile. "What are you two doing here?"

"Grandma dropped us off to get smoothies while she went to the store," Hope said, her facial expression not changing.

Faith smacked the table. "Are you two in trouble?"

"You do not need to be worried about us," Rebecca replied, smiling. "Besides, it's rude to eavesdrop."

Hope blushed, but Faith didn't give up. "You two are talking about meeting with a bad guy, aren't you? I mean, it has to be a bad guy if you're worried about getting beat up." Her eyes lit up with excitement. "We can help you!"

"No!" Rebecca and I replied firmly in unison.

"Why not?" Faith whined. "It sounds like you need help, and I'll bet no one else would help you." She stood up and marched over to us, her hands on her hips. "I heard what Jonathan said he overheard Matthew saying, and I've heard other people say that you two got in trouble with Mr. Truth. So, that means other agents probably won't help you." She tossed her braid over her shoulder. "Hope, Jonathan, and I are top of our class with our training. We can help you." She tilted her chin up confidently.

I smiled sympathetically. "That's very kind of you, but we really can't have you involved."

Her shoulders fell. "Not even to monitor tracking devices or something? I bet we could do it."

Rebecca's face was stern. "Faith, Hope, you two are not helping us. This is dangerous, and we don't want you to get hurt. So, forget you ever overheard this conversation. Okay?"

"Yes, ma'am," Hope replied. Faith just glared at us.

"And don't repeat anything you've heard to anyone, or you will jeopardize our mission," Rebecca said. "Understood?"

"So, in a way, you are helping us by not saying anything," I offered.

The sisters nodded in unison, their faces serious.

Rebecca smiled. "Thank you."

We said goodbye and hurried out of the coffee shop, not wanting to continue our discussion where Faith and Hope could overhear. Rebecca glanced over her shoulder as we left. "I sure hope those two don't say anything."

"I don't think they will," I assured her.

I just hope they don't try to jump in and help us on their own, I thought, worriedly.

CHAPTER 10

"Okay, looks good. Do you think you're ready?" Rebecca asked.

I glanced down at the outfit I was wearing. I had Rebecca's jeans and black shirt on. I wore my black boots that had a small heel because Rebecca was one inch taller than me. I wore my hair in a braid straight down my back instead of over my shoulder like I would normally wear it. We did a little bit of makeup to match Rebecca's, but we really didn't have to do much to my appearance. As others had often told us, we were "eerily alike."

"I think I'm ready," I said, checking my watch for the millionth time to make sure it was set to track my location.

My phone beeped. I grabbed it from my back pocket. "It's from Daniel!"

I glanced up at Rebecca to see her eyes light up. "What did he say?"

I read the text. "Sorry I didn't message earlier. Luke's surgery went well, but you probably knew that. Doctors assume he likely has a concussion, but the scans don't show any internal bleeding, which is good. Still hasn't woken up yet. I'm staying here all night in case he wakes up. I'll text you with more updates."

Rebecca sighed, still looking worried. "What's wrong?" I asked.

She shrugged. "If Luke were awake, he could tell us who attacked him, and we wouldn't have to meet with these guys tonight." She shook her head. "I shouldn't be so negative. He's doing well, so that's good." She tried to smile, but it looked forced.

"It will be okay. Remember Romans 8:28. God will work everything out for good," I said. *Lord, help me to believe it myself,* I prayed.

Rebecca nodded, glancing at the time. "We still have a few minutes before you need to leave." She looked me in the eye. "How are you doing?"

"Fine," I lied. I cringed inwardly, knowing it was wrong.

All day my mind had been flashing back to the memories of the last time I had impersonated my sister, when Mr. Zaiden captured and interrogated me. I hadn't stayed completely in character, and he figured out who I really was. I had been so sure I was going to be killed that day, but instead, Luke and Rebecca showed up. The memory of running upstairs after Luke freed me and seeing Mr. Zaiden holding a knife over Rebecca's face surfaced. I had no time to register my fear. I just ran forward and grabbed at his hand, giving my sister enough time to move out of the way. I still wondered about that moment. Just the memory scared me and had caused me to lay awake many nights wondering, "what if." *How could I have not been afraid in the moment but am afraid of that memory now?* I thought, frustrated at how wimpy I felt.

I looked up and saw Rebecca standing with her hands on her hips. "You're lying," she said matter-of-factly.

I sighed, running a hand through my hair. "I know. I'm terrified." I shook my head. "I don't understand how you and

Luke can be so brave. I keep thinking back to when Mr. Zaiden captured me, and just the memory scares me. And now I'm supposed to impersonate you again, and I'm panicking. What if I mess up again?" I took a deep breath, trying to calm my racing heart. "I don't know if I can handle this."

Rebecca stood silently for a minute. "Well, I've been learning from my Bible class that we're supposed to find strength and courage in the Lord. Psalm 28:7 says, 'The Lord is my strength and my shield; my heart trusts in Him, and I am helped,' and Psalm 31:24 says, 'Be strong and let your heart take courage, all you who hope in the Lord.' Something I've been learning is that I am not strong enough to do everything myself." She smiled and shook her head. "I used to think that I was so strong, but I've learned that I'm not as strong as I think I am. That's why I need God."

I smiled, silently thanking God for the transformation He had done in my sister's life. "I guess," I said slowly, "it's easy for me to know this stuff, but it's harder to live it. I mean, how do you do it? I guess I've always wondered if I'll never be as courageous and fearless as you and Luke because of my personality. It just seems a part of me to be worried and afraid."

Rebecca nodded, staring at the ground. "Courage is doing the right thing despite what our emotions say." She looked up at me. "Just because I can hide my emotions doesn't mean I don't have them. The Bible says that God is love, and perfect love casts out fear, right?" I nodded. "So, if you want courage and fearlessness, you've got to go to God. It doesn't mean we don't have emotions. It means we know where to take them, and we choose to believe God's truth, not our emotions."

I nodded slowly, allowing her words to sink in. *God, I don't want to be enslaved to my emotions anymore,* I prayed. *I want to believe Your truth, but I need Your help. Please cast out my fear.*

Rebecca glanced at her watch. "We need to get going. Are you sure you want to do this?"

I nodded. "Let's pray first."

Rebecca parked a few blocks away from the corner of 7th and 8th streets. She turned off the car and took a deep breath. "Sarah, I don't want you to do this," she said, shaking her head. "I don't want another person getting hurt because of me. It's not worth it."

"I need to. I think this is the right thing to do," I said. *God, please give me Your strength,* I prayed silently. "I know how to play you. Plus, we've got coms, and I'm armed. If I need help, you'll be there in a split second."

Rebecca stared at me seriously for a long second. Finally, she replied, "Okay. Stay in constant communication, understand?"

I nodded and opened the car door. I stepped out, glancing around to make sure no one was watching me. I noticed a car parked down the street, but it looked empty.

I walked down the street two blocks, then turned right onto 7th Street. At the end of the block was the sign marking the intersection of 7th and 8th streets. The streets felt eerie this late at night, the streetlights seeming too far apart for comfort. The lack of people made the usually cheery downtown feel creepy. I glanced at my watch as I approached the street corner. *11:23.* "Here," I whispered into my coms.

"Got it," Rebecca replied.

I stood up straight and mimicked Rebecca's confident

posture and movements, glancing around me as I waited for someone to show up.

"It's 11:25. Anyone?" Rebecca asked, her voice making me jump.

"Negative," I replied, turning in a circle.

"Keep waiting."

The longer I stood there, the creepier it felt. *Where is my contact?* I wondered. My heart rate was picking up, so I began quoting to myself the verse Rebecca had shared with me. *Be strong and let your heart take courage.* Repeating the verse started to calm my racing heart.

I felt like I had been standing by that street sign for an eternity. I glanced at my watch. *11:35. Ten minutes late?* I wondered. *This seems unusual.*

I was starting to feel bored and realized I was slipping out of character. I reassumed Rebecca's posture, listening for any kind of movement.

Five minutes later, I spoke into my coms, "It's 11:40, and still no sign of anyone."

"Fifteen minutes late. That doesn't seem right. Keep your guard up," Rebecca said.

It's already up, I thought, glancing around me.

A car drove past, causing me to jump. I watched as it turned right at the end of 8th Street, then let out my breath. *Was that the same car I saw parked behind our car?* I wondered.

A slight breeze blew through the streets, causing the leaves on the small maple trees lining the sidewalks to brush against each other, sending shivers up my spine.

I checked my surroundings again. Seeing no one, I glanced at my watch. *11:45.*

"If no one shows up in the next five minutes, then leave," Rebecca said.

Her voice made me jump again. "Okay." The breeze stopped, and everything was deathly still. "Rebecca, what if this was the wrong plan?" I asked, a new idea popping into my head. "What if this meeting is a diversion?"

"Could be. Stay for the rest of the five minutes just in case, though."

"I think I should come back," I began, then I heard Rebecca's car door open.

"What are you doing?" her voice rang in my ear. "Sarah, oof!" I heard a thud.

I took off down the street. "Rebecca, what's going on?" She didn't answer.

I rounded the corner, running as fast as I could. As I got closer, I saw two masked men trying to push my struggling sister into their car, the same one that drove past me earlier.

"Stop!" I cried, pulling out my taser and pulling the trigger. I hit the taller man, and he started shaking and fell over, letting go of my sister's arm. Before I could take aim at the second man, something hit the back of my head. I toppled over and hit my face on the sidewalk, and everything went black.

⚬

I woke up lying in the back seat of my car, my head pounding. I sat up slowly and glanced around, my head in a fog. There was a pounding sound that wouldn't stop. I put my hands on my head, trying to control the massive headache I was feeling. Suddenly, the pounding registered. I looked up to see Faith knocking on the window, Hope and their grandma, Melba, standing next to her. Their faces were full of concern.

I reached for the door handle, but it was locked. Looking

up at the front of the car, I noticed my keys were gone, and so were Rebecca's equipment, my taser, my watch, and my earpiece.

I crawled into the front seat and unlocked the car, noticing my black eye in the rearview mirror. I opened the door and stepped out of the car. "Sarah, what's wrong with you?" Faith asked in her usual, blunt fashion.

"Are you okay?" Melba asked, giving me a hug. "You don't look well."

I shook my head. "I'm okay, I just have a headache. But my sister is not okay."

"Where is she?" Faith asked.

Without thinking, I replied, "She's been kidnapped." I regretted the words as soon as they left my mouth. Faith's jaw dropped, her eyes wide with excitement, while Hope and Melba looked horrified.

"Were you knocked out in a fight?" Faith asked excitedly. Hope nudged her and gave her the look.

"Knocked out, yes. In a fight, not really," I said, remembering that I was hit from behind and fell on my face. *There were three attackers,* I thought. *It must have been Ethan, Ryan, and the guy contacting Carrie, maybe Braxton Niles.*

"Honey, why don't you come to my house so we can take care of your eye and give you some breakfast," Melba said.

I nodded. "Where are you parked? I'll meet you there. I want to check a few things first."

"Oh, don't worry about that," she waved. "I'll drive over here and pick you up."

They walked away, and I hurried to look through my car. Everything was gone from inside it, even my spare tire from the trunk. *Why did they steal all my stuff?* I wondered. I also noticed one of my tires was slashed. *They obviously didn't want me waking up and following them.* I glanced at the sky, noticing how bright it was. *Not that I would have, considering how long I was out.*

Melba pulled up, and I climbed into the passenger seat. I glanced at the time on the clock. It was almost ten. Seeing the time made my growling stomach register. I also became even more aware of my pounding headache.

The twins launched into a thousand questions at once. I leaned forward onto my hands, trying to still the pounding in my head as it matched time with Faith and Hope's cacophony of words.

Pretty soon, Melba hushed her granddaughters. "Save the questions till Sarah has some breakfast," she said quietly, her southern lilt causing me to smile.

Melba and her husband, Steve, had lived in Tennessee their whole lives, but when their daughter and son-in-law decided to join Truth Squad as special ops agents, they moved out to Oregon in order to see their kids, and later to take care of Faith and Hope whenever their parents were gone on secret operations. The sweet couple were like grandparents to everyone at Truth Squad and were affectionately called Grandma Melba and Grandpa Steve by many.

Before long, I was sitting at Melba's dining room table, sipping a glass of orange juice as she made pancakes. After taking some medicine for my headache, Faith and Hope sat down at the table with their own orange juice and looked at me expectantly.

I smiled. "What?"

Faith shrugged, her eyebrows raised. "Well? Are you going to fill us in? Who are the bad guys? What's the plan? How are we going to rescue Rebecca? What car—"

"Hold on," I said, shaking my head. "That's a lot of questions.

Also, did you say 'we' are rescuing Rebecca? Because you are not getting involved."

Faith crossed her arms. "Yes, I am." She leaned closer to me. "You need help, and I have skills."

Hope elbowed her sister. "That's kind of arrogant."

Faith sighed. "I guess that didn't come out like I intended."

Melba walked over with a plate of pancakes and set it in front of me. "Someone get Sarah some syrup and a fork," she said, walking back into the kitchen. Hope jumped up and ran to the fridge, returning with syrup while Faith grabbed me a fork.

"Thanks." I poured syrup over the stack of pancakes and started eating, trying to be refined and not stuff my face since I was starving.

Faith and Hope didn't sit in silence for long. "Please let us help you," Faith said, shaking her folded hands beneath her chin as she made a puppy dog face.

"Please." Hope grinned expectantly. "Who else are you going to ask for help?"

It's a good point, I thought, but shook my head. "These guys are dangerous. I don't want you two involved."

Melba walked into the dining room and sat down opposite me, her face serious. "Sarah, help me understand this," she said in her slow, southern drawl. "Explain to me the situation."

I glanced at the twins, took a deep breath, and launched into a quick retelling of the situation, starting from the threats, and recounting the training room hacking, the smoke bombs, Luke's attack, and finishing with Rebecca's capture. "We don't know what the motive is behind everything," I finished with a sigh. "That's really the worst part. And I need to rescue my sister before they get whatever information they need and are done with her."

I looked down at my half-eaten plate and suddenly didn't want to finish. *I need to go find my sister.* I stood up. "Thank you for the food, Grandma Melba, but I need to get going."

Melba shook her head. "Wait just a minute, young lady." She stood up slowly, a determined look on her face. "You can't rescue your sister on your own. That's clear."

I smiled, searching for the right words to sound convincing. "Thank you for your concern, but..."

"I'm not finished," Melba said, interrupting me. "We're going to help you."

"No," I said firmly.

"Don't argue with me!" Melba scolded. "You need help, and you don't know who to find for help. Well, my granddaughters do have skills, and I used to work at the sheriff's office years ago." She nodded decisively. "We're helping you."

I shook my head. "That's very kind of you, but these people are dangerous. And I don't know what I could ask you to help with."

"We can start with brainstorming," Melba said, grinning from ear to ear. "And, of course, the most important way we can help is by praying." She patted the table. "Sit back down, honey, and let's get started."

"Okay, you girls know what you're doing?" I asked as we walked through the front gate onto Truth Squad's campus.

Faith nodded. "Climb through the window into Matthew and Luke's lab and get the gadgets on this list." She waved a piece of paper.

"And try not to be seen by anyone," Hope put in. "If anyone sees us, we'll act natural, so they don't suspect anything."

Faith raised an eyebrow at me. "Do you know what you're doing?"

I smiled. "Yes. I'm sneaking into Luke's dorm and finding his laptop."

Since I couldn't convince Melba and her granddaughters to not help me, we came up with a plan to get Luke's laptop which tracked our watches to find out where Rebecca was. We also decided that if I was going to save Rebecca, I would need some gadgets and weapons. We decided to have Faith and Hope sneak into Matthew's lab since they would be less suspicious than me. Luke didn't have a roommate, so I knew I wouldn't have to worry about anyone catching me in his room, but getting into the boys' dorms was the tricky part.

"Meet you back at the front gate," I said, as we split ways. I hurried toward the girls' dorms first, needing some supplies from our room.

In our room, I found some climbing gloves Luke had invented. They used a vacuum to suction to the surface you climbed... at least that's what Luke said they were supposed to do. *I hope these work,* I thought, having never used them before. Luke had given a pair to Rebecca after he tested them, but Rebecca had never used them either. I grabbed our small tool kit and a holster for my belt, putting a few screwdrivers and a small hammer inside. I also grabbed an empty backpack to carry the laptop. My plan was to climb up the wall of the boys' dorm and get in through Luke's window.

I hope everyone is out doing things and not looking through their windows, otherwise I am toast, I thought, hurrying out of my room and down the stairs.

I jogged to the back of the boys' dorms and looked up at the windows. Earlier I had texted Daniel to find out which dorm was Luke's. It was on the second story, number 212.

Since their dorms were set up exactly like the girls' building, I knew that would be the third window to the right of the staircase. Positioning myself beneath the window, I pulled on my gloves and took a deep breath, trying to remember back to when Luke gave Rebecca instructions on how to use these gloves. There were two buttons near the thumb, one to create the vacuum to suction the gloves to the wall, and the other to release the vacuum so you could keep climbing.

This is going to take some serious arm strength, I thought nervously. I placed my hands on the wall at face height and pressed the top button. Nothing happened. I pressed the bottom button, and suddenly the gloves gripped the wall.

Top button releases, bottom button grips, I told myself. I braced my feet on the wall and pulled myself up with my arms. I released my left hand and quickly moved it up and regripped the glove. I repeated the process with my right hand, slowly making my way up the wall.

It's working, I thought, continuing my progress slowly upward. *Please, no one walk out of the back door right now.*

My arms were starting to ache. *Just four more steps, and I'll be able to open the window. Keep going,* I told myself.

Without warning, my right glove released its grip. A surge of adrenaline rushed through me as my hand slipped and my left arm tensed to hold my full weight. I quickly placed my hand back on the wall. *Please regrip.* I pressed the button. It started to grip, then released. *What is wrong?* I thought, panicking. I was barely out of reach of the window. *I can't keep going with just one glove. Lord, please let this work!* I prayed, frantically. I tried again, and it wouldn't grip. Suddenly, I noticed the release button was jammed in. I pressed it over and over with my thumb, trying to release it. *Come on!* I knew my left arm couldn't hold me much longer. Finally, the button released. I quickly placed my hand on the wall and pressed the bottom button. I breathed a sigh of relief as it gripped the wall.

Once I knew my right hand was secure, I slowly released my left glove and climbed higher. One more step, and I was in line with the window. I braced my feet against the wall and released my left hand, grabbing a flat screwdriver from the bag on my belt.

I pushed the flathead in between the trim and the window, trying to push it open. For a second, the window didn't budge. *I hope he doesn't have anything blocking it from opening,* I thought. Just then, it slid open an inch. I put the screwdriver back into the bag and pushed the window open with my hand. I popped the screen out and grabbed the ledge of the window. I released my right glove's grip and pulled myself through the window, tumbling onto the floor.

I laid on the floor, trying to catch my breath. My arms burned from pulling myself up the wall. *I'm so glad this is only a second-story room. I don't think I could have made it to the third story,* I thought.

I sat up and looked around the room, checking for signs of Luke's residence. *It would be terrible if this was the wrong room,* I thought, panicking for a minute. I noticed an empty doughnut box in the trashcan and felt fairly confident I was in the right room.

I stood up and began looking for Luke's laptop. I had hoped it would be sitting out somewhere, but it wasn't. Luke's room was surprisingly organized considering the state of his experimental lab he shared with Matthew. *He and Rebecca might be even more perfect for each other than I thought.* I smiled as I continued searching.

I opened the top drawer of his dresser and found a laptop. I opened it and looked at the lock screen. Seeing a picture of

Luke as a little kid, I knew I'd found the right laptop. I closed the laptop and stuck it in my backpack.

Suddenly I heard footsteps and voices outside the door. I couldn't make out the words, but I recognized the voice. *Matthew!*

I slung the backpack over my shoulder and hurried to the window. The footsteps stopped outside the door. I heard keys jingle. *I don't know how to put the screen back in from the outside!* I thought, and quickly shoved the screen behind a chair.

I climbed out the window, suctioning one glove to the wall while I used the other hand to pull the window. I tried to finish pushing the window closed completely, but I noticed the handle turning to the door of the room. *That will have to do,* I thought, grimacing at the still slightly open window. *Lord, please don't let Matthew notice,* I prayed, quickly moving down the wall and out of sight from the window.

As I climbed back down, I wondered what Matthew was doing in Luke's room. *Did Daniel tell him I asked for his room number?* I thought nervously. *Maybe Daniel did believe Matthew's story.* My heart sank at that thought, and I wasn't sure why.

I stood outside the front gate, waiting nervously for Faith and Hope. *Did they get distracted?* I wondered. *Or did Matthew catch them?*

I glanced at my watch, only to be reminded that I didn't have a watch on. I rolled my eyes in frustration. *Why did they take my watch?* I sighed. *More importantly, why did they take my sister?*

I heard some laughing and looked up to see Faith and

Hope headed my way, along with Jonathan. *Oh, no,* I thought nervously. *We can't have Mr. Truth's son mixed up in this.*

Faith smiled triumphantly as they walked through the front gate. "We've brought reinforcements!"

I tried to smile, but I knew it wasn't convincing. "That wasn't part of the plan."

"We know," Hope said quickly. "But, you see, we got into a pickle because Matthew showed up. He was about to ask us what we were doing sneaking into his lab when Jonathan showed up and distracted him so we could sneak out."

"Wow," I said, looking at Jonathan.

He shrugged. "I didn't know what they were up to, but I saw them sneak in and figured someone should watch their back."

"So, we decided it was only fair to let him help us," Faith finished.

My heart sank. *They told him what's going on?*

My face must have shown what I was thinking, because Jonathan said, "Relax. I do want to help. I know I told you I heard Matthew talking to my dad, but I think I believe your story." He shrugged. "I mean, my dad wasn't really buying everything Matthew was assuming, so I figure I shouldn't either."

I smiled. *Well, since he already knows what's going on, it won't hurt for him to join in the brainstorming, I guess.* "Let's go. I'm sure Grandma Melba has food waiting for us."

My guess was correct. As we walked into the house, I took a deep breath and smelled fresh brownies. We walked into the kitchen to find a huge pan cooling on the counter. Plates of turkey and cheese sandwiches were placed around the table with pickles and coleslaw on the side.

"Oh, we have one more guest!" Melba said excitedly. "Let

me make one more sandwich." She hurried about the kitchen and had another sandwich on the table in no time.

We each took a seat at the table, and after praying for the meal, Melba said, "Let's talk while we eat. How did the mission go?"

"My part was successful. How about you two, I mean three?" I asked, motioning to the friends.

Faith gave a thumbs-up. "Perfect. Jonathan helped us out, too."

Melba looked at me. "What's the plan now?"

I pointed to my backpack that was leaning against the wall. "I'll use Luke's computer to track Rebecca's watch. Hopefully, she still has it on her, and we'll be able to track her location."

"Then what?" Jonathan asked.

I took a deep breath. "I'll go find her."

Jonathan stared at me, his face blank. "You'll go find her? That's it?" He raised an eyebrow. "Come on, you've got to have a more detailed plan than that. This is a high-stakes operation, here! We've got to have a detailed plan A and a backup plan B!" Jonathan stood up and began pacing, reminding me of his dad. "We need times, we need locations, we need—"

"Yes, and we're starting with the locations," I interrupted. "That's what Luke's computer is for."

Jonathan shrugged and sat back down. "So, you're going to make a more detailed plan when you have the location?"

"Sure," I said, nodding slowly.

I have no idea what to do, I thought, staring down at my plate. *I'm not the plan maker. I follow the plan.* I shook my head and took a bite of coleslaw. *Lord, give me wisdom. I'm putting my courage in You, not me.*

We finished eating, and while Melba and the teens made brownie sundaes, I tried to figure out Luke's password. *I wish*

Rebecca was here. She has the software on her computer to solve passwords.

I tried common passwords, like "password," Luke's name, his name with some numbers tacked on, and his birthday, but no luck. I sighed. "I have to wait two minutes before it will let me try again," I said, stretching. "Does anyone have any ideas?"

"Something related to doughnuts?" Hope suggested.

I tried a few doughnut passwords after the two minutes were up, but nothing worked. "Oh, great. Now I have to wait five minutes." I shook my head. "If I don't figure this out soon, I'll be locked out forever."

And then I won't be able to find Rebecca. That thought scared me.

"Just a second," Jonathan said, texting on his phone. He stepped out of the room a second later when his phone rang.

A couple minutes later, he walked back into the room confidently. "I think I know it."

When the lock time finished on the laptop, Jonathan quickly typed in a password and hit enter, a smirk on his face. The laptop unlocked. "Yes!" I said, high-fiving Jonathan. "How'd you figure it out?"

He grinned. "I asked a friend. To be honest, it was an easy password if you'd thought about it."

What friend knows his password? I wondered.

"What was it?" Faith asked. Jonathan whispered something in her ear, and she started laughing.

"What's so funny?" I asked.

Faith didn't answer. She turned and whispered the message to Hope. Hope's face turned red, and she started giggling.

"It was," Jonathan paused, trying to suppress a laugh, "a

sideways V, a three, and then Rebecca." Jonathan burst out laughing.

Sideways V, three, Rebecca? I thought, lowering my eyebrows. *What does that mean?* I looked down at the keys, then realized what it meant: *heart Rebecca.* "Aww," I said, then joined in the giggling. "That's cute."

"Cute? That's hilarious! And now we all know his secret!" Jonathan said through his laughter.

Melba shook her finger at Jonathan. "Don't you tell the poor boy. He'll be so embarrassed if he finds out you all were here laughing at him."

Faith and Hope slowly stopped giggling and looked down at the ground, ashamed. "You're right," Hope said. "Sorry."

I found the watch tracking information on Luke's computer, and I started a scan for Rebecca's watch. As it scanned, I grabbed my brownie sundae off the kitchen counter and took a bite. "Delicious," I said, sitting back down by the computer.

The scan took longer than I expected. *We must have used a more high-tech computer last time we were tracking the watches,* I thought.

Fifteen minutes later, the laptop dinged. "It found it!" Faith said excitedly, looking at the screen.

I hurried back over from loading the dishwasher with Melba. The scanner located Rebecca's watch in a storage complex. "So, now we have our location."

Jonathan rubbed his hands together. "Let's get rolling on those details!"

CHAPTER 11

"Lord, we ask once more for protection and peace upon this group. I know You love them more than I do," Melba prayed, a hint of tears in her voice. "In Jesus' powerful name we pray—"

"Amen," we all said in unison.

I blinked back the tears that had formed in my eyes during Melba's prayer and looked up at the group with a smile. "Ready?"

Hope and Jonathan nodded seriously, while Faith grinned. "Oh, yeah!" she said, double-raising her eyebrows.

I turned to Melba. "Are you sure Grandpa Steve won't mind us using his van?"

Melba waved her hand. "Of course not. He's got insurance." She lowered her voice and leaned closer. "And between you and me, I think if something happens to his van, maybe he'll decide not to replace it and just retire already." She winked.

I laughed. "Well, okay, then." I took a deep breath. "And you're sure you want Faith, Hope, and Jonathan coming with me?" The butterflies in my stomach felt more like a tornado the closer we got to piling into the van.

Melba put her hands on her hips. "Sarah, you need back up. These kids are just staying in the van and calling the police when the time is right. Jonathan's got his permit and can drive them away if need be. And I will be in constant contact with them, too. I also know my Steve has a gun somewhere in that van, and the girls can find it if they need it." She nodded decisively. "Yes, I'm sure they can go."

"Okay," I said, wishing her assurance made me feel better.

I knew I couldn't keep stalling. *My sister needs me, and I am not going to show up too late to help her,* I told myself.

I turned to face my backup crew. "Hope, do you have the laptop ready to go with the coms?"

She nodded. "Yes, ma'am."

"Faith, you ready to be our eyes?"

"I'm going to watch for unusual activity or bad guys or any evidence that I can use to call the police." Faith grinned. "I'm also pretty good at acting, so if you ever need a distraction..."

"I don't think that will be necessary," I cut in. I looked at Jonathan. "And you're prepared to be the getaway man in case anything goes wrong?"

He saluted. "Prepared is my middle name."

"It's William," Faith said, raising her eyebrows. Jonathan just rolled his eyes.

"Let's get in the van," I ordered. We hurried out to the garage and piled in.

Melba pointed at Faith as she climbed in. "Don't forget to keep me informed. And I'll be praying for y'all." She hit the garage door opener.

I smiled as I buckled and started the van. "Thanks." I pulled the door closed.

I reached to change the vehicle to reverse when my smartphone beeped. I picked it up and noticed a message from Daniel. *Maybe Luke's awake!* I thought, opening the message.

Instead of an update on Luke, he wrote, "I thought you could use this reminder: Isaiah 41:10. 'Do not fear, for I am with you; Do not anxiously look about you, for I am your God. I will strengthen you, surely I will help you, Surely I will uphold you with My righteous right hand.'"

I smiled and replied with a quick thank you, then backed out of the driveway.

It was a twenty-minute drive to the storage complex. "Here we are," I said, pulling into the parking lot. I followed the fence along the perimeter to the back of the complex.

"Rebecca's tracker tells me she's in this building," Hope said, pointing out the window. "The green one."

I glanced at the green building. From my investigation of the storage complex's website and the images I found online, this building was the original office before they built a new office building on the other side of the complex closer to the main road.

"Alright, let's go rescue her!" Faith said excitedly.

"No. We're sticking to the plan, remember? I sneak in and rescue her, you three keep an eye out for any bad guys. Jonathan, if anyone tries to approach this van, you drive away. Got it?" I glanced around, trying to find a good place to park without being seen.

"But I'm not supposed to drive without an adult," he whined, staring at his phone.

"Emergencies are exceptions," I replied, parking between the fence and some trees. "Besides, you told me you were Mr. Prepared."

He rolled his eyes and put his phone down. "I guess I did say that."

I looked back at the green building. *Lord, give me strength,* I prayed quickly. I took a deep breath.

"Are you scared?" Faith asked, raising an eyebrow at me.

"You can tell?" I shook my head. "I am scared." I thought

for a minute before continuing. "But courage means trusting God and doing the right thing despite my emotions." I smiled. Despite my nerves, I felt peace wash over me.

Jonathan's face got serious. "I think this is a good time to pray."

🔫

After searching the outside of the green building, I found an air vent large enough for me to crawl through. The grate was near the peak of the building. *Good thing I brought those wall climbing gloves again,* I thought, pulling them on.

I ran my hand along the slick, metal surface. *I hope I'll be strong enough to get to the top,* I thought, knowing this would be more challenging than last time. I took a deep breath and started climbing.

About halfway up, my arms were starting to hurt. *Twice in one day was a bad idea,* I thought, willing myself to release the grips, lift my arm up, regrip, and pull myself up higher.

Out of nowhere, a bird flew at me. I stifled a scream and tried to dodge it. It flew away. I released my left hand and reached it up. Just as I pushed the button to regrip, the bird flew at me again. My hand slipped. My right arm felt like it was screaming at me as I dangled from it. My left hand banged on the wall as I tried to escape the attacking bird, and I froze. *Did they hear that?* The pain in my arm didn't let me stay frozen for long. Ignoring the bird, I regripped my left hand to the wall and leaned on that arm momentarily, allowing my right arm to rest.

What is wrong with this bird? I thought, ducking my head as it flew past again. I looked up. There was a barn swallow nest at the peak of the building.

Oh, no, I thought, a sinking feeling in my stomach. *I'm going to have to deal with these birds until I reach that grate.* I took a deep breath. *I guess the faster I get to the grate, the faster I get away from these birds.*

I continued my slow climb up the wall, trying not to scream as the swallow kept flying back around. My shoulders and biceps were aching. *Ten more steps... I hope,* I told myself, wondering if my arms would allow me to get there.

After what felt like an eternity, I reached the grate. Bracing my feet against the wall, I released the grip on my right glove and grabbed a screwdriver from my belt. I quickly unscrewed the bolts holding the grate in place. Pulling the grate off the wall, I looked inside. The air duct was barely large enough for me to crawl through. I lay the grate down inside the duct and placed my right hand inside the air duct, gripping the glove to the side. Slowly, I released my other hand and quickly gripped it inside the duct. With a grunt, I pulled myself inside.

I breathed a sigh of relief, feeling something solid underneath my feet. I put a finger on my com. "I'm in," I said. I paused, waiting to hear an answer. *Is Hope not paying attention?* I wondered.

I grabbed the grate and tried to prop it up by the entrance, but it wouldn't stay. *I hope that swallow doesn't try to follow me in here,* I thought, and started crawling through the duct.

The duct seemed to stretch on forever. The cold air rushing through it felt good on my burning arms, but my nose soon felt frozen.

I wonder if this was a bad plan, I thought. *I haven't seen any openings to the ground below.*

Suddenly I heard a bunch of activity through my earpiece. "No, I don't think that's it. Just let me do it! Oh, wait, it's on." Hope cleared her throat. "Copy that."

"Thanks," I whispered, grinning.

"Sorry about that," Faith's voice boomed in my ear. "We were having trouble figuring out how to turn our mic on. But we figured it out now."

"Copy that." *I hope they don't talk too much,* I thought, continuing my trek through the air duct. *I'll need to be able to hear when I find Rebecca.*

I saw light coming through a grate up ahead, and I felt a wave of excitement rush through me. *Finally!*

I slowed down as I neared the grate, being extra cautious about making noise. I looked down and saw a pile of flattened cardboard boxes in the middle of a concrete floor. Near the wall was a pile of junk. There were rusted tools, empty paint cans, and a few pieces of broken furniture.

Hmm. This is not what I expected to see, I thought. I put my ear down near the grate, trying to listen despite the noise from the air rushing through the duct. I could hear what sounded like someone talking, but I couldn't make out their words.

I looked up, spotting what looked like more light from another grate. I started crawling toward it. I reached the grate and looked down. This time I saw people. My heart skipped a beat when I saw my sister tied to a chair in the middle of the room, Ethan standing next to her. Ryan stood a few steps away, shifting back and forth on his feet. A third, short man with dark hair and wearing sunglasses paced around the room, coming in and out of my view. *That must be Braxton.*

I leaned down next to the grate to hear what was going on. "Are you ready to talk?" Ethan asked, sounding frustrated.

I could hear Rebecca mutter something, but I couldn't make out her words.

Ethan slapped her face, and I cringed. "Get talking! Tell us the codes already!"

"Which one?" Rebecca asked, sounding bored.

I crawled back to the first grate. I looked down through the grate again, watching to see whether Braxton would walk into view. A second later he barely walked into view, spun on his heel, and walked back out of view. *He's far enough away from the pile of junk, I think if I time this right, I can hide behind it without being seen,* I thought.

I knew I couldn't jump from the grate to the concrete without risking breaking my legs. I opened the small bag on my belt and grabbed a hook with a magnet on the end. Noticing how small the magnet was, I grabbed another one. *Just in case.* I placed the two hooks on the wall. The sound of the magnet against the metal was louder than I expected. I glanced back through the grate. No one was coming into view. *Hopefully, they didn't notice.* I grabbed a rope off my belt and tied it in a circle, looping it over the two magnetic hooks.

I took a deep breath and closed my eyes. *Lord, give me strength.*

I grabbed the screwdriver again and began prying at the grate. Once I had it loosened, I pulled it up into the air duct and set it to the side. I grabbed onto the rope and watched for Braxton to walk into view. Once he turned around, I threw the rope down the opening, making sure the knot was at the bottom, and quickly slid to the ground.

I glanced in the direction of my sister and her captors. The only person facing me was Ryan, and he was staring at the ground, fidgeting with his hands. I untied the rope, pulled it down, and dashed behind the pile of junk.

I could hear Ethan yelling. "I'm tired of your games. Start with the codes in the messages."

"Let's see," Rebecca said sarcastically, "I distinctly remember that you sent email messages that would disappear after we read them. Can't help you there."

I looked around the pile of junk just in time to see Ethan sock Rebecca in the stomach. "Stop it!" His voice cracked as he let out a frustrated scream.

Braxton marched over to Rebecca and pulled her hair back so that she was looking him in the eye. "Listen to me," he said, his New York accent coming through, "You start telling my man what he wants to know, or I will shoot you." He let go of her hair and pushed her head forward.

"Look, you can't kill me until I give you the info, and I don't know what in the world this info is, so it looks like we're at a stale-mate." Rebecca maintained her sarcastic attitude.

Ethan slapped Rebecca again. "Don't mess with me," he said, but he sounded perplexed.

I glanced around the room, trying to find a way to get closer to Rebecca without being seen. I noticed two doors off the opposite side of the room, and leaning against the wall near Ryan was another pile of flattened cardboard boxes. There was nothing else to hide behind.

This building is poorly lit, I thought, noticing the shadows along the opposite wall. *Maybe I could get over there fast enough to not be seen, then I could make my way over to the cardboard boxes.*

I peeked out from behind my cover, seeing a heated discussion between Ethan and Braxton. Ryan was still fidgeting with his hands, so I decided to go for it. I followed the wall backward toward the front door, then ran across the room to the opposite wall. Staying in the shadows, I edged my way toward the stack of boxes. I felt a glimmer of hope as I got closer and closer to the boxes, the captors seeming too involved in their argument to notice me.

Just as I stepped in front of the second door, Ryan took a step forward and looked up, making eye contact with me. "Hey!"

Before he could say anything else, I drew my taser and shot.

"What was that?" Ethan roared, watching Ryan start shaking and fall over. He whirled around.

I took aim at Ethan, but a shot echoed through the building, causing me to freeze. I looked at Braxton, who lowered his gun from pointing at the roof to pointing at Rebecca. "Don't move, or the next shot goes through her, and this isn't a dumb taser like you Truth Squad people use."

"Drop the taser," Ethan said. I dropped it.

I could hear some commotion in my earpiece. "Sarah, what happened? Did you get shot?" Faith asked. I didn't dare answer. I gritted my teeth as they continued peppering me with questions that I couldn't answer. *Just call the police,* I thought, hoping they would stick to the plan.

Braxton pulled a knife off his belt and cut the ropes holding Rebecca to the chair. He pulled her to her feet. "We'll be going now—all of us! Ethan, grab the twin."

Ethan grabbed my arm and pulled me toward the first door at the side of the room. "Sit at the table," he said. He yanked the door open and pushed me into the room with a large wooden table surrounded by metal chairs. The back wall was lined with upper and lower cabinets, and the windowless room was lit by two old sconces.

Ethan pushed me into a metal chair. "Put all your tools on the table," he said with a growl. *This did not go as planned,* I thought, my heart sinking as I took off my tool belt.

Rebecca was slammed into a chair next to me, and Ethan put a hand on each of our shoulders.

Braxton rummaged through the cabinets. He grabbed a roll of duct tape from a cabinet and slammed it shut.

As the two men duct-taped us to the chairs, I felt a

glimmer of hope, knowing Faith, Hope, and Jonathan were still listening in through the coms. *They have enough evidence. They should be calling the police,* I thought, praying they were sticking to the plan.

"What's this?" My heart sank again as Ethan pulled my com out of my ear. "Braxton." He held up my earpiece.

Rebecca was right about him being the third guy, I thought.

Braxton turned the com over in his hand, then threw it on the ground and stomped on it. "Tell us," he said, moving in front of my face, "who was listening."

I shook my head. "I'm working alone." *It's half true,* I thought, hoping I sounded convincing.

Braxton laughed. "No one who wears an earpiece is working alone. Who was listening?"

I shook my head but didn't say anything. Braxton opened his mouth but was interrupted by a groan from outside the room.

Ethan rolled his eyes. "Ryan?"

Ryan stumbled into the room. "That's the second time," he said, his voice muffled from the numbness in his face.

"Ryan, go get the van ready. We need to get out of here." Ethan threw some keys at him.

"Why?"

"Because someone knows our location." A slow grin spread across Ethan's face. "Plus, we need somewhere to dump their bodies."

Ryan's jaw dropped. "Wait, what?"

Ethan folded his arms. "They're getting in the way. You know what I do for a living, right?"

"You told me no one was getting killed!" Ryan said, his eyes wide.

"I said you weren't killing anyone," Ethan replied. "Now, go get the van."

Ryan shook his head. "I'm not being a part of killing people."

"You're not," Braxton jumped in. "We hired you to do computer work. You can focus on doing your job, and we'll focus on ours. Otherwise, you can join these twins in being tied up."

Ryan stood still for a moment, glaring. Slowly, he turned around and walked away, muttering something about the van.

Braxton leaned down in Rebecca's face. "I hope you heard that. Even if you don't give us information, we will still get rid of you." He looked at Ethan and nodded toward the door. "Let's go get things ready."

They walked out the door and slammed it shut, locking it. I opened my mouth to say something, but Rebecca shook her head, mouthing, "Listen."

"I think you're wrong," Ethan was saying. "We aren't supposed to return without those codes. She's the only one who has them."

"I don't see how he would need some dumb codes this bad. We are supposed to get rid of defectors. End of story." Braxton sounded confident.

"You need to pay better attention," Ethan scolded. "MAX specifically said we bring back those codes, or we're dead."

Their arguing died off as they walked away. I looked at Rebecca, wide-eyed. "MAX?"

Rebecca nodded. "He's the guy Zaiden worked for. But what do I know that he needs? What do I know that only I know?"

"And he wants your training codes?" I asked. "Why?"

She shrugged. "I don't know. I mean, why would the training codes be something that only I know? And if they're not just training codes, then what are they?" Rebecca shook her head. "I don't understand it." We sat silently for a moment before Rebecca asked, "So, who was listening to your coms?"

I grinned half-heartedly. "Faith, Hope, and Jonathan."

"What?" Rebecca's jaw dropped. "I thought we agreed they weren't getting involved."

"There was no one else. Besides, Grandma Melba was okay with it."

"Mr. Truth won't be."

I sighed. "Well, Jonathan was a last-minute addition, and he insisted on joining in since he helped save the girls from a run-in with Matthew."

Rebecca raised an eyebrow, shaking her head. "So, where are they right now?"

"Hopefully, they have called the police and driven away," I said. *Knowing them, they probably didn't drive away,* I thought. *Lord, please keep them safe.*

Rebecca let out a small chuckle.

"What?" I asked.

"I'm just impressed that you got in here undetected and took on these three guys by yourself." She smiled. "I think you have more courage than you know."

I looked away, feeling my face grow warm. "Thanks, but I've been thinking about what you said..." I was interrupted by the door being unlocked.

"Okay, girls. Time to go," Ethan said. He pulled out a knife and cut the duct tape off from around my chair.

I don't think he knows my hands aren't tied, I thought as he moved over to Rebecca.

I waited until he began putting the knife away, then I jumped up and punched his jaw. He staggered backward. I picked up my chair and swung it at him, knocking him to the ground. "Let's go!" I cried, motioning for Rebecca to run.

We took off. "Can you untie my hands?" Rebecca asked as we rushed for the door.

I pulled at the knot as we ran and got it slightly undone before reaching the door. I pushed it open. Braxton stood at the van just outside the door. "What's going on?" he cried, running toward us.

"Quick, follow me!" I said, running around to the other side of the building. Part of me hoped that my backup crew had disobeyed me, and the van was still waiting for us.

I rounded the corner and looked over to where I'd parked the van. It was gone. "The one time they actually obey me," I said, shaking my head.

"We'll just have to outrun him," Rebecca said, finally pulling her hands free from the rope. "Let's head toward the front building."

I followed Rebecca as she ran in the opposite direction toward the new offices. As we dashed between storage units, I glanced over my shoulder. "He's not behind us anymore," I called to Rebecca.

Suddenly, Ryan shot out in front of us in the van. "Turn around!" Rebecca called, running back in my direction.

I ran back in the direction we'd come from, willing my legs to go faster despite the burning in my lungs. Just as I rounded the corner, Braxton jumped out at me. I barely ducked in time to miss his blow.

Rebecca was there in a flash, and it was two against one. Every time Rebecca took a swing and Braxton dodged, I tried to swing at him from the other direction. Braxton was fast. We got a few punches in, but he dodged most of them.

Rebecca looked at me from the corner of her eye and tilted

her head back. *We're going to run.* I nodded to let her know I understood.

Rebecca took one last swing, then shouted, "Now!"

We took off running. She was headed toward the fence. "Are we going to climb it?" I asked.

Rebecca shook her head. "Let's keep heading toward the offices."

We reached the fence and turned to follow it toward the front of the complex. The van shot out in front of us, blocking us. I turned around and saw Braxton coming from behind us and Ethan coming from beside us. "We're trapped," I said.

"Climb the fence," Rebecca ordered. She grabbed hold of the chain link and started pulling herself up. I followed.

"Stop right there!" Ethan yelled, and a shot rang out. The bullet whizzed past us and hit a tree on the other side of the fence. I froze. "Get down, or my next shot hits one of you."

I looked at Rebecca. She sighed and nodded. We both dropped to the ground. "Put your hands up where I can see them," Ethan said.

I raised my hands above my head. Suddenly, I felt a sharp pain in my shoulder.

I turned to see Braxton pull a dart from my shoulder. "Sweet dreams," he said, an evil grin on his face.

I raised an eyebrow. "What are you talking about?" I asked, although I could already feel myself growing dizzy and my vision blurring.

I heard Rebecca ask, "What did you do?" Her voice sounded miles away. I felt my body go limp as I fell backward, and Braxton caught me. Then everything went black.

I woke up as the van bounced over a large pothole. "Be careful, Ryan," Ethan scolded.

"I didn't choose the route," he retorted.

I tried to open my eyes, but they felt like they had bricks holding them shut. I could feel pine needles and scratchy carpet beneath me and decided I must be lying on the van floor. My hands were tied behind my back this time. My left arm was numb, having lost circulation from laying on it.

I listened as Braxton talked to Rebecca. "You know, we might let you live if you give us the codes."

Rebecca replied with a muffled, "Uh, uh." *She must be gagged,* I thought.

Braxton laughed. "Okay, so the easy way is you tell us the codes, you die, we'll let your sister go free, and that's that." He paused. "The hard way is we take you to MAX, and he'll make you talk one way or another. And trust me, that will be a lot worse than the easy way."

I finally forced my eyes open and looked around me. Ryan was in the driver's seat. We were driving through a tree-lined road, and from the many bumps and potholes, I assumed we were in the middle of nowhere on a country road. The back of the van had bench seats along the sides with storage underneath. Braxton and Ethan sat on one side, and Rebecca sat on the other, tied up and gagged. Ethan kept glancing nervously out the back window.

Braxton glanced at me. "Ah, you're finally awake." He stood up just as Ryan hit another pothole. He lurched forward but regained his balance. Grabbing my arm, Braxton hoisted me up onto the bench next to Rebecca.

Sitting up made me feel even more like a sack of bricks. Braxton tied my hands to a handhold on the wall, then tied my feet together. *It's not like I would be fighting anytime soon*, I thought, struggling to keep my eyes open.

Ethan sighed. "Ryan, what does our GPS say?"

"Forty minutes. You know, you asked for the time five minutes ago."

"Whatever." Ethan folded his arms and glanced back out the window. He shook his head. "I wonder if we should veer off our route."

"We're not being followed," Braxton said. "We're on a country road with no turn offs for the next three miles. Seriously, just stay calm."

Ethan frowned and looked back out the window.

I turned my head, trying to see around Rebecca, but with my hands tied to the handhold, I couldn't move far enough to get a good look. "Where are we going?" I asked, my voice sounding like a frog's croak.

Braxton laughed, sounding sinister. "Somewhere we know we can convince your sister to talk." He stretched, sighing with satisfaction. "I'm so glad you decided, foolishly I might add, to rescue your sister. We now have a reason to get her to talk."

I wanted to panic, but whatever Braxton had injected me with made me feel zero emotion. *Lord, please help us to get away somehow*, I prayed. *I don't have my coms anymore, and I have no clue where Faith, Hope, and Jonathan went. Please help the police to find us.* I felt like smiling, but I couldn't do it. *Well, Rebecca said she's good at faking not feeling emotion. Right now, I can't show emotion even if I wanted to. How ironic.*

Ethan shook his head. "I think we're being tailed."

"Stop saying that!" Braxton said, sounding annoyed, but his face betrayed his worry. "Ryan, pull off at the next side road we find."

We rode in silence for a minute. Suddenly, Ryan spoke up. "Guys, I don't want to be a part of this anymore. When we get to our destination, I'm dropping you off and leaving."

"You will do no such thing!" Ethan said.

"Why? You don't need a computer expert anymore. You're done hacking Truth Squad. You've got the girl you were after. I'm not needed anymore. Just give me my money and let me go." Ryan sounded upset. "I don't want to be a part of this anymore. You said all I had to do was hack, not help you kidnap and murder people."

"Then leave without your stupid money," Ethan replied.

Ryan gasped. "No way. I've spent months helping you."

"Then don't bail on us."

"But you told me we weren't hurting anyone," Ryan whined.

"Shut up," Ethan said. "You knew perfectly well that I am a hitman. What did you think you were signing up for? A walk in the park?" Ryan didn't reply. "You didn't squirm about hitting Luke."

"I told you I thought we were going too far," Ryan replied tensely.

"Let me shoot you straight," Ethan said slowly. "I was hired to get the information needed from Rebecca and then get rid of her. What did you think 'get rid of' implied?"

"I don't know!" Ryan yelled. "I just know I don't want to be a part of this anymore."

Braxton pulled out his gun and pointed it at Ryan. "So, now you have a choice. You keep helping us, or I'll shoot."

Ryan closed his mouth. The van was full of tense silence. No one moved. Finally, Ryan said, "We're coming up on a side road. Do you want me to turn?"

Braxton slowly lowered his weapon. "Yes."

The vehicle pulled off onto the dirt road. Ethan stared out the back window. "They turned!" he cried. "We're being tailed!"

"Ryan, gun it and do a U-turn. I want to get a good look at these people," Braxton ordered.

The van sped up and whipped around, causing us passengers to slide. My shoulders ached from being pulled on in such an awkward position.

I glanced over my shoulder as we drove by, trying to see who was tailing us. I couldn't see anyone's faces, but the glimpse of the vehicle made my heart jump. *Is that Grandpa Steve's van?*

"Did you recognize them?" Braxton asked Ethan.

Ethan shook his head. "I didn't get a good look. Step on it, Ryan. We've got to lose them!"

The engine roared as Ryan pulled back onto the main road. "What is that?" Ryan yelled, pointing out the front window.

A small smile crept onto my face. A police barricade blocked the road. *Thank You, Lord!*

"Turn off onto that road." Ethan pointed to the left. Ryan whipped the van off down another dirt road and sped up.

We sped down the bumpy road until Ethan spotted a run-down barn. "Drive over there and park inside."

As soon as we stopped, Ethan and Braxton untied our legs and untied us from the van's handholds. Braxton grabbed a bandana from the front seat and gagged me. "No funny business, or you're both dead!" he whispered, pulling me out of the van.

"What are we doing?" Ryan asked, jumping down from the van. "This will be the first place they look." His eyes were wide with fright. "Look, I don't want to be a part of this."

"Then don't be." Before the words even registered, Braxton pulled out his gun and shot Ryan.

I screamed, but it was muffled by the bandana.

Braxton slapped my jaw with the butt of his gun. Pain shot up my jaw to my head. "Don't do that again." He nodded at Ethan. "Let's go."

I stumbled along as Braxton pushed me to the edge of the barn. After looking around, he nodded at Ethan and hurried toward the forest.

Where are we going? I wondered, trying to keep up with Braxton. My legs felt like I was wearing concrete shoes, but the effects of the medicine were wearing off enough for me to raise my eyebrows questioningly as I glanced at my sister. She just shrugged in return.

My heart was pounding. It was hard to keep up such a pace with a gag in my mouth, and I was starting to feel my emotions again. *God, I'm scared. We need You. Save us!*

Ethan and Braxton marched on and on as Rebecca and I stumbled along to keep up. Not only was it hard to breathe, but having my hands tied behind my back made balancing difficult.

We came to a fallen tree, and Ethan slowed his pace. "Let's stop for a minute and get our bearings." He sat Rebecca down on the log and looked at his watch.

Braxton shoved me next to Rebecca and walked over to Ethan. "How far have we gone?"

"About a mile and a half." Ethan looked around. "We're in the middle of nowhere, man."

"Yeah, and that's what we want. It'll be harder for the police to get us." Braxton crossed his arms. "What direction do we need to head to get to our pick-up spot?"

Ethan looked at his watch then looked up again. "That way." He pointed away from us.

I noticed Rebecca was wriggling a lot. I glanced over and saw she was rubbing the rope around her wrists on a broken tree branch sticking out from the log. *Smart thinking!* I thought, winking at Rebecca. She grinned slightly and kept working.

I don't know if she'll get that off in time, I thought, watching our captors as they deliberated their next move.

A glimmer caught my eye. I turned to see a piece of broken glass on the ground. *Thank You, Lord!* I glanced up and watched Ethan and Braxton, waiting for them to turn their backs to us. They kept talking, not moving. *Please turn!* My heart pounded, and my muscles tensed, ready to move. Finally, they turned their backs.

I jumped up and lunged for the piece of glass. Sitting down on my backside, I felt around with my hands until I felt something sharp. I grabbed it and leaned forward onto my toes. Struggling to get my balance, I glanced back at the two men. They hadn't turned around yet, but I knew it wouldn't be long till they did. I quickly pushed myself onto my feet. I sat back down on the log just as Ethan turned back to look at us. He raised an eyebrow.

Did he see me? I thought, trying to keep a straight face.

He kept staring, my heartbeat racing faster the longer he stared. Finally, he rolled his eyes and turned back to Braxton.

Breathing a sigh of relief, I began sawing at my ropes with the piece of glass. Slowly, I felt the strands start to break. Rebecca grinned slightly, noticing my work.

Suddenly, Braxton whirled around. "Let's go," he said, heading our way.

I stopped moving. *What if he notices the frayed rope?* I held onto the glass, not wanting to let go until the last possible second.

"I think it would be better to wait out here until the police leave," Ethan said, crossing his arms.

Braxton turned back toward him. "That's foolish. They'll just wait us out."

"Do you know how many miles it is? Our rendezvous is forty minutes away by car, not by walking. Plus, we don't have any water."

"We could find some water. There's got to be a stream around here somewhere."

As the two continued arguing, I slowly continued cutting my ropes. Suddenly, I felt my ropes go slack. I moved my hands, and the rope slid off. *Yes!*

Ethan and Braxton had taken a few steps away and were whispering. I slowly slid closer to Rebecca and untied my gag, then hers. As I worked on untying her hands, she whispered, "You need to get out of here."

"Not without you." The knot on her ropes was tight, so I began sawing at her ropes with the glass.

"Sarah, you heard them. You're here because they want to make me talk. They won't kill me until I give them the codes they want. If you get away, you can get help." She grabbed the glass from my hands. "Seriously. Go while they're not looking!"

"Rebecca, I didn't do all this to run away," I argued. "I did this to save you." I pulled the loosened ropes off her hands.

"It's better that one of us gets away than both of us dying!" She glanced at our captors. "They're coming back. Get down!" She pushed me over the edge of the log.

I landed on the ground with a thud. I heard Rebecca stand up and run.

"Hey, what are you doing!" I heard Ethan yell. "Don't move or I'll shoot!"

"Where's the other one?" Braxton asked.

"Tell us where your sister went. And how did you get untied?" Ethan sounded panicked.

"She's running back to the police," Rebecca replied. "And trust me, they will find you two, and you will get what you deserve."

"We've got to find Sarah," Ethan said.

"No. We've got who we're after. Let's just go to the meeting place," Braxton replied.

"We can't let her get away. She knows our identities. She could jeopardize everything!" Ethan argued.

"You could split up," Rebecca offered. "One of you look for Sarah, and the other can take me to your rendezvous."

"That's a good idea," Braxton said.

"Don't take advice from our prisoner!" Ethan yelled. "She's only saying that because she knows with only one person on her back, especially since we don't have more rope to tie her with, she could take us out. She's highly skilled. You know who she trained under." Ethan huffed. "We're sticking together. Sarah couldn't have gotten far. That tranquilizer takes a long time to wear off fully, so there's no way she's running. Let's go."

I listened as they stomped off in the direction we came from. I waited until my surroundings were silent.

Slowly, I sat up. *Now what?* I looked in the direction they went. *I guess I'll follow them.* I stood up. *Just don't get caught,* I told myself.

It felt good to be able to breathe as I hurried back in the direction we came from. I tried to watch for landmarks to make sure I wasn't getting lost, but I was surrounded by trees, and the shadows were growing longer with the setting sun, so there weren't many landmarks to look for. *Just keep going this direction and don't stop.*

I heard Ethan's voice and slowed my pace. *They must be up ahead,* I thought, darting behind a tree. I slowly picked my way forward, dodging from tree to tree. As I got closer, I saw Ethan holding onto Rebecca's arm, but I didn't see Braxton.

"She probably got lost," Ethan said, sounding irritated.

"Doubtful. Sarah has a good sense of direction," Rebecca replied.

Ethan shook her. "Would you stop making sarcastic remarks? I don't want to hear another word out of you!" He looked around. "Anything, Braxton?"

Suddenly, a hand clamped over my mouth. I tensed, stifling a scream. Yanking the hand away from my mouth, I noticed the size of the hand. *This isn't Braxton.* I whirled around, and my jaw dropped. "Faith?"

She put a finger to her lips. "Here," she whispered, handing me a taser. "Wait for the signal."

"What are you doing here?" I whispered.

She rolled her eyes. "Saving the day, of course. Now stay here." She stealthily worked her way over a few trees, giving me a wink as she pulled out her own taser.

What is going on? I wondered, but I didn't have much time to think about it.

I heard Braxton yell, "Hey, who... Ethan... oof!"

"Braxton, what is going on?" Ethan yelled. Just then, a whistle blew.

That must be the signal, I thought, jumping out from my hiding place.

Ethan was caught off guard, and Rebecca flew into action. She grabbed his wrist and twisted his arm until he dropped his gun, then kicked it away. Ethan grabbed Rebecca's arm and flipped her over his shoulder, slamming her to the ground.

"Hey!" Jonathan yelled. Ethan looked over at him. "Put

your hands in the air and walk away from our agent." His commanding stance and voice matched that of his dad, only in a voice that hadn't quite changed yet.

"I don't take commands from a kid," Ethan said, stepping toward him.

"I wouldn't think about that if I were you," Faith said, stepping forward. "We have you surrounded."

"Give it up, Ethan," I joined in.

He whirled around and faced me. "I should have known you would stoop so low as to involve children in your plot," he said, his stance faltering.

"Actually, I'm thirteen, so I'm not a kid," Faith said, flipping her hair.

"I'm not afraid of your stupid tasers," he said, making a break for an opening in the circle.

Just before I could shoot, a deep voice said, "I don't think so." My breath caught as I saw Daniel step from behind a tree, holding onto Braxton with a gun trained on Ethan. "This one's not a taser."

Ethan's eyes widened. Rebecca got up from the ground and grabbed Ethan's gun, walking up behind him. "And this one's not, either."

"Get on your knees and put your hands behind your head," Daniel ordered, shoving Braxton toward Ethan. Pushing a button on his watch, Daniel spoke into it, "We've got our men. Sending you coordinates."

"Truth Squad doesn't use guns," Ethan said, thoroughly confused.

"Sir, I am an independent detective, and I use real guns," Daniel replied. "So, stay where you are."

Ethan looked even more confused. "But I've seen you at Truth Squad."

"Yup," Daniel said. "But right now, you'd better be careful what you say, because anything you say can and will be used against you in court."

Moments later, our group was surrounded by police officers. Relief washed over me as I watched Ethan and Braxton get handcuffed and read their rights. They were then escorted by the police to their vehicles.

"I'll meet your group at the station, Detective Reid," the officer said, nodding before walking away.

"Yes, sir," Daniel replied. He walked over to me and put a hand on my shoulder. "You okay?"

Without warning, all of my pent-up emotions came flooding out in tears of relief. Daniel enveloped me in a big hug. "It's okay," he whispered. "You did it." He slowly released our hug and smiled at me.

I smiled back, not wanting to say anything. *My voice sounds ridiculous when I cry,* I thought, suddenly feeling embarrassed.

"Yes!" I turned to see Faith high-fiving Jonathan.

"That was awesome!" they said in unison.

"I can't believe we just did that," Hope said, her hands on her head and her eyes wide.

Faith had a huge grin. "I know! We just did a for-real mission! Can you believe this?" She jumped up and down. Jonathan did a victory lap.

I looked over at Rebecca. She sat on the ground with her eyes closed. I joined her. "You okay?"

She looked up at me, tears glistening in her eyes. "I'm okay." She giggled, blinking away the tears. "I told you I feel emotion."

CHAPTER 12

"How did you find us?" I asked Daniel as we drove to the police station. "Also, how did you know what was going on?"

"I can answer that," Jonathan piped up from the back seat of the van next to Rebecca. Faith and Hope sat in the third row, calling their grandma on the phone. "When I asked him for the password to Luke's computer, he asked what was going on, so I told him."

I raised my eyebrows. "You're the friend he texted for the password?"

Daniel grinned. "Yeah, and don't tell Luke I gave that password away. He would be very embarrassed."

I grinned. *No kidding.* "So, how did you find us?"

"That's a longer story," Daniel said. He merged onto the freeway before replying. "You know when I sent you that Bible verse earlier today?" he asked, blushing a little. I nodded. "Well, to be honest, that was an encoded text. I used it to track your location to the warehouses."

"Really?" I asked, a little shocked.

He nodded. "It maybe didn't need to be encoded because Jonathan was texting me updates the whole way there."

I looked back to see Jonathan shrug. "Hey, I was feeling

a little nervous, okay? I thought we could use some more backup."

I smiled, looking out the front window. The sun was almost completely set, and stars were starting to appear. I knew it would be a long night at the police station. "Where did you go after I got caught?" I asked, remembering that the van was gone.

Jonathan smiled sheepishly. "You said I was supposed to be the getaway driver if anything went wrong. We heard you get caught, so we decided to drive away in case they came looking for us. Daniel told us to meet him at the restaurant across the street, and then he took over the driving part." He shrugged. "I only drove across the street without an adult, and it was for an emergency, and you told me to do it, so I'm going to say it was okay."

I giggled. "I did give you permission."

"So, you guys tailed the van, but how did you find us in the woods?" Rebecca asked.

"Well, we found the van in the barn, and Ryan." Daniel shook his head. "Once we notified the police that we found the van and told them about Ryan, I decided to look for footprints. We found some leading into the woods."

"Daniel wanted to go rescue you guys by himself, but we wouldn't let him," Jonathan said, sounding a little cocky. "Also, I would like to point out that we spotted the footprints first."

Daniel nodded. "Yes, you did. Thank you for reminding me." His tone made me wonder how many times Jonathan had reminded him.

"So, you just followed our tracks until you ran into us?" I asked, stifling a yawn.

Daniel nodded. "We lost the tracks after a while, but then

we heard some commotion and came up with the plan to surround you all." He glanced at me, smiling. "I'm just praising God that we were able to find you."

I smiled back. "Me, too." I looked back out the window at the sunset, then leaned my head back and closed my eyes, still smiling.

"Sarah. We're here." Daniel was gently shaking my shoulder.

I opened my eyes and looked out the window, realizing we were at the police station. "Oh, did I fall asleep?" I asked, embarrassed that he had to wake me up.

Daniel smiled. "Yes, but it's okay. We just got here." He shrugged. "It'll be a long evening as we fill out police reports, so it was probably a good idea to get a nap in."

We got out of the car and walked into the station. Rebecca was already inside, filling out paperwork. Faith and Hope were still on the phone with their grandma, filling her in on the details. Jonathan stood nearby, adding his own commentary.

I quickly got to work filling out my part of the report. Not long later, an officer walked up to us. "An FBI agent is wanting to talk to you," he said, pointing his thumb over his shoulder. I glanced up and saw Agent Brandon, Truth Squad's FBI contact, walking toward us.

"Good evening, sir," I said, shaking his hand.

Agent Brandon nodded as he shook Rebecca's hand. "Good evening." He looked back and forth between us. "I understand you two helped apprehend a man we've been after for a long time. Goes by the name of Braxton Niles."

Rebecca nodded. "Yes, sir."

"From what I understand from Detective Reid, he was after you, Rebecca, and this was related to your work with Zaiden. Is this correct?" He raised an eyebrow.

"Yes, sir," Rebecca repeated. "But it was mainly Ethan Cole who we interacted with. He infiltrated Truth Squad along with a guy he hired to do computer work for him."

"If you don't mind, I'd like to have a word with you two. We have one of our guys interviewing Cole and Niles to try and learn what we can about the case. We'd like to hear what you know, as well. Since this appears to be connected to the Zaiden case, we are very interested in finding out what's going on," Agent Brandon explained.

We agreed, and soon we were sitting in a conference room across from Agent Brandon and his colleague, recounting the story of everything that happened from the moment Ethan showed up to the moment we were rescued.

"What information were they wanting?" Agent Brandon asked.

Rebecca shrugged. "They kept asking for the codes. I'm not sure what they're for, but I think all the codes Mr. Zaiden taught me when I was training under him were something this MAX guy needs for some reason."

"So, MAX has come up again?" Brandon said, scratching his chin. "Interesting. You know, we tried to look into him with the last case, but it didn't go anywhere. We'll have to look into him again." He raised an eyebrow. "What codes did you learn?"

"Mr. Zaiden would teach me a phrase and attach it to a number," Rebecca explained. "They were phrases that had to do with good undercover work. For example, Code One was 'your cover is only as good as your facial expression.' He quizzed me on them all the time, so I know them like they're a part of me."

Agent Brandon crossed his arms. "Interesting. How many codes were there?"

Rebecca thought for a moment. "One hundred and ten."

"Codes one, fifteen, and forty-five were the ones that they specifically included in the threats we got, if I remember correctly," I said, glancing at Rebecca.

She nodded. "That's right."

Suddenly, I remembered an important detail. "There's also a hostage situation," I said, quickly.

Agent Brandon raised his eyebrows. "What?" I quickly told him about Carrie's brother.

Agent Brandon stood. "I'm going to join the interrogations and find out where this hostage is. I'll also see if either Cole or Niles knows anything about MAX."

While Agent Brandon conducted his interrogation, Rebecca and I finished filing our police reports. Grandma Melba showed up and took Faith, Hope, and Jonathan home.

"You girls stop by my house. I don't care how late it is. I just want to make sure you're okay. Plus, I have your favorite cookies waiting for you," she said, giving us both a hug.

"You're too sweet. Thank you," I said, waving to her as she left.

Agent Brandon joined us a few minutes later. "What did you find out?" Daniel asked.

"Braxton Niles won't talk. He asked for a lawyer immediately," Agent Brandon said with a sigh. "Ethan Cole, on the other hand, confessed to everything. He said if he was going down, he was taking other people down with him. Apparently, he's from Canada but does hit jobs for MAX. He confessed to holding Carrie's brother hostage and gave us the location. We passed the word onto Truth Squad since their base is close by. They should be on that by now. Cole also confessed to being hired to get the codes and take out Rebecca. He said he was told Rebecca knows too much, but she has codes that only Zaiden knew."

Daniel lowered his eyebrows. "That's weird that the information would be split up like that."

"Yeah, Cole didn't have an explanation," Brandon said. "He gave us names and locations of his contacts, but he's never met MAX. He thinks some of his contacts know who MAX is, though. He also told us he's been hired by MAX before to take out other 'defectors,' as he calls them, and to gather stolen weapons." Brandon shrugged. "Whatever MAX has going is quite an operation, and we need to keep an eye out on his activity."

He shook our hands. "Thank you for your information. We will stay in touch. Goodnight!" He waved and headed out the door.

Daniel checked his watch. "Wow, it's past eleven. Are you sure Grandma Melba wants you two stopping by?" We started walking toward the door.

I nodded. "Trust me. She would be angry if we didn't stop by." I pointed my thumb toward the van. "Plus, we have to return that thing."

Daniel shrugged. "True. Maybe she'll let me stop by with you for some cookies, because I'm starving."

Rebecca grinned as we climbed in the van. "Maybe we could stop for fast food first, because I am even more starving than either of you. I haven't eaten since last night before I was captured."

"Yikes," I said, frowning. "Why didn't you say something? We could have had food brought to us at the police station."

She shrugged. "I don't know. Let's just get some food, please!"

"Rodger that!" Daniel said, starting the van.

⚓

I woke up the next morning to the sound of my phone ringing. Groggily, I picked it up off my nightstand and swiped to answer the call. "Hello?" I glanced at the clock. It was only seven.

"Hi, Sarah, it's Daniel." His voice sounded excited.

"What's up?" I asked, not sharing his enthusiasm. We got to Melba's house around midnight and stayed up till two in the morning since she wanted to hear all about what happened from our point of view.

"Luke's awake!"

I shot out of bed, suddenly full of energy. "He is? How's he doing?" I ran out of my room and pounded on Rebecca's door. I didn't wait for her to open it and barged in. "Rebecca, Luke's awake!"

She sat up quickly and threw the covers off. "Let's go!" she said, grabbing clothes from her closet.

I remembered Daniel was on the phone and put the phone back up to my ear. "Sorry, I was passing on the news to Rebecca. Can you repeat what you said?"

Daniel laughed. "I didn't say anything because I heard you yelling at your sister."

"Oh." I felt my face grow red as I hurried back to my room and grabbed my outfit for the day.

"Anyways, Luke's doing great, and he wants you two to get over here and see him. He says he can't believe you aren't here right now, and he wants you to sneak him doughnuts because he's supposed to be only eating ice chips right now, and he's mad about it."

I rolled my eyes. "I am not bringing him doughnuts."

Daniel repeated my words away from the phone. I heard Luke's voice but couldn't make out what he was saying. Daniel spoke into the phone again, "He says he'll trade you ice chips for doughnuts."

I laughed. "Hmm, doesn't sound like a fair trade. No deal. See you soon!" I hung up and got ready to go, feeling a mixture of relief and excitement.

Rebecca, as usual, was ready to go before I was. She tossed me a pop-tart as we headed out the door. I grinned. "I hope pop-tarts don't become our usual."

We started walking toward the parking garage when I remembered that my car was still parked downtown with a slashed tire. *It's probably been towed by now,* I thought. "I'll call Grandma Melba and see if we can borrow the van again."

Faith answered instead of Melba. "Hello, how may I help you?"

"Hi, Faith. We were going to visit Luke at the hospital, but as you know, I can't drive my car right now. We were hoping your grandma would let us borrow the van again."

Faith gasped. "I want to visit Luke, too!"

I heard excitement on the other end of the line. "So does Hope. And I'll bet Jonathan does, too. Hope, text Jonathan and ask if he wants to go." Faith started yelling for her grandma, so I pulled the phone away from my ear. I nodded toward the gate. "Let's start heading that direction," I said to Rebecca.

Pretty soon, Faith was talking to me again, "Okay, grandma says you can take all of us. We have to wait for Jonathan because he's coming, too."

"Sounds good." I hung up.

Not long later, we were all piled into the van and headed to the hospital.

"Are you eating pop-tarts?" Jonathan asked as we drove.

"Yes," Rebecca replied, grinning.

Jonathan sighed. "My mom doesn't let me eat pop-tarts." He stared longingly at our breakfast. "I can't wait till I'm an adult and can buy my own food."

"That's probably the best part of being an adult," Rebecca joked.

I laughed. "I'm not sure pop-tarts are the best part of being an adult."

Jonathan shrugged. "It's got to be close, though. Very close."

Mr. Truth met us at the entrance when we got to the hospital. "Hi, Dad!" Jonathan said, trying to give his dad a high-five instead of getting a hug. Mr. Truth managed to meet his high-five and give him a side-hug, making Jonathan roll his eyes. "Can we go see Luke, now?"

Mr. Truth nodded. "Daniel's inside the door. He'll take you to his room." As the trio hurried inside, Mr. Truth looked at us. "Can I have a minute?" We nodded in unison, following him into the building.

We stood next to the sliding door, waiting for Mr. Truth to speak. He seemed to be gathering his thoughts. *Am I going to be fired for real?* I thought, noticing the seriousness of his face.

Finally, he cleared his throat and faced us. "I was informed by Agent Brandon, and by Daniel and Jonathan, about your adventure yesterday. And," he took a deep breath, "well, I would like to formally apologize for the way Matthew and I handled the situation. We didn't take you seriously in the first place, and we should have. We could have saved a lot of trouble by not jumping to conclusions. I am truly sorry." He paused.

"Sarah, I understand that Matthew revoked your Truth Squad membership?"

"Yes, sir."

He smiled. "Well, I am officially reinstating it."

I breathed a sigh of relief. "Thank you."

"I spoke to your parole officer, Rebecca, and he will be stopping by later today to get everything straightened out." Noticing the concern on Rebecca's face, he continued, "Don't worry. I will make sure he fully understands the situation and make sure you can stay on at Truth Squad."

Rebecca's face lit up. "Thank you."

He cleared his throat. "I would also like to say that you three proved that our security system needs some upgrading."

"Proved?" I said, nervous about that term.

He nodded. "Yes, proved. Both by solving the case yesterday and by your crazy sneaking around our campus to do so." He smiled. "While normally I would not let such behavior go unreprimanded, I have chosen to overlook it since you helped catch two important men who slipped past our security. I wanted to know if your trio would be willing to help upgrade our security. I know that you specialize in that sort of thing, Rebecca. And I figure if I get help from the people who can beat our current security, they can help input a better system that even my best three agents can't beat."

A huge grin spread across Rebecca's face. "I'd love to!"

"I'm willing to help, too," I agreed.

He smiled. "Great! Also, we had some of our guys in Canada on the case to rescue Carrie's brother, and I just received word that they completed the mission. He's fine, and Carrie's headed home today to see him."

"That's a relief," Rebecca said.

Mr. Truth smiled. "Now, go visit Luke before he gets mad at me for stalling you."

We hurried to the elevator and rode up to the third floor. As we stepped off the elevator, I noticed Matthew walking toward us. Instantly, I felt my body tense.

He looked up from watching the ground and made eye contact, his face reddening. "Excuse me," he said quietly, "I know you're here to see Luke, but can I have a word with you two?"

Rebecca sighed in frustration. "I guess so."

Matthew raised an eyebrow. "What, did Mr. Truth just stop you two?"

I nodded. "What is it?" I hoped I sounded friendly, because I still felt mad at him.

Matthew took a deep breath. "I wanted to apologize to both of you. Not on behalf of Truth Squad or anything else, but personally." His face grew redder as he talked, and he kept his eyes trained on the ground. "I realize I jumped to conclusions when I shouldn't have. And I jumped to conclusions because I have not trusted you, Rebecca, since you first came to Truth Squad. When I heard Agent Brandon's report, I realized that I was wrong in the way I treated you all. I have been a horrible friend and a horrible leader. I'm truly sorry." He looked up at us. "I promise to never jump to conclusions about either of you like that again."

"We forgive you," Rebecca said.

"Yes," I agreed.

He shook his head. "You shouldn't."

Rebecca's face was serious. "No, we should. That's what Jesus did for me, and if He has forgiven me of everything I've done, how can I not extend that to others?"

Matthew blinked rapidly and swallowed. "Thank you," he whispered, then hurried past us toward the elevator.

I looked at Rebecca. She smiled seriously, then took a deep breath. "Well, are we finally ready?"

I nodded, and we walked down the hall. Daniel stood outside the room and waved us inside.

Luke was sitting slightly upright in his hospital bed, somehow his usual energetic self despite being in the hospital. As we walked in, he interrupted Jonathan's story and called, "Hey, it's Rebecca and Sarah! About time you two showed up!" He glanced at an imaginary watch. "I've been waiting for forever!"

I laughed, and Rebecca rolled her eyes. "Forever is an exaggeration," she said, but she was grinning from ear to ear. She hurried over to him and gave him an awkward side-hug.

"Well, it felt like forever," he said quietly, looking up into her eyes for a moment. Then he grinned. "Time always goes slower when all you can eat are ice chips." He raised his eyebrows at me. "Did you sneak me any doughnuts?"

"No," I said, raising my hands. "Why would I do that?"

Luke ran a finger down his cheek. "You see that? That's a tear. For my doughnuts."

Jonathan snorted. "Do we need to pause in a moment of silence?"

We all laughed. "Nah," Luke said. He looked back at Rebecca, then at Daniel, who was standing at the foot of the bed. Daniel was nodding his head toward Rebecca, his eyebrows raised.

Luke took a deep breath and cleared his throat. *Something's gonna happen,* I thought, excitement bubbling up in me.

"Rebecca, I have something I'd like to ask you," he began. He took another deep breath and looked nervous. "Well, let me back up. Rebecca, it has been a joy to get to know you and to see you grow in your walk with Christ. It has been an honor to be your friend." He paused.

Daniel faked a cough.

Luke sighed in frustration, glancing at Daniel. "I'll be honest, I had a speech prepared, and I forgot all of it after this point."

Rebecca glancing at me in confusion. I grinned at her, pretty confident about where this was headed.

"Anyways, since I forgot my speech," Luke said, talking quickly, "I was wondering if you would be willing to go to dinner with me sometime... after I'm out of the hospital and not eating only ice chips. I mean, you could eat ice chips with me if you want, but that sounds pretty lame." He winked.

Rebecca raised an eyebrow. "Go to dinner with you?" she said slowly. "You mean, like a date?" She still looked confused. I looked away, trying not to laugh.

Luke took another deep breath. "Yes, like a date. But I don't mean just like a for-fun date or whatever. I mean, like, I want to get to know you better. You see, I've been praying for a long time that God would lead me in who He wants me to date and who He wants me to marry. And I've been praying about this for a while—"

"He really has," Daniel cut in, nodding.

Luke glared at Daniel. "Seriously, dude?"

Daniel raised his hands in surrender. "Sorry. I'll stop."

"So, you've been praying?" Rebecca asked, motioning for him to continue. She had a small grin on her face, her eyes bright.

"Yeah, I've been praying for a while about, well," he paused, his cheeks growing red, but his voice remained confident, "about you. I've liked you for a long time, and God has given me peace about asking you if you'd be willing to date me." He paused. Rebecca didn't reply. He stared at her for a minute. Finally, he said quickly, "So, basically, I'm asking, will you be my girlfriend?"

Rebecca started laughing. "I can't believe you're asking me."

Luke's face fell. I covered my mouth, trying not to laugh. *Come on, Rebecca, keep talking.* I knew she had more to say.

When Rebecca composed herself, she continued, "It's just ironic."

"Why?" Luke asked, raising an eyebrow.

"When I first met you, I thought you were annoying," Rebecca said, shaking her head. "You were always so cheerful and goofy, but it was really the fact that you could throw me off my game that annoyed me." She smiled. "But I needed that, because you and Sarah pointed me back to Christ. And now, you're one of my best friends. So, yes," she said, laughing again. "I would be glad to go on a date with you."

Luke's face broke into a huge grin. "Yes!" he said, doing a fist pump.

I quickly turned my head and wiped at the sudden tears that came to my eyes, my heart full of happiness at seeing these two finally admit to liking each other.

Jonathan faked a cough. "This was an awkward moment to be a part of," he muttered.

Hope's jaw dropped. "No, it wasn't."

"I'm so excited!" Faith exclaimed. "I always knew you two liked each other."

Daniel stepped over to me and grinned. "Do you want to leave these two love birds and go get some coffee?" he asked quietly.

My eyes widened, and my heart skipped a beat. "What?" A thousand butterflies seemed to take flight in my stomach.

"I happen to know you love coffee," he said, winking.

"Are you asking her on a date?" Jonathan asked loudly, a sly grin on his face. I felt my face flush.

Faith elbowed Jonathan. "Don't say that. You're ruining the moment."

I laughed nervously. "I'd love to get coffee with you, whether it's a date or not," I said, my face feeling like it had burst into flames.

Daniel shrugged, looking away with embarrassment.

Luke cleared his throat. "Do you need help remembering your speech?"

Daniel glared at Luke. "Seriously, dude?"

Luke grinned. "Just returning the favor."

Daniel looked back at me, his face growing red. "I wanted to be a little more casual about it, but I guess I was kind of wanting it to be a date." He cleared his throat. "I don't really have a speech prepared—"

"But he's liked you for forever."

"Luke!" Daniel looked like he wanted the floor to swallow him. He looked me in the eye and swallowed. "I do like you."

My jaw dropped. "You do?" *How did I not see this coming?* A huge grin spread across my face.

"Shall we go get some coffee then?" Daniel asked. I nodded, too excited to say anything.

"Ah, that's so sweet," Hope said, holding her hand over her heart. Faith rolled her eyes.

Jonathan cleared his throat. "Hey, don't you need some chaperones?"

Faith's eyes lit up. "Yeah! We could be your chaperones... for a price."

"Coffee sounds amazing," Jonathan continued, nodding.

"We don't—" Daniel started, but Faith cut in.

"Sarah, you owe us! We saved your life yesterday." She put her hands on her hips. "What do you say?"

I laughed. "I guess I do owe you." I glanced at Daniel.

Daniel shook his head. "Why don't you all come along, then!"

Luke piped up, "Hey, bring me back one, too!" He pointed to Rebecca. "And one for her, too. The usual, of course."

I waved as we walked out the door. "Will do! For Rebecca, that is. You're still eating ice chips."

Hope ran up and put her arm around me. Faith and Jonathan stepped in between Daniel and me. "We'll stay between you two, you know, since we're your chaperones and all," Jonathan said, grinning.

Daniel shrugged and grinned at me.

I smiled back, my heart so happy and light, I felt like I might either levitate or explode. *Thank You, God!*

THE END.

Printed in the United States
by Baker & Taylor Publisher Services